Burgundy: Twisted Roots

Books by Janet Hubbard

The Vengeance in the Vineyard Mysteries
Champagne: The Farewell
Bordeaux: The Bitter Finish
Burgundy: Twisted Roots

Burgundy: Twisted Roots

A Vengeance in the Vineyard Mystery

Janet Hubbard

Poisoned Pen Press

Poisoned Pen Press

First Edition 2017

10 9 8 7 6 5 4 3 2 1

Library of Congress Catalog Card Number: 2016955796

ISBN: 9781464205590 Trade Paperback

Poisoned Pen Press
4014 N. Goldwater Boulevard, #201
Scottsdale, Arizona 85251
www.poisonedpenpress.com
info@poisonedpenpress.com

Printed in the United States of America

Acknowledgments

I raise a glass to Barbara Peters and Robert Rosenfeld, editor and publisher of Poisoned Pen Press, their staff, and to the "posse," the authors at PPP who provide so much support.

I celebrate my agent, Kimberly Cameron of Kimberly Cameron Associates, every day.

Deepest gratitude to the women who offered me a home away from home: Shannon Gilligan (Vermont), Colette Buret (Paris), and Nancy Ebersberg (Burgundy).

In the U.S., Courtney Jenkins edited the early drafts, and Linda Tyler was my computer teacher. Kevin van Schaick taught me about guns. Heidi Gardner is my "girl on the red Vespa," and Barbara Ensrud (b-e wine.com) and Honora Horan of HH Communications in New York were great connectors.

My children, Luke and Ramsey Brown, are a constant source of inspiration, courage, and love.

My French team went beyond all expectations. *Remercier vivement* to food and wine expert, Meg Bortin (www.everyday-frenchchef.com), and to winemakers Jean-Marie Chaland of Domaine des Chazelles, and his wife, Evelina; Esther Prunier of Domaine Michel Prunier et fille; and Marc Jessiaume of Domaine Chanzy. Tom Kevill-Davies was an entertaining and knowledgeable host in Auxey-Duresses.

A highlight of my stay in Beaune was a private wine-tasting with Robert Drouhin of Maison Joseph Drouhin, and Ursula

Bouchard, empress of Beaune. Valerie Drouhin was a gracious host. I am also grateful to French friends Simon Buret, Astrid Latapie, George Guthrie, and Jo Ann Landsman.

For my granddaughter,
Camille Aurora Katharine Brown

"Those cries rose from among the twisted roots
through which the spirit of the damned
were slinking to hide from us...."
—*Dante Alighieu*

Chapter One

As the plane began its descent into Paris, Max Maguire peered down through the frothy clouds hovering over the city and, catching a glimpse of the Eiffel Tower, felt a frisson of excitement. Her mother, Juliette, seated in the aisle seat, dozed with her head against her husband's shoulder. Hank sat scrunched in the middle, reading a book on Juliette's tablet. The family was on their way to meet up with Juliette's mother at her summer house in Burgundy. Mid-October was not considered an ideal time to visit; it could get quite cold and many of the second homes weren't equipped for winter, but so far it had been unseasonably warm, and the prediction was that it would continue.

It had been Max's dream, after meeting her maternal grandmother the year before, to spend time with her in Burgundy, where her mother had spent her summers growing up. Hank, who had just retired from the NYPD with too many accolades to count, had been disgruntled about the trip. "I cut off my roots a long time ago," had been his response when Max had first brought up the subject of reconnecting with her mother's family. "Besides," he had said, "her parents were rotten to her when she married me. They disowned her, for Christ's sake." Juliette had taken Max's side, telling Hank that she and Max would go without him. She added that just because they had lost their roots didn't mean Max had to lose hers. He'd laughed at that and said, "Neither of you are fooling me. Olivier Chaumont will be in Burgundy with his family, and has invited Max to visit."

Max closed her eyes, aware of the sensation of being in a time machine, rushing toward her future at five hundred miles an hour. In an hour she was going to be in Olivier's arms again. He had postponed his vacation in order to have a month with her in Burgundy, and if she were being honest with herself, which she rarely was, she was hoping he would propose.

They had met two years before at a wedding in Champagne, where the aunt of the bride was murdered. And last year they were thrown together again when an American wine critic, whom Max was hired to guard, was murdered. It was then that Max knew she wanted to commit to the man who everyone agreed was essentially her opposite—that is, if he proposed. The six-month separation had felt like an eternity at times, and mercurial at others. At thirty-two, Max felt ever more aware of what a trickster time could be.

Although Olivier had responded succinctly and lovingly to her texts and e-mails, it was his long, handwritten letters that convinced her of his devotion. Until then, she had had no idea of the power of language to sweep one into a state of longing or love very far removed from the stress-inducing, staccato beat of a text pinging in on her cell phone.

Max's first attempts at responding in kind to Olivier were frustrating. She wrote about her latest arrests, and told him about winning a jiu-jitsu competition. But how to write about her feelings? Eventually she stopped shaking her foot and hopping up for a cup of tea or snack every few seconds and held still, pen in hand, until something came. In her last letter, written two weeks ago, she had responded that she could not imagine her life without him, and that she counted the days and hours until they were together. He'll think I'm on crack, she had thought, after rereading it. Frustrated, she texted him: no time to write. see you soon.

Hank interrupted her thoughts. "I hate these gadgets," he said. Max asked him what the problem was. He complained that he couldn't bookmark a page on the Kindle, and Max showed him how. "What are you reading?" she asked.

"Your Ma thought I'd like this Bruno, Chief of Police, mystery series. She said he reminded her a little of me."

Max knew the series by Martin Walker set in the Périgord and smiled. "That's flattering. Bruno's a pretty romantic guy, though."

"And you think I'm not?" Hank turned off the Kindle.

"Let's just say it's not obvious. Burgundy might give you a new perspective. Good food and wine. Fire in the fireplace. Long walks."

"I thought we were supposed to be focusing on *your* romance."

"Funny."

They fastened their seat belts and prepared for landing. She felt certain Olivier had been on the verge of proposing in New York when they were summoned to the airport to track down a serial killer. He had come to the point of reaching into his pocket, but was he pulling out a ring or a handkerchief? After the case closed, by chance they found themselves opening a bottle of a fabulous wine, a 1945 Mouton Rothschild, a perfect moment to propose, but the ring never emerged. Now she had these handwritten love letters with a few lines suggesting a future together.

The plane gently bumped the runway. Hank said, "You know, I gave Olivier a lecture last year about patience not always being a great virtue, like everybody thinks. If I had been patient with your Ma we wouldn't be in this plane right now."

"Oh, God, Dad. Why tell me now? He obviously didn't grasp the meaning since there was no hint of a proposal six months ago when he came to visit."

"He got the meaning, alright. My hunch is he got cold feet."

The plane came to a halt. Juliette leaned over and said to Max, "Your feet are cold?"

Hank barked a laugh, and Max turned her face back to the window.

Chapter Two

Olivier Chaumont stood in the Gare de Lyon in Paris with his assistant, Abdel Zeroual. They had driven together to Paris from Bordeaux a few days before, and now Abdel was on his way to Lyon. If all went as planned, Abdel would be transferred to Paris to continue as Olivier's assistant after his final interview with the Police Nationale. Abdel's grandmother, who arrived in France after the Algerian war ended in 1962, had served as both housemaid and nanny to the Chaumont family. Once Olivier became a *juge d'instruction*, or investigating magistrate, one of the youngest ever to have achieved such status, she decided to accept his offer to work for him in Bordeaux. Olivier had become a mentor to the boy and was at least partly responsible for Abdel's decision to become a police officer. Olivier was aware that a few of his peers questioned how he managed to manipulate the powers-that-be in order to have Abdel as his assistant whenever he was transferred, but so far no one had officially complained.

Olivier looked around the station. "We have time. Let's have a coffee upstairs in Le Train Bleu."

"*D'accord.*" They walked up the flight of stairs, and entered the restaurant that had been built in 1900 for the World Exposition. It was like entering a palace with the vast ceiling covered with frescoes, ornate chandeliers, and paintings. "*Mon dieu*, what is this place?" Abdel said. The *garçon* led them down an aisle to a smaller room enclosed by a wall of windows, where people sat sipping drinks or coffee.

"It's amusing," Olivier said, "how tourists go to the Left Bank to sit where some of the great artists and writers hung out, but this restaurant was a haunt of Coco Chanel, Jean Cocteau, Colette, and Brigitte Bardot."

"I adore Bardot," Abdel said, "and don't give a shit about the rest."

Olivier laughed. He ordered *deux express* and turned to Abdel. "How long do you plan to spend with your cousin in Lyon?"

"Two weeks. He agreed to come to Paris to help me move into my new apartment."

"And where exactly is it?"

"The *neuf-trois*. Infested with immigrants." Olivier made note of the anger on Abdel's face, though he spoke calmly. "My apartment is near where some of the Paris attackers holed up waiting to commit murder last November."

"I wonder if you will be conflicted about your new potential job of arresting jihadists, or would-be jihadists."

"Monsieur, pardon, but I consider your comment racist. I have never had a problem arresting criminals, and they are criminals."

Olivier was taken aback.

Abdel didn't wait for a response. "The term jihad has been hijacked by the media as a blanket term for terrorists. When in fact the word refers to one's personal struggles, be that with one's own fears, or with a flat tire."

Olivier realized they were dealing with a different vocabulary in these troubled times. A different reality, too. France was under siege, which was why he had applied to work with fellow investigative magistrate Jean-Louis Bruguière, who had handled some of France's most famous terrorism cases. The decision had come after the attacks on the offices of the satirical magazine *Charlie Hebdo* in January of 2015. The final death toll was fourteen people. He had marched in the streets with his fellow citizens, which was a first. But even that paled when over one hundred young people were murdered in the Paris attacks in November. A few weeks ago he was accepted as an antiterrorist magistrate, and from then on it all felt like a blur. Depression had been offset by action, but what had been put aside was his personal life.

"I'm not convinced, Abdel, as I have been under the impression that the murderers call themselves jihadists. And when I use the term, I'm not referring to Muslims."

"I admit to being sensitive on the subject."

Their attention was drawn temporarily to an elegant woman who had stood up to slide her arms into her coat. Olivier said, "I think when France created the law in 1996 against "*association de malfaiteurs en relation avec une entreprise terroriste*—establishing guilt by association—it was a mistake."

"I agree. Proof was not always established when young suspects were arrested. They were put in prison for participating in a group intent on creating an act of terrorism. This crime carried a maximum sentence of ten years. Many became radicalized in prison, served their time, and are now free. They will seek revenge."

"It's interesting to me how they seem to have no strategy."

Abdel leaned forward. "What few understand is that Sunni jihadists—and okay, we will use that term—don't reason like the French. Western terrorists would have an objective, acquire the means, and only after they were organized around their goal would they take action. For these terrorists the target is often chosen very late in the mission."

"Almost impulsively, right? They were clever to strike in several places at once during the Paris attacks." Olivier glanced at his watch. "Time for us to go down to the train." He beckoned to the waiter. "Did you read that they want to build a glass wall about the Tour l'Eiffel? As if that's going to solve anything!"

Abdel grinned. "The politicians want to protect the tourists. Maybe they'll hire immigrants to build the wall."

Olivier ignored the sarcasm, but it reminded him to be diligent that no wall be allowed between him and Abdel. He turned to his assistant as they walked toward the train. "The cousin you're visiting in Lyon? He's a mechanic, right?"

"Yes. And I'm going because family rumor has it that he is on opioids. My grandmother wants me to check."

"I hope that's not the case. Drug use has reached epidemic status in the U.S. We mustn't let that happen here."

"I did some research. Abuse in Europe is highest among those in a low socioeconomic status, which automatically puts the problem on the back burner. It was declared a major public health issue in 2015. The focus today is on twenty thousand general practitioners prescribing buprenorphine to treat the opioid-dependence cases, and now that's an entry drug for many."

"It makes me think of a sci-fi film. Entire populations on drugs. It doesn't sound as if you'll have much of a vacation."

"On a positive note, I get to see Max and meet her famous father." They stood in line, waiting for the signal to board. "Which reminds me, what does she think of your new position with the counterterrorist office?"

"I didn't include her in the decision. When I mentioned my interest six months ago, she was concerned that it would activate my depression gene. She hasn't forgotten that awful spell I went through in Champagne."

"You wouldn't be alone today. Everyone I know is depressed."

"I promised her that Burgundy is the place that restores my soul. It will be okay."

"You are always better around Max, I've noticed."

Uh-oh, thought Olivier. He knew where the conversation was headed. "No comment."

Abdel smiled. "Allow me to pass along something my grandmother told me. She said there is a small window of time when everything will work perfectly and we intuitively know when that is. Many ignore the open window, and when it slams shut, regret often follows."

"Hank Maguire told me that patience is not a virtue. I think he was encouraging me to propose."

Abdel laughed. "So propose."

Abdel vanished into the crowd before Olivier could respond.

Olivier drove to Charles de Gaulle Airport. He hadn't seen Max in six months when he had gone to New York for a brief visit. Marriage had not come up, though he still had the ring he had bought at Cartier's for her when they were solving the Bordeaux counterfeiting ring. Twice he had come close. The pursuit of a serial killer had interrupted his first attempt, and the second time he was drinking the finest wine imaginable, a 1945 Mouton Rothschild, which had overshadowed the intention to propose. In other words, he had lost his nerve.

He and Max were in almost constant touch daily through texting, the addictive tendencies of which he loathed. Max's humor in short snappy sentences had won him over, though he realized early on that he didn't have her skill. He sent letters instead, and though she teased him about it, after a few weeks he received a five-page letter from her, written in large letters with many words crossed out and affectionate epithets interspersed throughout. They had also attempted FaceTime, which he thought made her features look slightly distorted. He didn't think he came across well, either, speaking louder than usual, and self-conscious about being on camera.

Her last text had been preemptory, which made him wonder if she might be experiencing the same uncertainty he was. As they had only spent time together solving murders, he was interested to see how they would be together, without the adrenaline flowing. What better place than Burgundy, where, other than a few thefts, crime didn't exist? She liked to play Scrabble, and he had picked up the French version. She had expressed her intention of rereading *War and Peace*—the greatest novel ever written in Olivier's mind. As far as he knew, her other hobbies were action-packed. She participated in jiu-jitsu competitions and went on long runs through Central Park. She had begun taking salsa dancing lessons with her new police partner, Carlos, and showed Olivier the latest moves on FaceTime. Another favorite activity was drinking beer with her buddies at a bar on Amsterdam Avenue, evidence of which arrived regularly in the form of selfies.

He used his ID to park in an illegal zone, and rushed five minutes late in to the arrivals section of the airport. Max's tall silhouette filled the doorway leading from customs; pausing to scan the room, then striding with long legs to him, a big smile on her face. She wrapped her arms around him, and squeezed him in a bear hug, after which she bestowed kisses on each cheek, and then his lips were on hers. Max was back. All doubts dispelled in one breathtaking moment.

Chapter Three

Isabelle Limousin de Laval stood in the doorway of her stately home in the village of Auxey-Duresses, ten miles from the ancient walled town of Beaune, the wine capital of Burgundy. Tall and regal, she kept her penetrating blue eyes fixed on the passengers who emerged from the car. Max was the first out; she ran to her grandmother and merged the French and American traditions of exchanging kisses on each cheek, then enveloped her in a warm embrace.

"Can you believe we really pulled this off?" she asked her grandmother in French, but her grandmother's attention was riveted on her daughter, who was walking up the sidewalk.

"You look well, Maman," Juliette said, exchanging cheek-to-cheek kisses with her mother as though they had seen each other the week before, when it had actually been two years, and a thirty-year lapse before that.

Max saw her grandmother's chin tremble, the only display of emotion. "I am glad you have come home, Juliette."

They turned at the sound of Hank swearing. He had already lifted two suitcases from the trunk of the car, and was struggling with a third. Olivier, who was waiting to greet Madame Laval, rushed to help him.

"Do you think the two of them can manage?" Isabelle asked in French, and Max looked to see if she was being sarcastic, and saw that she was. "Come inside," Isabelle said to Max and

Juliette. "Hank will surely find other things to do to prolong meeting up with his old nemesis."

"Maman!" Juliette chastised her mother. "We've just arrived and already…"

Isabelle turned before Juliette could finish her sentence, and mother and daughter followed. The house was hundreds of years old, with *pigeonniers*, or dovecotes, on either side of the open gallery along the front of the house, and a beautiful stone staircase leading to the front hall. The entrance hall was vast, with stone steps elegantly winding up to the first floor. "Your childhood room awaits you," Isabelle said to Juliette.

The heavy, carved wooden front door opened and Hank and Olivier entered. Max thought this might be the first time she had ever seen her father look intimidated. He shook Isabelle's hand, and said *"Bonjour, Madame."* Max imagined them as hawk and crow as they stood there assessing each other.

"Bienvenu," Isabelle said coolly. "Juliette will show you where to take the suitcases." Her gaze turned to Olivier. "Lunch will be in one hour. I do hope you are staying. Now if you'll excuse me, I must see to preparations." She vanished through a door Max had not noticed.

"She hasn't changed in thirty years," Hank said. "She must be at least seventy-five now, right?"

Juliette smiled, "Seventy-six. The stroke two years ago took a toll on her."

"You kiddin' me?" Hank said. "I meant her attitude hasn't changed."

"Neither has yours," his wife said.

Olivier picked up Max's suitcase and asked "Where to?" Juliette pointed upstairs to the guest room. Max took the stairs two at a time. "I feel like I'm in a fairy tale," she said when they entered her room.

"Fairy tales are horror stories," Olivier said. "At least the ones I know. They are how I learned about evil."

"And all that evil led you to become an examining magistrate, right? You needed to set the world aright."

"That's the short version."

She laughed.

They looked around at the high-ceilinged room with windows overlooking the undulating fields of vineyards of the famous *Côte-de-Beaune*. Max rushed to the window to look out, suddenly feeling self-conscious. He had been formal since their arrival. After dropping their bags at the apartment the day before, Olivier had driven them around the city, stopping for a light lunch in a café near the Eiffel Tower. Hank told Olivier he had been following the news and wished he could have been there to take down some of the attackers in November. From there they spoke of the American soldiers and friends who had stopped a terrorist from blowing up the train from Amsterdam to Paris. Olivier had nodded, but said very little.

After Juliette and Hank went off on their own to see Juliette's sister, Max and Olivier strolled along the Seine. He had looked thrilled to see her at the airport, but she hadn't broken through his reserve. He had taken her to dinner at one of his favorite restaurants in the Sixth Arrondissement—Bouillon Racine, a brasserie built in 1905, which today boasts a fabulous interior of engraved mirrors and beautiful walls. The waiter rushed to greet them when he saw Olivier. "You will only find Parisians here," Olivier had said. He gave a sardonic laugh. "Actually, you will only see Parisians in the city these days."

She had tried to bring up the attacks again, and he had said, "Let's wait on that discussion. I'm happy just to sit here and look at you."

After dinner they drove to the hotel and met her parents for a nightcap. He apologized after an hour and said he would be off. She had gone for a run early the next morning, and then Olivier arrived to drive them to Burgundy.

"Let's drive up to the village of Saint-Romain," Olivier said, and soon they were on a road that Max would describe as a bicycle path leading up, up to a cluster of beautiful stone houses. Hardly anyone was about. Olivier parked the car, and they ventured down a path that led to a park overlooking a valley in the distance.

The sun shone through the clouds, casting the valley into a mirage of light and shadow. Max stood transfixed. "It's weird, Olivier. I am standing here looking over a magnificent corner of France, and instead of being happy, I feel regret that I'm such a stranger to it."

"I think I understand that."

"I also feel like I'm a stranger to you. We've been apart too long, and I regret that, too."

He reached for her hand. "I'm sorry if I seem tenuous."

"Tenuous, I can handle. Aloof, I can't." She wanted to add that depression was on her list of things she couldn't handle, too, but didn't. Instead she said, "You're probably in hangover mode from the attacks in November. Hank says it took five years for New York City to return to normalcy after 9/11."

"They predict there is more to come. If not here, then Belgium or Germany. Hangover is a good word for how many of us are feeling. And on that note, let's go sip a glass of white wine." He pulled her to him and kissed her on the lips. Max's heart raced as she reminded herself that Olivier moved at a snail's pace compared to her. He drove her around to see the countryside covered with vineyards, though the vines wouldn't be lush until summer. "I'd like to work in the vineyards one day during the harvest," she said.

"I'm glad I had the opportunity when I was younger. The work is backbreaking, but the rewards far outweigh the pain. The dinners alone make it an unforgettable experience." They stopped at a little café and sipped white wine. Their conversation veered from Hank's retirement to Olivier's brother's success in Australia. Nothing to arouse emotions.

As they drove into Isabelle's driveway, they saw Juliette sitting on the low stone wall in front of the house, looking out onto the rolling hills. "I feel like I am completely back in my childhood," she said, "as though the past forty years never happened. I am walking with my father across that field to visit Isabelle's friend, Anne, and her husband, Gervais. It was an idyllic time."

A bell sounded and Juliette joined them on their trek to the house, where a round table was set in an alcove off the kitchen. A bottle of Puligny-Montrachet Le Caillevet 1er cru, had been opened, and was waiting to be poured. Juliette studied the label, and explained to Max that here the labeling was quite different from Bordeaux and other areas. Each label is a *petite histoire*, she said, and Max could appreciate the analogy, noticing the amount of printing on the label. "The village wines are allowed to take the names of the famous wineries, and so it's important to understand the differences."

Olivier tasted, "Fresh. A good nose of summer flowers. Excellent."

Juliette sipped. "I love tasting the minerals from the soil. It sets our chardonnays apart."

Jeannette brought a dish of *feuilleté d'escargots à l'oseille,* snails in a puff pastry with a creamed herb sauce, to the table. Hank said he didn't know when he had tasted anything so delicious, and Isabelle looked pleased. The conversation was desultory, as they settled in, catching up on each other's news. Juliette mentioned that she had been making a list of places they had to visit, and people, too. Olivier invited them to a dinner at his parents' house, an hour south, in the village of Viré, the date to be announced once they were settled.

The next dish to arrive was *poulet à la moutarde,* and Juliette said that it had been her favorite dish when she was a child. Isabelle's housemaid, Jeannette, brought in a bottle of red wine to accompany it. "It's a local wine made by the Prunier family," Isabelle said. "The daughter, Estelle, has taken over and is doing a magnificent job."

Olivier asked Hank how he was enjoying retirement, and Hank admitted he wasn't used to it yet. "I've been volunteering a bit in a couple of the public schools where Juliette is teaching French."

"He teaches these middle school children that crime doesn't pay," Juliette said, "and they listen to him."

Hank chuckled. "They're so relieved to be out of French class they'll believe anything I say." Turning to Isabelle, he said,

"I read in a magazine about the guy who tried to poison the famous Romanée Conti vineyard for extortion purposes in 2009. What a scandal."

"An entire book was written about it," Juliette said. "By an American, of course."

Isabelle shrugged. "Most people here don't even know about it. Only two grapevines were damaged. The extortionist was a man who stewed in prison after bungling a house robbery and decided to try extorting money from a famous *domaine*, but was picked up and put back in prison."

"He hanged himself in his cell in 2010," Olivier said. "Case closed permanently." He smiled, "Surely it's been made into a movie in the U.S. by now?"

They laughed. Isabelle said, "I'm certain the highly esteemed owner, Aubert de Villaine, would be happy for the story to disappear. He would be much happier to put the focus on the *climats*, or vineyards here, being listed as a UNESCO World Heritage Site."

"What is it about his wine that deserves such attention?" Max asked.

Olivier said, "The British wine critic, Clive Coates, said it best: It's the purest, most aristocratic, most intense example of the pinot noir grape, and I agree. You would be fortunate to get a vintage bottle for ten thousand dollars."

"Supply and demand," Hank said. "Everybody wants what they can't have."

"Thieves have been breaking into a few cellars, stealing certain bottles," Isabelle said. "Because the bottles are numbered and can be traced, the theory is that unscrupulous collectors will go to any length to get a certain rare bottle."

"It can't be anything like the scale of thefts and counterfeiting that we uncovered in Bordeaux," Max said.

"Oh, no, nothing like that," her grandmother agreed.

Olivier said, "Some of the finest vineyards produce no more than fifty cases, as opposed to the four thousand cases a famous winery in Bordeaux makes."

"And the grapes that grew a few meters away will bring in half of that," Isabelle said. "Because they are not designated *grand cru* or *premier cru*, the income is much less for the producer."

"That must create some fights," Hank said.

"Most people accept the system that was put in place in the 1930s," Isabelle said. "Though some work hard to change their appellation. My good friend Anne's son-in-law should have a better rating for his wines, but he is a rebel and doesn't adhere to the rules of the ruling body, the AOC. They dictate how many plants you can have, and how far apart they have to be, for example. They have existed for as long as I can remember, but not until recent years, when prices have skyrocketed, have they become like spies, checking to make sure no one produces one liter more than his allotment. It's absurd."

"And this is the same woman who produces the most extraordinary chardonnay in the land?" Olivier asked.

Isabelle smiled. "One and the same. She has worked very hard to prove her father and brothers wrong about her, and happened to surpass them all with her skills."

Juliette said, "Wasn't there an old myth that women tainted the vineyards?"

Isabelle scoffed. "Not the vineyards, but the presence of a woman entering the room where the wine was fermenting could damage the wine. Women here in Burgundy are finally being recognized for their fine wines, but there are far fewer than there should be. With my few vines, I joined their organization called Femmes et Vins de Bourgogne. There are only forty-eight of us, and I barely produce a glass. But at least we can support each other." Lunch was drawing to a close when Hank said, "Juliette told me that Anne's daughter died."

Isabelle's face drooped. "Caroline died last year of breast cancer at age thirty-eight, leaving behind her husband, Jean-Claude, and a son, Luc. A tragedy. And now Anne is finding the time to fight with Jean-Claude because her daughter left him one hectare of *grand cru* land that her father had bequeathed to her."

"But the inheritance laws are quite specific as far as the children and the spouse are concerned," Olivier said. "Any property governed by French inheritance law cannot be disposed of by will. The two classes of heir who possess an inalienable right to a proportion of the property are the surviving descendants and, if there are none, to the surviving spouse."

Isabelle said, "Yes, and in this case, Luc inherits a share, which means Jean-Claude would need his agreement to sell or even rent out his house. But Jean-Claude can set up a special clause to deal with that. As for Anne and Jean-Claude, in the end you hope to have a good *notaire*, for the last word rests with them and their interpretation of the law, which can differ."

Max wanted to ask why her mother had not inherited from her father when he died, but knew this wasn't the time to ask. Isabelle suggested that everyone get some rest and said they could make plans after. "Dinner will be at nine," she said. Jeannette began clearing the table as they moved outside from the kitchen.

Isabelle approached Olivier. "Monsieur Chaumont," she said. "I wasn't going to bring this up, but Anne telephoned before lunch and I felt that I should speak to you."

"*Bien sûr*," he said. "Shall we go back inside?"

"*Non, non.* She accepted a young grape-picker, a girl from the U.S., who showed up on a beat-up red Vespa to help with the harvest last September. Anne, like many vineyard owners today, no longer hires pickers from other countries because of the bureaucratic demands, but she was so taken by this girl that she accepted her. Soon the girl was living with her, and the next thing we all knew, Anne had asked her to stay through the winter. Of course she is trying to replace her daughter by..."

Olivier tried to disguise his impatience over Isabelle not getting to the point. "And the problem?"

"The girl took off a few days ago, and hasn't returned. Jean-Claude saw her at a party with some unsavory people a couple of nights ago, and Anne is frantic."

Olivier didn't think it sounded out of the ordinary, and said so. He was met with a strong stare from Isabelle, indicating that she would not have brought the subject up if she agreed with his quick assessment, which led him to say, "There's nothing to say unless it is known that she left against her will. Why don't I stop by later and listen to what Madame Bré has to say about the missing girl, who, I assume, must have a *prénom*?" What he didn't add was that he relished the opportunity to meet the woman who made wine that turned the senses upside down.

"The girl's name is Lucy Kendrick. I've invited Anne to join us for dinner. You will be here, of course." She turned and walked up the slight incline to the house.

"What do you think?" Max asked him when her grandmother was out of hearing.

"What do I think? I think Burgundian women are formidable to the point of being intimidating. It is daunting to imagine sitting at table with those two *grandes dames!*"

Max laughed. "I meant the girl on the red Vespa."

"I'm sure it's nothing but the imagination of two women suffering from ennui."

"Speaking of boredom," Max said as she watched her father approach. "Hank doesn't know what to do with himself, and he's only been here a few hours."

"It's the country. One doesn't have to do anything."

Hank was upon them. "Your mother is settling for a nap. I'm going to drive to the café for a café."

"Don't expect anyone to speak English."

"I'll manage." They watched him walk across the lawn.

"I have to sleep," Max said.

"Good. I'll return for dinner." She gave him a light kiss, said *à toute*, and within half an hour she had sunk into a deep sleep. She awoke to the sound of her father's voice drifting up the stairs. It was dark outside. She propped herself up against a big pillow and listened. "An American girl is missing," he said. "A couple of guys were talking about it at the café."

"What did they say?" Isabelle asked.

"A guy who spoke English explained it to me when I asked. He said that she had created a bit of a sensation in the village because of her odd appearance. Dyed white or silver hair, pale skin, and blue eyes that make you feel singed when she looks at you. He picked grapes alongside her up in Chablis. He said she stayed the winter with the old lady on the hill, but rumor had it she had run off with an Arab in Lyon. The bar patrons speculated that something bad has happened to her."

Max climbed up out of her dreams and headed to the shower as a way of avoiding hearing any more of the story. Both of her trips to France, first to Champagne, then to Bordeaux, had ended up with her solving a murder case—in each case the murder of someone either she or Olivier knew. The last thing she wanted to think about was a girl gone missing.

Chapter Four

Olivier drove up the narrow, cobblestoned street leading to his mother's childhood home in Viré, a latecomer to the fame of other Burgundian villages. The drive brought on a rush of fond memories. He and his brother could run freely through the streets of the old village when they were children. A favorite path led up to the cemetery, overlooking the village and sometimes, far beyond, Mount Blanc was visible. Above the cemetery was another, mostly unused, road where they raced their bikes, veering off onto trails through the vineyards.

His parents had kept a car there, and the family traveled back and forth to Paris on weekends. His maternal grandparents were alive back then, and they sent their teenaged grandsons out to work in the vineyards during the harvest. It was intense labor, but both boys looked forward to spending a couple of weeks with a diverse group of people who came from all parts of the world. His brother became passionate about winemaking, and after graduating from the university, went to Australia to work, and ended up staying there.

Olivier passed Alain Milne's house and thought he might give him a call. Alain's father and his father before him had made a regional white wine. As the area was handed no appellation until a decade ago, the growers were just starting to catch up to the explosion of global wine culture that existed an hour north.

He and Alain had worked together in the vineyards, and stayed in touch until a few years ago. The last Olivier knew,

Alain had become director of one of the local co-ops, where wines were created from grapes sold to them by many farmers in the area. The majority of his yield were lovely white wines that held their own with the more famous whites from further north, but because the area had not become classified until the nineties, prices were still affordable. Viré, the cooperative, had the generic name "Mâcon-Village," but most of the wines they produced had the appellation Viré-Clessé, quite well-known now, with prices that were competitive, depending on the plot where the grapes were grown. Olivier had followed Domaine Chaland Viré-Clessé and the well-known producer Domaine Michel. He was looking forward to sipping a local wine tonight.

The late afternoon air was chilly. He entered the two-story house that had large-tiled floors and dark beams running across the high ceilings of the kitchen and salon, and immediately got the fire going in the kitchen stove, then went upstairs to prepare his room. He stood for a moment, allowing his eyes to adjust to the darkness, before opening the shutters to allow sunlight to flood the room. His earliest paintings, mostly landscapes, were on the walls. Several pieces of sculpture sat on top of a bookcase filled with hundreds of books. His parents had traveled extensively when he and his brother were adolescents, and picked up artifacts from various countries in Africa, which were displayed on additional shelves.

He returned to the salon and sat quietly, enjoying the solitude. The walls were adorned with old, framed family photographs and paintings that varied from oil paintings of ancestors to pastoral watercolors. He had pulled a photograph album from a shelf and sat down to peruse it when a knock at the door startled him. He answered it and was surprised to see Alain. "I was just thinking about you when I drove in," Olivier said, extending his hand. "*Comment ça va*?"

"You've stayed away too long, Olivier," Alain said. "Is your wife with you?"

"I divorced several years ago. And you?"

"Still married to Yvette. You remember her from high school." The image of a tawny-haired girl with a bossy attitude fluttered into Olivier's vision, then vanished. "Twenty years we've been together. Our son Roland is eighteen."

Olivier wondered how to recap his adult life, but didn't have to, as Alain continued talking. "The co-op keeps me busy. And with land prices near Beaune reaching two to four million euros a hectare, our land here in the south is becoming more appealing. I wish we could stay exactly as we are."

"Eh, *bon.* You are producing reds and whites?"

"Mostly whites. The same stuff I started out making."

Olivier led him to the kitchen, then disappeared into the cellar and brought out a bottle from the young neighbor who was achieving international success with his wine. "Let's sit," he said, motioning to the kitchen table. "I'm interested in the guy who made this wine. I knew his parents. He's married to a beautiful Polish woman...."

"Sure. Stéphane. He's younger than we are. You remember we picked for his parents a long time ago?" Alain smiled and took the glass offered him.

Olivier swished the liquid around in his mouth before swallowing. "*Pas mal,*" he said.

"You prefer Stéphane's to the co-op wine?"

"My parents must have purchased it," Olivier said. "It was in the cellar. But, yes, he's doing a good job."

"Stéphane is now producing fifty thousand bottles that are being exported to places like the U.S. and Germany. He thinks he's above the rest of us. I've stopped asking him to donate cases to our annual local wine festival. His dad used to give generously."

Olivier detected jealousy in Alain's voice. "Burgundy is about the independent, young winemakers these days, both men and women," he said. "I was just reading about that in a magazine. Even if they have no land, they want to be creative and purchase grapes in order to make a few unique cases. They share facilities."

Alain made a face. "It's the new Burgundy, alright. These are wealthy guys in the Beaune area who talk the Americans into investing in them. They do it all for the tourists now up in the Beaune region. The grapes must be handpicked. No machinery is to be used. No chemicals. And they try to dictate to the rest of us."

"And Roland? Is he among the new and upcoming *vignerons*?"

The silence that followed made Olivier assume that he had said something wrong.

"Nah, he likes hunting a lot more than working in the vineyards. And video games. No one can beat him."

"That's a world I know nothing about."

"You think I do? His mother has catered to his every whim. It's not like when we were growing up."

Olivier thought it sounded like Yvette had the upper hand in this family.

"You hope for the best, that's all I can say," Alain said. "Which reminds me, I hope your mother will continue to let me purchase the grapes from her vines."

Olivier pretended ignorance. He knew his mother had a contract with Alain, but that she was seriously considering Stéphane's request to purchase her grapes. He thought she had another year before their contract expired. "As you know, I am rarely here. I can put in a word, though."

Alain finished his glass. "I'll bring a couple of the co-op bottles over while you're here. You can compare."

Olivier wondered if his old friend had really just happened to stop by, or had he something on his mind. Alain sat stiffly, his hands clasped. Olivier didn't have to wait long. "I didn't just see your car in the driveway," Alain admitted. "I want to talk to you about something."

"Of course."

Alain stood and began to pace. "There was a girl who showed up here last fall on an old, red Vespa to pick grapes. She wanted to start in this area and then move up to Beaune, then go up to Chablis country in the far north corner of Burgundy. She had a way about her. She got Roland out in the fields, and next thing she was taking him here and there with her. He has an old scooter, and they would take off."

Olivier felt a slight surge of curiosity. "What do you mean, a way about her?"

"Weird silver hair and eyes blue as a Burgundy sky." He glanced at Olivier. "Yvette never allowed girls to pick here, and she was mad at me for saying yes to Lucy. I didn't have to send her away because she went on her own. I heard she moved in with Madame Anne Bré for the winter. Roland went up often to hang out with her. But now he tells me she's vanished into thin air."

"I heard the same story from friends in Auxey-Duresses. Madame Bré is looking for her, too."

"She was a damn good picker. Skinny, but all muscle." Now it was Alain's turn to shrug. "Maybe Madame Bré fell under her spell the way Roland did. He hasn't shown up for a couple of nights, and my hunch is he's looking for her. I have a tiny parcel of land up there, and I hunt there with her son-in-law. I may go and see what's going on."

• • ● • •

The only way to combat the illogical, Olivier thought, *is to focus on the logical.* "She's gone," he said. "And there is no proof that there is anything to worry about. She isn't a child, right?"

"She told me she was twenty-one, but I checked her passport and she's seventeen. Turning eighteen sometime in November."

"She allowed you to see it?"

He paused, "She left it lying around and Yvette found it. It's natural to have a look, right?" He sipped the last of his wine. "I decided when I saw your car that you might be able to help, now that you are a powerful man in Paris. You were in all the papers when you broke open the counterfeit ring in Bordeaux."

Olivier was in a congenial mood. "I am helpless, though, when it comes to teenagers. As you may recall, I didn't understand them when I was one."

The clock struck eight and Olivier realized he just had time to drive back to the Beaune area for dinner at Max's grandmother's. "I'm sorry, Alain, but I must leave soon. Your son is eighteen, correct? France has ended all missing persons searches for adults, you know. As for the girl, I'd have to check."

"I guess people have to show up dead in order to be counted as missing."

Olivier didn't think he was joking.

"Yvette blames everything on the girl. Roland's a farm boy, and easily led astray. Tends to follow the wrong crowd."

" But you see her as a positive influence. Love is at its worst and it's best when a young man is eighteen, don't you agree? My first time falling in love I recall as torture."

Alain chuckled. "I thought I'd die if I couldn't have Yvette. I'm lucky she's stuck with me."

Olivier wondered what it would have been like had his first love, Sophie, stuck with him. They were eighteen and he had fallen ill for a month after she left him for somebody else. Until Max, he had not felt lucky in love at all. His wife had left him for a horse-trainer and then his model girlfriend, Véronique, turned out to be an addict, and would have ruined his career if she could have. He saw her photo splashed across various gossip columns all the time, and each time felt relief. She had tried to come between Max and him, but he had managed to dodge that bomb.

"I'm going to hunt *sanglier* up north over the weekend," Alain said. "The wild boar are becoming a nuisance, showing up in neighborhoods and eating the ripe grapes from vineyards. They need to be thinned out. If I go up, I'll see if you can come along. Remember when we used to hunt?"

Olivier remembered all too well the sight of the boar as it tore through the field chased by dogs, then was shot and flew into the air, and landed beside him with an impact that shook the ground. He recalled telling his father that seeing the boar brought down was more like a car crash than anything having to do with nature. "Who will you be hunting with?" he asked.

"Jean-Claude Villemaire. Madame Bré's son-in-law."

Olivier smiled. "I am soon to be engaged to an American woman who is half-French and her grandmother and Anne Bré are good friends."

"An American, eh? You get around, Olivier. I just remembered, the missing girl babysat for Jean-Claude. He worried that she was a gold-digger."

Ah, so there is a gossip mill, Olivier thought.

Alain continued speaking, and it struck Olivier that his childhood friend was lonely. "He thinks she's preying on his mother-in-law after learning that her daughter had died. But Madame insists the girl has an extraordinary nose for wine, and should be trained."

This sounds like a fable, thought Olivier. A stranger enters a village, creates minor chaos, and a fascinated curiosity develops among the townspeople. "She's a teenager who sounds a bit lost. Not very different from your son, perhaps."

Alain stood and pulled a business card from his pocket. "Here's my mobile number if you want to hunt. They don't allow women in the hunt club, but your fiancée could help with the food. Yvette will be in charge. She feels like it's her God-given responsibility to look after Jean-Claude since his wife passed."

An uncomfortable silence followed, as Olivier once again couldn't think how to respond. The two men said good-bye.

Olivier's phone rang and he picked up quickly when he saw it was Abdel. "*Ça va*?"

"*Oui.* I am with my cousin in Lyon."

"Oui?"

"It's probably nothing. My cousin sold a Vespa, back in early September, to a friendly American girl who chatted him up while he was doing the paperwork. He said she told him she needed the Vespa to travel at sonic speed, as she was dodging a man who might be intending to murder her."

Olivier couldn't believe his ears. "Red Vespa? Silver hair?"

"Ring in her nose. *Oui.*" Pause. "You know her?"

"She is everywhere. Like the cold fog that descends and stays on our skin here in Burgundy. Only, at the moment, the general opinion is that she has disappeared."

"That's odd. She stopped in yesterday at my cousin's to have something minor fixed on the Vespa. She told my cousin that she has been living in Auxey-Duresses, but when she heard her uncle had learned her address, she took off. He told her he was glad she had not been murdered, and she laughed and said, 'it's always a good day when you're not murdered.'"

Olivier wondered why it seemed everyone was objectifying the people in their lives. Even Abdel was speaking of "the girl" and "my cousin." "What's your cousin's name, Abdel?"

"Ali. The girl is Lucy."

Olivier felt impatient. By now he was driving through the elegant village of Meursault next to Auxey-Duresses. "An old friend of mine from Viré stopped by earlier and said his son is a Lucy follower, and he's going up to see if he can find them. The woman she was staying with in Auxey-Duresses wants to declare her missing."

"Ali will be upset to hear this."

"How is he?"

"He's a pain in the ass. Swears he's not on opioids, but has friends who are. I'm keeping a close eye on him."

"What about Lucy? Any drug use there that you know of?"

"Ali wouldn't tell me if she was."

"She's too young to be roaming all over creation. If she's not back in Auxey by tomorrow, let's pick her up and see what's going on."

"*D'accord.*" They said good-bye, and Olivier realized that his efforts to learn what was going on with the girl were time-consuming, and done to appease two women who suddenly seemed to have a lot of control over him.

Chapter Five

Max looked up as Olivier entered the salon where she was enjoying an *apéritif* with her family. "You look beautiful," he said softly in her ear as he kissed her cheek, then greeted everyone else. She was wearing a one-piece black jumpsuit. Simple and elegant. A fire was going in the fireplace. Hank and Juliette sipped a kir royal, a champagne and cassis combination. Isabelle greeted Olivier warmly, and Max knew from a remark she had made that she, like everyone else, was expecting Olivier to propose. She watched as her grandmother introduced him to her friend Anne Bré, who stood all of five feet, and was dressed in black pants and sweater, and black high-heeled boots. Her light brown hair was pulled back in a ponytail, and the bangs that grazed her eyebrows, along with the strength and vitality radiating from her, gave her a gamine-like quality. *Exactly how I want to present at sixty-five*, Max thought, *though at five-ten I'm hardly the gamine type.*

Anne was curious about Olivier's opinion about a certain Bordeaux wine and he gave a lengthy explanation. "Will you be remaining in Bordeaux?" she then asked Olivier, who hesitated a second before saying, "No. I will be joining the antiterrorism magistrates in Paris."

So that's what's going on, Max thought, *but why didn't he tell me?* The answer felt obvious to her: he had decided to carry on without her. She felt a slump within.

"The defense attorneys are publicly criticizing the judges for removing the rights of suspected terrorists," Madame Bré said. "It will be a tough job."

"I'm prepared for the criticism. Change is underway, and I want to be a part of it. Sixty-seven percent of our citizens have lost faith in the government's ability to protect them."

"And Max," Anne said, "where are you in all this?"

"I'm in New York City, just promoted to sergeant."

"Congratulations, Max," Olivier said. "I didn't know."

"Nor did I know of your dramatic change."

Isabelle excused herself and disappeared into the kitchen, followed by Juliette and Hank. Anne turned to Max, "The arrival of her family has given your grandmother new purpose."

Max sighed. "I watch my mother with my grandmother, and feel sad that they missed so much of each other's lives."

"Your grandfather, Frédéric, was the type who could never admit when he was wrong. Or apologize. In my mind it was his only character defect. But it prevented him from reuniting with his daughter, or knowing his grandchildren, which is a tragedy. Isabelle has deep regrets, but she will never admit them."

"You were a friend of my grandfather's?" she asked Madame Bré.

"Of course. We have lived in this village for many years. Frédéric was from a very old family here, an aristocratic family who ended up losing their vineyards to the inheritance laws that were created by Napoleon after the Revolution. The land gets divided up, which divides families, and the taxes, on top of all that, are prohibitive. This was the case with my son-in-law, Jean-Claude. In the end, eighty winemakers were sharing fifty hectares of vines."

Max knew from her grandmother that Anne herself had been in a family squabble, and was finally ousted from the board of her family's company. She then started her own vineyard, eventually making some of the most famous wines in the world.

Isabelle called them to the table, and Anne left them to enter the kitchen. Olivier, who had sat listening, said, "I wasn't sure that I would be accepted. And when I mentioned it to you after the attacks in Paris, you brought up my old nemesis, depression."

"And so you decided not to say anything?"

"I thought it best if we talked about this in person."

"What? Your depression? Your new job?"

Max knew everyone was waiting at the table. She strolled into the dining room ahead of Olivier, and sat. Madame Bré's *grand cru* wine was on the table, so distinguished that it required only Domaine Bré to appear on the label. Olivier took the seat beside her. A sideward glance told her that he was unhappy.

"I'll be interested to hear your opinion of my wine," Anne said to Hank, who finished his beer and said he'd be happy to try it. "I never ask the opinions of the oenophiles," she said. "They're always asking me about the pH balance. It's ridiculous." She turned to Olivier, "Will you do the honor of pouring?"

Max could see that he was only too happy to oblige. Hank sipped and said, "It's got some zip."

"Just what I wanted to hear," Anne said, and they all laughed. "What you are doing really, Monsieur, when you sip this," she said, "is tasting the *terroir*, a word that was invented here in France. We can learn to identify a wine from the soil in which it was grown. The vines may cover less than a hectare…"

"That's two and a half acres," Juliette interjected.

"But that wine will taste differently from the wine produced one hundred yards away."

Hank leaned forward. "But the winemaker, meaning you, adds your essence to the *terroir*, right? It's your method of making the wine that helps to create its fame."

"My wine contains everything I have learned since I was a child…my philosophy, if you will, and in that sense you are correct. It begins with the harvest, and choosing which day to pick, which grapes are selected, then fermentation happens, all carefully monitored on a daily basis. We never really know the results of all this until we sip the wine." She paused. "There is a French expression that compares winemaking to a symphony, in which case the *terroir* is the composer or composition, and the conductor is the *vigneron.*"

"And you'll be passing this philosophy along, I hope," Hank said.

"My daughter, who had a keen interest in wine, passed away last year," she said. "There is a young girl who came to me this year as a laborer, who has a fantastic nose, meaning she is a natural. But…" her voice drifted off.

"I'm sorry to hear about your daughter," Hank said. "I know what it's like to lose a kid." He paused, "I talked to a Brit earlier today who sings the traveling girl's praises. Her name is Lucy, right?"

"Oh, I know the B&B guy. Tim Lowell. I was planning to call to see if he knows Lucy's whereabouts. She's with him every opportunity she has." She sipped her wine. "I have to say, this isn't bad."

"It's superb," Olivier said.

Max said, not wanting to get off-topic, "Don't take this the wrong way, but is this Lucy a seductive type?"

Madame Bré smiled. "Not at all, in the traditional sense. I would say she is androgynous. But she has great *élan. Esprit de corps.*"

Isabelle said, "I saw quite a lot of her over the winter. It's not fair what we are doing to her reputation. She has spunk, and a certain charisma, but she is a normal girl, who—to my mind—has a difficult path to navigate. She glanced at Anne and continued, "Her mother, now dead, convinced her that her biological father is here, which is why she came to Burgundy, and she lives in constant fear that her step-uncle is coming to claim her."

Everyone shifted their attention to Anne. "She adored her mother, but I think she was pretty much on her own as a child. She's like a vine that veers off in the wrong direction, following the light. It will wither if the roots are not deeply set." She looked at the faces around the table. "I'm with friends, I know, and so will speak freely. I feel Lucy was sent here by my daughter."

Everyone grew stone-still.

"It sounds strange, I know, but I was at such a low point after Caroline's death, I really didn't want to go on, and this girl arrived at my door, radiating vitality or strength, I'm not sure which, and I thought, 'She is part of my destiny.'"

Juliette, who had been quiet, said, "I believe you. We don't always know the reason for someone having such an effect on us, but when it happens we must pay attention. I, too, receive messages from my son Frédéric."

Max had never heard her mother speak in this manner, although she, too, was sure her brother had been with her time and again, as when she had nearly lost her life during the Bordeaux case.

The slightly awkward silence was broken by Anne, who smiled and said, "That makes me feel ever so much better, just to have shared that."

Max knew Hank was keen on bringing the subject back to grounded reality when he said, "The fact is, the girl is elusive as hell, and maybe running from someone. Somebody needs to have a talk with her and find out what's going on and stop pretending she's some wraith."

Anne looked to Olivier. "We have already instructed Olivier to find her."

He nodded, wanting to end the subject, Max knew. She could see from his clenched jaw that he did not like the idea of being instructed, but he was also too civil to be rude. "She was seen a couple of days ago in Lyon."

"Well, then, why is everyone in such a tizzy?" Isabelle asked. "Anne, are you certain she didn't tell you where she was off to, and you forgot?"

It was obvious that Anne was offended. "Absolutely positive, Isabelle."

Max looked over and saw her father's lopsided grin, and winked at him.

The first course arrived, a *tarte a l'epoisses*, or cheese tart made with epoisse, one of the great Burgundy cheeses. Juliette smiled at her daughter's exaggerated expression of bliss upon her first sampling of the tart.

Olivier said that he had been invited by Alain to hunt wild boar over the weekend and wondered if Hank wanted to go.

"I'm in."

"But you don't hunt," Juliette said.

"I can walk across a field. I can shoot a gun. What else is there to know?" Everyone laughed.

"I'd like to try," Max said.

"They have a women's hunt club," said Olivier, wishing he could avoid the issue. "According to Alain, his wife and the other women prepare and serve food on the day the men hunt."

Anne said, "My son-in-law hunts with them. It might take a little coercion on my part to get you in, Maxine, mainly because these men don't take to outsiders, much less women, but I'm willing to try."

Isabelle said, "And why should they want women in their club? France is not the U.S., where no one must ever be excluded."

Juliette chimed in, "Maman! Women have had to fight for every inclusion in the U.S. You can't imagine what it was like for Max at the NYPD when she started."

Hank looked from mother to daughter. "It wasn't that bad, was it?"

The question broke the ice as everyone laughed, and Hank looked befuddled.

The main course arrived, and attention shifted to food. *Onglet de veau*, or veal steaks accompanied by a pumpkin gratin and wild mushrooms sautéed with garlic and parsley, received raves from everyone. The wine that accompanied it, a rich, deep, dark red from Domaine Billard Gabriel, was a *premier cru* Pommard wine, and Max thought perhaps her favorite of all pinot noirs she had sampled.

Anne said, "This *domaine* is owned by two sisters whom I support every chance I get. *Pas mal, eh?*"

Olivier, after sipping, said, "Victor Hugo said of the Pommards, 'It is night in combat with day.'"

Max felt his hand on her thigh, and turned to click her glass gently against his. For a moment it was only the two of them in the room, and doubt subsided as she saw the warmth radiating from his eyes.

The main course was followed by a *salade de cresson*, watercress salad. A *tarte aux pralines roses* was brought in for dessert, and by then the merriment of the group was at full tilt—except for Max, who tried valiantly, knew she wasn't succeeding, unable to rise above her insecurity.

When she refused dessert, Olivier whispered to her, "Please come home with me tonight?" His hand encircled hers and she nodded.

Chapter Six

"It's unfair of me to pull you away from your family, Max, but with so much family about, I thought we should seize any moment to be together."

"I took a nap and feel fine."

The hour was late, but Olivier was happy to be driving to his parents' home in the south. It had been exactly the kind of evening Olivier enjoyed most, the kind that made him feel like a *bon viveur*. The company and the wine had been scintillating, the meal superb. And having Max by his side had made him realize how lonely he had felt over the past year.

He said, "Do you really want to hunt?"

"I prefer hunting to hanging out in the kitchen with Yvette."

Olivier laughed. "I'm the one who doesn't want to hunt. I said yes to Alain because I thought your father would enjoy the opportunity."

"You were right. He jumped at it."

"Alain seems bitter about his life. Jealous of the neighbor who is making better wine, disappointed in his son, and I think worried about his marriage. It's like he's reached a dead-end, but he's still young."

"I see this with some of my friends. Education finished. Marriage. Decent jobs. Good money. A kid or two. Yet they complain. The marriage feels flat. The job is boring. Daycare expenses are prohibitive."

"I don't know how Americans manage with the high costs of education and health care. It must feel like they are on a sinking ship."

"And Europeans, we read, are feeling overwhelmed by over a million migrants flooding in. Look how much has changed since you and I met, Olivier."

Olivier listed out loud the attacks that had occurred: the one on *Charlie Hebdo* last January, the attempted attack on a popular train from Amsterdam to Paris in August; the Paris attacks in November, with over one hundred dead and many more wounded; and only a few weeks ago, the attack on the Bruxelles-National Airport. "And more anticipated," he added. "People are traumatized, and the randomness of the attacks make everyone more fearful."

"I get why you wanted to switch to the anti-terrorism unit."

"It was stupid of me keep my plans a secret. I wanted to make sure I was accepted before I announced it. I'll be honest and say I did feel depression gnawing at me after the first attacks, but then I decided that I would be acting in this new role, not reacting. All of my training has led to this, Max." They were off the highway now, and entering Viré. He smiled at her. "I can assure you that tonight I'm not depressed. You look ravishing, by the way."

She laughed. "I was just thinking the same thing about you."

He led the way into the country kitchen that contained a wood-burning cookstove; a large, wooden farm table in the center; homemade jars of jam on a tray. The French put furniture in their kitchens, which made them cozy. She followed Olivier into the salon, a room filled with books, comfortable sofas, and art on the walls. A small office adjoined this room, with more books resting on shelves.

"I like imagining you here as a boy," she said, as he built a cozy fire in the fireplace.

"And I like having you here with me now."

"Olivier."

He turned to her. "*Oui*?"

"We have to talk. I feel awkward as hell saying all this, but here goes. We are surrounded by our loved ones who are expecting you to propose to me. It is obvious, to me at least, after a few hours together that you and I are moving toward our futures in solo mode."

He poured a glass of Armagnac for each of them. Since he had bought the ring for Max and failed to propose, he'd overthought the whole thing. It wouldn't be fair to take her from her parents. It was thoughtless to ask her to move to a country where attacks were constantly happening. He, too, worried about the depression that had threatened to cripple him. So many reasons to remain a bachelor, none of which, he reminded himself, had to do with another woman. There had been only Max for a long time now. And though she had just arrived, the thought of her leaving created a well of sadness.

He handed her glass to her, and sipped from his. "Max, I am ready to discuss this, but first I must retrieve something. Don't go anywhere." He went up the stairs and opened his suitcase, the same suitcase he'd had in New York. The ring had lived in a little corner of the suitcase all this time. He fumbled around and put his hand on the little box.

She sat exactly as he had left her, perched on the edge of the sofa, the cognac untouched. He had never seen her look quite so sad when he entered the salon again. "What could you possibly not live without for an hour?" she asked with a smile on her face.

"This." He pulled the ring from his pocket. "I have had this since the counterfeit case in New York. It was bought for you, and somehow I started thinking it was unfair to ask you to marry me. But, really, I was terrified. I think I have never loved anyone until you, Max." If he hadn't felt so much concern about her answer, he would have laughed at the expression on her face. A mixture of shock and disbelief and finally a wisp of a smile. He took both her hands and pulled her up and said, "Will you marry me?" She nodded, and he slipped the engagement ring onto her finger.

"Olivier." The heat from the fireplace filled the room, and this time there was no holding back as they shed their clothes and slid down onto the rug and made love.

They'd pulled pillows off the sofa and sipped brandy, talking about logistics—and who would live where, when—when Max suddenly said all that practicality bored her tonight. She began to caress him, her body moving like a wave on top of him, her eyes molding into his. This time there was no hurry, no attempt to make up for lost time, no anxiety about the future.

"I am enraptured by you," he whispered to her, and she kissed him again. And again.

It was four in the morning when she yawned and said she needed to sleep.

"*D'accord.* I thought we could marry in two weeks. We could marry here."

"Olivier, are you drunk?"

"I've been intending to propose for two years."

"Are you referring to the night at Restaurant Veritas in Manhattan?"

"That was the day I bought the ring. Yes. We were interrupted by our teammates coming to escort us to the plane."

"And then in France, the night we drank the '45 Mouton Rothschild?"

He laughed. "*Exact.* The wine overwhelmed my senses."

"That's the strangest excuse I've ever heard."

He put his arm around here. "I admit to being callous. It was running from attack to attack that made me realize how lonely I was. I spent hours thinking about the victims, reading stories of how they had kissed loved ones good-night and rushed out to a concert, or to a meet up with friends, and never returned. I had visual images of what they had left behind: a hairbrush left on a dresser, the note that never got sent, the empty wineglass left by the sink, a lover asleep on newly laundered sheets."

Max squeezed his hand. "I'm here." He pulled the quilt that his grandmother had made for him when he was a child around them, and they drifted off to sleep.

Chapter Seven

The sound of a cell phone ringing woke Max. She was still wrapped up in a beautiful old quilt on a rug, enjoying the heat coming from a wood stove. She held her hand up. The ring was elegant, simple, and perfect for her. She listened as Olivier spoke softly in a different room. She got up and slipped her arms into the robe he had placed beside her, and went into the kitchen.

"A private investigator named Yves Laroche either fell or jumped to his death two nights ago in Lyon after hosting a party."

"I assume it was Abdel who called?"

"Somehow his cousin is involved."

She moaned. "Tell him we just got engaged and are taking a month off."

"The American girl was also at the party."

"Which explains why she didn't come back to Anne's. I guarantee you she's in trouble. I'm off to shower, then I'll go with you."

She stood under the hot stream of water, going over in her mind the story of the girl who had gone from victim to potential suspect overnight. She knew Abdel wouldn't have called for Olivier to come in if he didn't think he had some kind of case.

Olivier greeted her with a kiss, then poured coffee into the bowl in front of her. I was thinking about wedding venues," he said. "And thought it would be simple to marry in the town hall here. Or perhaps here in this house."

"I don't think for a minute that my mother and grandmother are going to agree to that. Sorry to change the subject, but has Abdel picked the girl up yet?"

Olivier frowned. "The police are searching for her. We could also just marry and then tell them."

I keep thinking we've reversed roles. After all this time, what's the hurry?"

"Our families are together. I'll fly your partner and anyone else you want from New York to France." A ping, and he looked down at his phone. "It's Abdel. Let's go."

"Okay, okay." She walked with him toward the car, but when he got a call and stopped to answer, she paused to look at the vineyards on the side of the house and across the narrow lane where tiny shoots were emerging from the twisted roots that jutted into the air. "It looks like a graveyard coming to life," she said, entering the car.

"That's not a bad description. We'll return at harvest, when the landscape turns into a sea of green." He started the car. "My gut tells me this Laroche death could turn into a murder investigation, and I promised myself that I would not conduct another one. I don't want any part of it."

"I'm feeling slightly drawn to it because of the American girl."

"I know. You're a born detective, Max. I'm not."

"You're better than you know."

"We could marry, then leave to visit my brother in Australia in two weeks, and I would start my new job in May."

"You have it all sewn up. The only problem is that I wasn't consulted."

He glanced over at her, surprised. "But you don't want all the falderal that goes with weddings, do you? I don't think of you as that type."

"Please don't pigeonhole me. Deep inside, I adore the idea of a beautiful wedding dress."

His laugh was a hoot. "Perhaps we can find a way to compromise." He grew serious. "We'll be in Lyon in an hour. By the way, the dead P.I., Laroche, harvested grapes at Anne Bré's this year, a tradition that started a decade ago."

"Not good. I wonder if he and Lucy hooked up. Maybe she rejected him and he jumped."

"That sounds a bit Tolstoyan."

"Or maybe she pushed him when he tried to hook up with her. Even I find that a strange term. Meaning he tried to get into her pants."

"Does anyone use the term 'falling in love' anymore? These expressions like 'hooking up' conjure up such unattractive images."

"Hooking up has nothing to do with falling in love. And in my parents' day it was all about one-night stands. Same idea."

Max realized that she and Olivier had developed the kind of bantering that cops used to cover up anxiety. She thought it must be similar to the way surgeons told jokes while operating. Olivier explained that they were entering the tunnel de Fourvière that leads into the heart of Lyon. Sunlight glinted off the buildings overlooking the Saône River. Looming over the city on the other side of the river was a cathedral. "What a beautiful cityscape," Max said. "The ornate bridges remind me of Paris. From here, I could be standing along the Seine, looking across at the Musée d'Orsay."

"I wish we had more time here," Olivier said. "Lyon is the gastronomic capital of France. I will make sure you visit the Halles Paul Bocuse, which is on the other side of the Rhône River." They crossed the bridge onto Rue Octavio Mey, passing many signs for couscous restaurants and then pulled into an empty parking space. Abdel emerged from a nondescript apartment building and Max leapt out of the car to embrace him. "You're the first to know," she said. "Olivier and I are getting married."

"About time! When?"

Olivier had joined them. "Soon." Abdel glanced at Max, who rolled her eyes, but she was smiling.

Glancing behind him, Abdel said, "My cousin is inside."

Max thought Olivier was right, this was going to turn into something nasty. They entered the small bachelor's lair, and sat on a small sofa after Abdel introduced them to Ali. "I have already spoken with the police," Abdel said. "They're awaiting the results from the medical examiner, who initially declared the cause of death to be suicide. But my fellow officer who is local said that Yves Laroche landed in such a way, splayed out, his face hitting the pavement, that he changed his mind and suspected that he was pushed. The case will be put before the prosecutor if there is any suspicion, of course."

"If they determine murder, the girl is a definite suspect?"

"Witnesses saw her. She stands out, you know."

"No, I don't know at all. She could easily become a scapegoat."

"The police are interviewing neighbors, and examining the video camera outside the building. Laroche was hosting a party so people were coming and going all night, according to other tenants."

Max said, "Lucy must be close by. Not that hard to find." She turned to Ali, who was studying his smartphone. "She stopped here yesterday?"

"Yes. At my garage. I told Abdel."

"What time?"

He shrugged. "Maybe noon."

"Was anybody with her?"

"She had a guy with her; at least I think he was with her. He went for a slice of pizza while I fixed her Vespa, then lurked around in the parking lot until she was ready."

"What'd he look like?"

Ali shrugged again. "You know, like any guy. Young. Wore jeans and had on a hooded sweatshirt and a wind jacket."

"Why didn't you tell me about him?" Abdel asked, giving him a remonstrative look.

"You didn't ask." Ali grew defensive. "I think you're on the wrong track. That girl wouldn't hurt anybody. Hell, she's no bigger than a *puce*." A flea, Max translated.

"You don't know anything about her," Abdel said, a stubborn expression on his face.

"With all due respect to Abdel," Ali said to Max and Olivier, "the police here like to jump to conclusions." He leapt up off the couch and paced in a small circle, looking from one to the other. "Aw, come on, guys. Don't link my name to this. I've been arrested twice. They've been watching me. In no time, they'll label me a co-conspirator or something. These are tense times."

"Did you know Yves Laroche?" Max asked.

"No."

Max thought he was lying.

Olivier turned to Abdel and Max. "It's not a case yet. Let's hope the poor guy jumped. Why don't we go for a walk and then I'll take you both to a restaurant I remember from a lifetime ago? Authentic regional food."

Max and Abdel exchanged disbelieving stares, yet she knew, as did Abdel, that good cuisine and wine were Olivier's antidote to the human condition.

Ali grabbed his coat. "I have to get to work." Olivier stepped aside.

Max said, "Ali, one more question. How did you hear about Yves Laroche dying?"

"Lucy told me."

They all stopped.

Abdel said, "When?"

"Last night. She called me."

Olivier said, "What did she say?"

"Her exact words were, 'Some nasty shit is going down. You'll see it on the news. I'm lucky to be here.'"

Abdel said, "You weren't at that party, were you?"

"For half an hour."

"*Pourquoi*?" Abdel grabbed Ali by the arm. "Did you buy drugs?"

"Mais, non!" He shook Abdel off.

"You are all idiots!" Abdel shouted. "Do you know if she has a cell phone?"

"I never saw one. She carries around a banged-up laptop." He marched out the door.

"This is what I have to deal with all the time with my own people," Abdel said, walking alongside Olivier.

"The girl could be a sociopath," said Max. "Charming, woos everybody into trusting her, then bam!"

They followed Olivier across the bridge to the Vieux Lyon, and soon were at the restaurant l'Apostrophe. Olivier entered the bar area and looked around. "This is it," he said. "Nothing has changed." Checkered tablecloths covered the tables. A little sign advertised a Côtes du Rhône for three euros and a glass of white for the same. A waitress led them to a table, and after much discussion on Olivier's part, Max ordered, against her better judgment, the *tablier de sapeur,* or tripe, and Olivier and Abdel had the *boudin aux pommes*, which Max knew was a blood sausage, which was made up of pork, dried pig's blood, and suet.

Olivier said, "This is the three of us celebrating Max's and my engagement. No crime talk until after the meal. *D'accord?"*

"Why don't I take a few photographs of our engagement luncheon and put it on Snapchat?" Max said, and was pleased that she got a laugh out of Abdel.

Abdel explained to Max how he had applied to the police department in Paris because he wanted to continue working with Monsieur Chaumont, and said that he was surprised to have been accepted so quickly. "You have a good reputation," Olivier said. "Saving my life last year went into your report, though that may be a mark against you." They laughed. Max couldn't believe the three of them were together again.

Abdel said, looking at his boss, "Monsieur, happiness becomes you."

"I am happier than I have ever been. At almost forty, I am getting married to the woman I love, I am moving back to Paris, and I will be doing work that will be deeply gratifying." He looked at Abdel. "My brother is unable to come all the way from Australia for the wedding on such short notice. I want you to be my best man."

"But, Monsieur…"

"No buts. You must do this for me."

"Of course. I am honored."

Abdel looked at Max. "Who will stand with you?"

"My sidekick is coming from New York. Carlos. And Chloe and Ted, of course."

Olivier reminded Abdel of their friend whose wedding he and Max attended in Champagne a couple of years ago, and he nodded. "That was a sad day when the bride's aunt was killed."

The plates arrived, and were placed in front of them. Max thought her dish looked like a sizzling chicken-fried steak.

Olivier was now caught up in the food. "How is yours?" he asked Max.

"Fine, if I don't think about it being the stomach of a cow," Abdel laughed.

"Mine is really quite wonderful," Olivier said, offering a bite of the sausage, which she declined. They sat conversing over coffee, and Max glanced around the restaurant that had not changed its décor or its menu in decades. She'd been told that people came here knowing they would be in a cozy, familiar atmosphere, eating traditional French food. She turned her attention back to the conversation, which was winding its way around to the millions of refugees arriving in Europe from Syria, Iraq, Afghanistan, and God-knows-where-else, seeking an environment free of war and persecution. "I was in their shoes once," Abdel said, "Or at least my parents were. I hope we can keep the borders open."

"The same is true for my father's family," Max said. "They came to America to escape the potato famine in Ireland."

Olivier said he had grave concerns, especially for Germany, where because Chancellor Merkel was allowing such a flood of refugees in, there could be backlash. Europe was changing in front of their eyes, Max realized, and looking from Olivier to Abdel, she was aware that the three of them were facing big transitions, due to consequences of recent terrorist activities.

Eventually, it was time to leave. As they stepped out into the bright sunlight, Olivier's cell rang and when he saw it was Hank he put it on speaker. They stopped to listen.

"I took Isabelle's car and drove to a medieval village where there is a monastery," Hank said.

"Oh, yes, I know it," Olivier said. "Le prieuré de Blanot. A Roman church, originally built in the tenth century."

"I'm not calling to tell you I had an epiphany or anything. Or maybe I did. As I was leaving I stopped in at a little café and ordered a beer. After my eyes got used to the dim light, I looked around and knew that the girl huddled in the corner was that girl Lucy. The hood of her sweatshirt fell off when she shifted position, and she glanced up from her laptop, and looked directly into my eyes. There was only one other patron, and the waiter-bartender. I got up and walked over to her table and said, 'Hey, people are looking for you. They're worried about you. I'm on your side.' I told her I was a detective in New York, and gave her my card. She suddenly yelled in rapid French to the waiter who rushed over and told me in broken English to leave. I followed him to the bar and tried to explain. When I turned around, the girl was gone. I rushed out the door, and she already had the Vespa running. She had put on sunglasses. She said, 'I know you're with Uncle George,' in English, and roared off. She's definitely acting like a fugitive."

"I need an accurate description."

"Easy. Five six, slender like a young Patti Smith, cropped hair that's more blond now than silver, dark blue intelligent eyes with heavy, arched eyebrows, ears close to her head, long neck, full lips, no makeup. Not beautiful in the classic sense, but a magnet. Now that we know Uncle George exists, I might do a little homework. I'll call a couple of my cronies in New York to see what they can find out. Over and out."

"Meet the other member of the team," Max said to Abdel. "He's bored in the country."

Abdel laughed. "And yet, there's still no case?"

Olivier said, "Not until we know how Yves Laroche died."

Abdel's cell rang; he picked up and was off in ten seconds. "Pushed."

"*Merde!*" Olivier said. "Abdel, can you give up your vacation and lead this investigation?"

He grew quiet, then said, "Where will you be?"

"Australia. You can do this. I will speak to the judge here and ask him to put you in charge, or at least here in Beaune."

Max held her breath watching Abdel, sure he would say no, but after an interminable silence, he nodded. "We won't be able to nose around without permission once this is official," Olivier added.

They parted ways and Olivier and Max began the drive back to Auxey-Duresses. "Abdel might have a conflict of interest with his cousin somehow involved," Max said.

"He will need an informer. This will be good for him."

"I haven't seen a dark-skinned person since I got here. That isn't a problem?"

"What is that supposed to mean? You're suggesting people will be prejudiced against Abdel?"

"Marine LePen is stirring things up with all the refugees flooding in. I guess that's what I'm saying."

"France is not Germany, where over eight hundred thousand have been invited in. Holland has only okayed fourteen thousand, if I remember correctly. The French hate prejudice of any kind."

"Hank was outwitted by Lucy," Max said. "That doesn't happen often. He won't let it go now."

"He can play backyard detective if he finds it entertaining. We won't be here."

"Maybe we should set a date. Most couples do that."

"You have a point. April twenty-eighth?"

"Suits me. Let's make a bet," Max said. "We haven't done that in ages."

"What are we betting on?"

"Lucy will be my bridesmaid."

Olivier spluttered. "I don't want to bet on something so absurd."

"Come on, *chéri,* admit it, you're worried I'll win."

"Okay, whoever wins gets to make the final choice on which apartment we take in Paris."

"Great one! High five!" She held a splayed hand up.

"I'm driving."

She laughed gustily, as though she had already won.

Chapter Eight

The maid came to the door and invited Olivier and Max into Anne's living room. Dominated by a massive stone fireplace where flames shot skyward, soaring ceilings with intricate moldings, parquet floors covered with worn Persian rugs, and furnished with sofas and chairs arranged to create intimacy, the room could otherwise have been overwhelming in its stateliness, yet greeted them warmly.

Hank was sitting at attention in a cushioned chair. "About time you got here. Anne and I scoured Lucy's room, and found a journal in the armoire."

He handed it to Olivier who read aloud, *In the event of my death, here's the story.*

Hank said, "Lots of notes about picking grapes. But on one page she wrote that she was excited that her friend, Yves, had offered to help her find her father. On another she wrote about being held under lock and key in a loony bin in Westchester County, which is where she was when her mother died. The docs said the cause was an aneurysm, but Lucy writes that her uncle George Wyeth, who owns the hospital, was responsible for her mother's death."

"How awful," Max said. "He had control of her, it seems. Her mother must have given permission, as she is a minor."

Anne took over. "Lucy told me about her search for her father. Her mother attended a semester at the University in Dijon in 1995, and while there had a brief affair with a married man who was, according to her, a successful merchant and *vigneron*. Lucy says she is the result of that liaison, but her mother had promised not to reveal the name of her lover until his death. Evidently he was quite a bit older. Hank and I think that finding her father must have been Lucy's only hope once her mother died, as she made her way all the way to France."

"Let's not over-romanticize the situation," Olivier said. "Lucy is seventeen, and could be delusional. We don't know what she did to get placed in a mental hospital. Did she tell you, Anne?"

"No."

"I can find out the cause of her mother's death," Hank said. "At least what was written on the death certificate. And I can check out this George guy." Before Olivier could reply, Hank said, "To satisfy my own curiosity."

Anne said, "My concern was that Lucy was too much of a free spirit. She comes and goes as she pleases, but this time when she left she didn't tell me anything, which is not like her." Anne grew quiet for a moment. "She was somewhat besieged by men wanting her attention. The boy from the south, the one I don't like, Roland, I think his name is. He's perfectly harmless, of course, follows her around like a puppy, and our local Brit who runs the B&B nearby calls to take her into Beaune to meet up with his friends...nice guy that one. Then there is Yves, who has been coming here for years to pick grapes. He was gaga over Lucy, but he is the age of my son-in-law, Jean-Claude. I thought his behavior grew unseemly, and I told him to leave. Everyone was having a falling-out with him, even Jean-Claude."

Olivier and Max exchanged glances, then looked to Hank, whose face said he had not mentioned the death of Anne's former worker. Olivier said, "Pardon for the interruption, but Anne, I have unfortunate news. Yves Laroche fell to his death a couple of nights ago."

Anne looked stricken. After a moment, she spoke in a low voice. "How does one fall to one's death, Olivier? They either jump or they are forced, isn't that so?"

"The theory is that he was pushed."

Anne's face was grim. "Then who did it?"

"The police are investigating," Olivier said. "He hosted his own birthday party the night he died, and Lucy was seen leaving there."

"I knew something like this would happen!" Anne said. She stood up in an act of impatience. "There was a group of… singles…who hung out together. All ages. Tim is the Brit, and his inn is where they all congregate. I've seen them when I drive by, or go for a walk. That god-awful wife of Alain Milne's…what's her name…Yvette…took to going there, and you can imagine the scandalous news that suddenly started making the rounds. Jean-Claude denied being in a relationship with her when I confronted him, but I think he was lying. She's been married just long enough to know she's bored. He has a child to raise, and he was setting a horrible example for Lucy."

Olivier was shocked by the degree of hostility in Anne's voice, and saw that Hank and Max were as well.

She continued. "Jean-Claude has changed since my daughter's death. He's drinking too much, and hanging out with people Caroline didn't care for. Oh, some of them are old diehards around here. Men who haven't entered the twenty-first century, who put women down with their insipid jokes, whose politics are right of Le Pen, who would love to see me ruined." Her face became distorted by ragged emotions. "Look at me," she said. "An old fool if ever there was one." The doorbell rang and she gave them an imploring look, hastily wiping tears. "Oh, that will be Jean-Claude dropping off my grandson. Please do not discuss any of this with him."

They shook their heads in unison, as if to say "never."

She went to the door. They heard her speaking to a child, who followed her into the room and shook hands with each guest. Jean-Claude followed behind. Olivier figured him to be in his mid-forties, judging by the grey streaks in his hair. A man who spent a lot of time outside. Unquestionably attractive, though he hadn't smiled once since entering the room.

"Sit, sit," Anne said, but he begged off, saying he had work to do.

The little boy, Luc, ran over to a shelf, fetched a Babar book, and sat down next to Max, who whispered something that made him smile. Max watched him and thought, he's too young to lose his mother.

"How old are you?" Max asked him in French.

"Huit ans."

"Eight," Max translated for Hank, who was studying the child.

Jean-Claude said to his mother-in-law, "Did you see on the news that a guy fell off a balcony in Lyon? Turns out it was Yves Laroche."

Anne sniffed the air. "Yes, I know about his terrible accident."

Jean-Claude continued standing, forcing Anne to look up at him. "I wonder if Lucy knows." He turned to the others. "Monsieur Laroche worked here during the *vendanges* and was crazy about this American girl who showed up. I warned her about hanging out with him."

Now irritated, Anne said, "Surely, she hasn't seen him since I sent him away?"

Her question hung in the air as Jean-Claude took a seat, finally, realizing he had an audience. He turned to Olivier. "He was a snoop. A P.I. They have to hold a degree now in France, but they're still snoops. He kept Lucy in a state of hope about finding her father. I told her that if her father wanted to be found, he'd have looked for her. She needed a dose of reality."

"Yves was inappropriate with her, which is why I fired him. But that didn't keep him from showing up at Tim's inn. I saw his car there."

Max thought Anne was sounding like a first-class spy.

Luc piped up. "Papa, Lucy sent me a postcard from Lyon, right?"

Jean-Claude smiled, and Max noticed his dimples. "Luc heard from her, this is true."

Olivier thought Lucy's act of writing to a lonely little boy was a solid act of compassion. He said, "I wonder if Monsieur Laroche stuck his nose where it didn't belong."

Jean-Claude said, "He was proud of the fact that he had dossiers on a lot of people who didn't know he had them. He was a double-agent in the domestic world, the way I saw him. It was greed, pure and simple. He would promise Lucy information on her father, but at the same time he was in touch with Lucy's uncle, who was looking for her. I got suckered in by him on some information I was seeking, then he turned on me." Jean-Claude looked accusingly at his mother-in-law. "No one was immune."

"He's gone," Anne said. "I hope all the gossip dies with him."

"You're working the Yves Laroche case, Monsieur Chaumont?" Jean-Claude asked.

"No. I'm requesting that my assistant, Abdel Zeroual, be a part of the investigation." He felt no need to explain that he wanted him to direct it.

"You don't trust the officials here to do a thorough job?"

"The tradition is for judges and prosecutors to cooperate with each other."

Jean-Claude clearly had no intention of backing down. "I've already spoken with the prosecutor in Lyon, Emmanuel Caron, who buys my wine, and told him that I stopped by Yves' birthday party earlier that evening. I had a date and so didn't stay long."

"Did you notice anything unusual?"

"Yves was strung out on heroin. He had also started dealing, I heard." The clock chimed nine times. "I am running late." He leaned down, kissed his son, and told him to be good.

Anne took her grandson's hand and led him into the kitchen, asking Max and Olivier to join them. Anne's *employée de maison*, or housekeeper, had set the table for six. Anne reached into the fridge and brought out a bottle of chilled white wine. "This isn't from my top tier of wines, but I like it."

They sat, and Anne said, "The Laroche guy sounds like a monster. And we fed the monster. I'll admit, I went to him to talk about the land Jean-Claude and I are in dissent over. Yves Laroche was coming here when Gervais was alive, and one harvest season—1995, I think it was—Gervais and I were having a terrible go-round because of his philandering. Yves had an indelicate habit of pointedly reminding me of my husband's transgressions. This year he put the daffy idea in my head that Lucy could be the result of my husband's affair with Diane, Lucy's mother. He recalled a pretty American woman coming to pick grapes, he said."

Olivier blurted, "And…?"

She shrugged. "He was going to run a DNA test. I don't know if he did, or not, because I fired him."

"I'm surprised the land boundaries aren't clearer with the parcel you were speaking of," Olivier said.

"It wasn't my husband's to bequeath. It was part of an inheritance from my father. I let it go because my darling Caroline was so pleased that her father had left something specifically to her. But after her death, Jean-Claude came up with a paper she had signed bequeathing that same parcel to him."

"But it will go to Luc eventually, anyhow," Olivier said.

"I assume. But what if Jean-Claude marries again, which he most likely will? If he has more children, it could become very complicated, though it is supposed to be passed down through bloodlines." She sighed. "It's in the right location on the hillside to become a *grand cru* vineyard, a gold mine for Jean-Claude and a chance for him to prove his skill at crafting a truly fine wine. Caroline always felt sorry for him, as his father had lost their family vineyard. A giant investment company bought it, and Jean-Claude tried working for them but it didn't last. He's been at loose ends ever since, working a tiny piece of land that he managed to buy, that has no appellation, and helping others."

"It doesn't sound like it was his fault," Max said.

Anne shrugged. "It's quite common, unfortunately. Both our land laws and our inheritance laws are too strict, if you ask me. I've been conferring with a wine dealer named Hugo Bourgeot, who is interested in buying it."

Olivier couldn't hide his shock. "Everyone knows him, in one guise or another. Big landowner here and in the American northwest. His is the only private *négociant* firm left standing. He must be approaching eighty."

"He wants this piece for a personal reason and that's all I can say."

"Does Jean-Claude have any idea that you're doing this?"

"There is no reason for him to know. If he wins our legal battle, which is doubtful, I will offer to buy the land back from him at a price he can't refuse. If he loses, I can do what I want with it."

Luc, who had left the table with his grandmother's permission to play Legos, returned. She put her arm around him. "Let's read a Babar book." He nodded and ran off to retrieve it.

Olivier took this as their cue to leave, and stood up. He and Max, Juliette and Hank, bid Anne good night.

Hank had arrived at the door when he turned back to Anne. "What would you do if the DNA matched up and Lucy turned out to be your husband's child?"

She smiled, as though he had uncovered a secret. "I like your boldness, Hank. I would have no choice. Lucy would be entitled to a portion of everything I have." She smiled, "I am coming around to the belief that it could be my destiny. And Lucy's."

Olivier said, "I wonder if Jean-Claude knows any of this is going on. Yves Laroche was the last thing from discreet, and they drank together."

"I'm concerned about that. I wonder what Jean-Claude was doing at that party. He's not a kid. He must have been nosing around for something. Olivier, I think you would be wise to destroy every file Yves had. Start fresh."

"There are laws about that, Anne. They will be used as evidence, if need be."

Olivier, Max, and Hank bid Anne good-bye, and headed back to Isabelle's. "Whichever prosecutor is chosen to handle this case must be diligent about sticking to the facts," Olivier said, "and not get led into these tales everyone is weaving."

"I keep going back to that piece of land she's negotiating over with Hugo Bourgeot," Max said. "What is she getting in return?"

"I wouldn't dare name a sum. A million, at least."

Hank said, "She doesn't need money. When we know what she does need, we'll understand why she wants to sell that parcel."

Olivier said, "Who knows what anyone needs, much less Madame Anne Bré?"

Chapter Nine

Max bustled around in Isabelle's kitchen, helping with the dinner where she and Olivier were to officially announce their engagement. Isabelle had decided on the traditional dish of *boeuf bourguignon*, which demanded three separate cuts of meat that needed to simmer for hours. The aromas of red wine, onion, and bacon wafted up into the atmosphere. Max joined Olivier in the cellar where he stood studying the wines, carefully selecting the ones that would work with the meal.

"This is perhaps the most pleasant task I've ever been assigned," he said, selecting a bottle and putting it back, then picking up another. "Your grandmother has a rather remarkable collection. She's told me that over the course of many years, she simply bought a few bottles from every vintage." He smiled, "Of course she had neighbors making fine wines."

The doorbell chimed, and Juliette called down that Olivier's parents had arrived. Max hurried upstairs and looked into the warm, intelligent eyes of Olivier's father, who delivered kisses on each cheek to his future daughter-in-law. Olivier was his father's clone. His mother was of medium height, trim, and exuded a quiet elegance. Hank introduced himself and Max observed Olivier's mother appraise the tall man before her. "Olivier didn't get your looks, which is too bad," Hank said to her, and Max thought she saw a trace of amusement cross the woman's face.

For the first time, Max's impending marriage felt real. Images from the evening began to merge one into the other as her gaze went from her grandmother, both haughty and warm; to her mother, who was elegant in black; to her father, who sipped a glass of *cremant*, the Burgundian equivalent of champagne, content to observe the group; to Anne, who spoke animatedly to Olivier's parents; and finally her eyes landing on her fiancé, who was completely at ease. At Isabelle's command they entered the dining room and sat, with barely a lull in conversation as the transition was made.

Olivier said, "Jean-Claude called. The wild boar hunt is scheduled for tomorrow morning. Max will be allowed to come and observe."

Max gave a mock, exasperated look. "If a boar attacks me, I have no weapon?"

"I'd be more worried about the men shooting you," Isabelle said. "Make sure you wear orange. Let's see, my husband's hunting jacket is upstairs, which may be perfect a perfect fit for Hank. I'm sure I can come up with something for you, Maxine. Have you ever been hunting?"

"Only for criminals in New York City. Wild boars should be easy after that."

"She'll be okay with me," Hank said.

"You don't hunt, either," Max said.

"The Army wanted to keep me on as a sniper back in the day, but I said no. I've gotten so I hate killing anything. These boars might change my mind."

Everyone laughed. Max reminded herself to ask Hank about that period in his life she knew so little about. She felt Olivier's mother's eyes on her and glanced in her direction, relieved to see that she, too, was amused. Olivier reached over and took her hand and she felt herself blush. Isabelle noticed, too, and smiled. She raised her glass. "We are here to celebrate the engagement of Max and Olivier," she said. "May I be the first to welcome you into our family, Olivier."

The diners clinked glasses. Olivier's father spoke next. "We could not be happier to make the acquaintance of our future daughter-in-law. Welcome to France, Max."

"There is something we haven't told you," Olivier said, smiling. "Max?"

"The wedding date is April twenty-eighth."

The room went silent, then all the women were talking at once. "This is not possible," Isabelle said. "We have only two weeks. Not even." She and Juliette exchanged wild glances. "Olivier," Juliette said, focusing her attention onto her future son-in-law, "I know Max talked you into this absurd notion. Please, you are a reasonable man."

"We are together on this," Olivier said. "What is the point in waiting? We know what we want. I'm moving to Paris and want her to help me select our new apartment. We will begin immediately after the wedding, if not before. She will be putting an application into Interpol before we depart for our honeymoon."

Juliette's eyes filled with tears. "I'm not prepared for her to move across the ocean."

Max jumped up and threw her arms around her mother. "You'll have time to get used to the idea, Maman. And you can come to Paris any time you want."

Isabelle said, "My apartment is big enough for a family of six. Really, Juliette, you and Hank must consider it home."

"Oh, Maman," Juliette said. *"Merci."*

"I want to offer my house for the wedding," Anne said. "But what about flowers? Wine?"

"And what will you wear?" Juliette exclaimed.

"We'll find something," Max said.

"Your grandmother and I will take you into Paris."

Anne said, "My wedding dress is in storage. We can alter it to fit you. My daughter also wore it."

"Okay," Max said, breathlessly. "Dress problem solved."

Olivier's mother said she would host a dinner the night before, Isabelle circled the date on her calendar, and Hank, who had not said a word, held up his glass to propose a toast. "I told Olivier that patience is not always a virtue, as I thought he was lollygagging with his proposal, but now I will tell them both that patience is the key to keeping a marriage together. For now, that's all I have to say." And everyone responded, "Hear, hear."

Max leaned over and planted a kiss on Olivier's cheek. She caught, out of the corner of her eye, her grandmother's housemaid Jeannette, discreetly beckoning from the kitchen. Isabelle glided gracefully out to the kitchen, her absence barely noted. She re-entered the room and said, "Olivier, your assistant wants to see you."

Olivier walked out to the front hall, closing the door behind him. "It sounds ominous," said Anne to the group. "I hope everything is alright."

Max wanted to say that it is rarely "alright" when the police arrive at your door, but held her tongue. Olivier returned with Abdel. "I'm sorry for interrupting," Abdel said. "But there was some business that couldn't wait."

"Oh, join us," Isabelle said, motioning to Jeannette to bring another plate. "We're celebrating Max and Olivier's engagement news, which I'm certain you already know."

"Only for a moment," he said.

"Any word about Lucy?" Anne asked.

Abdel explained that Lucy's guardian had arrived from the U.S. and had gone directly to Beaune. The uncle had hired a private investigator in Lyon to help him find his missing niece. Of course, the man he hired was none other than Yves Laroche. The fact that the uncle had arrived in Beaune meant that Yves Laroche had informed him of his niece's whereabouts. The uncle put out an alert to the police that Lucy was unstable, that she had escaped from a psychiatric institution."

Isabelle and Anne expressed outrage at this, and Abdel found himself in the middle of a flurry of questions.

Lucy is back in the forefront, Max thought.

Max was impressed with her grandmother, who didn't flinch when Abdel entered, but in fact insisted that he join them. She knew this would not happen in most households in France, not in the upper-crust families, anyhow. It wasn't considered rude or prejudiced to act biasedly toward other races, for theirs' was a society based on class, and everyone knew his place in it. She thought of the millions of people who had come to France seeking a better life, in many cases as refugees, and the surprise of many when they realized they could only advance so far. Even middle-class French families did not hold high hopes of climbing the corporate or political ladders, as they did in the United States, because leaders were manufactured in a certain select few schools.

After dinner they were ushered into the library. Abdel, Olivier, and Max found themselves huddled in a corner. Soon Hank joined them, and Abdel said, "It is an honor to get to know you, sir."

"You, too," Hank said.

"I've always wanted to meet one of New York's famous detectives."

"I'm an unemployed detective," Hank said. "And everybody in New York gets five minutes of fame. I'm interested in the P.I. who died in Lyon."

Abdel acted happy to oblige. "The Laroche P.I. Agency was started by Yves' parents in 1960, a very different era, where they literally went on foot seeking evidence, rifling through trash cans, photographing unsuspecting people, and conducting their own interviews. Today the agencies are more regulated, but back then it was open season. His parents had a reputation for their doggedness, and their success, I might add. Yves took over almost a decade ago, and upgraded the agency with state-of-the-art computer technology. He focused more on corporate accounts, but he also liked to work for private customers, as his parents had done. He accumulated a large number of files on people in Lyon, and that expanded to this area when he started picking grapes twenty years ago. Those files are on his computer, but he also kept physical files, and he had a tendency to pit one person against another."

Hank said, "In other words, he had something on most of them."

"*Exact.*" He paused, "He became obsessed with Lucy Kendrick after meeting her in September. We found a trove of photographs of her, perhaps taken by your neighbor, Tim Lowell, who was presumed to be a friend to both of them. But her files are missing, both the computer version and the hard copy."

"As is she," Olivier said.

Abdel continued, "She is a suspect, of course, because she was at the party, but now that her uncle has arrived and notified the police of her escape from a hospital, the police are doubly focused on her."

"No sign of her?" Max said. "No sightings?"

"Someone called in yesterday, who thought he saw her in the café of a train with a friend, heading to Paris mid-afternoon."

The doorbell chimed and Olivier looked at his watch. The library door opened and a slight, blond man entered, obviously comfortable in the great house. "Hello, Anne," he said, in a clipped, British accent. He went directly to her, and bestowed *baisers* on her cheeks. "I'm here to let you know Lucy's okay. We returned from Paris earlier today. She's a bit on the lam, as you surely know from television, but there is an explanation. Or explanations, as it were." He was smiling and at ease, as though it were perfectly normal to drop in at ten at night. When the maid approached, he said, "I'd adore a cognac."

Tim looked around the room, realizing that it wasn't an ordinary gathering of neighbors. "I'm sorry for imposing," he said. His face brightened when he saw Hank. "You must be the American she bumped into in the café. She described you perfectly." He grew serious. "I'm surprised she didn't show up here this evening, Anne, but she'll return tomorrow, for sure. She left because she was certain she was being followed, and that the person after her was sent by her uncle."

Abdel spoke, "I represent the police. She has been with you these past few days?"

"Yes. I took her into Paris yesterday and we spent the night at a friend's place on Place des Vosges." He smiled, and Max could see that he wavered between anxiety and being in the throes of new love, a state of mind she was familiar with since meeting and falling in love with Olivier.

"You didn't take her to that party Yves gave, did you?" Anne demanded.

"I stand accused. She was determined to go, and I saw no harm."

"Now it's a scandal," Anne said, "and Lucy's name is mixed up in it."

"She's with her friend, Roland."

"Him! The last person I want her to associate with!"

"He is loyal to her, and she is a good influence on him." He finished his cognac. "Look, I promise she will be back here tomorrow. I had work to do, and she wanted to make sure he went back to his family."

Abdel was firm. "She's a suspect in Monsieur Laroche's death. This is a serious charge."

"We are both innocent, and we can prove it."

Max introduced herself and then asked, "What kind of work did you have to do this evening?"

He hesitated—a few seconds too long, in her estimation. "I'm developing rolls of film for a magazine shoot I did. It has to be sent tomorrow."

Olivier said, "Some of us have an early morning hunt. If Lucy isn't here by noon tomorrow you will be arrested, and so will Roland Milne."

"I'm going, too," Tim said. "The hunters allow me to go with my camera sometimes. Okay, she will return by noon tomorrow."

Max didn't know why he didn't just come out and say he and Lucy were staying together tonight.

"The police will be working through the night," Abdel said. He handed Tim his business card, and told him to call if anything came up.

Anne said, "I didn't know you two were a couple, as it were. Why wouldn't she have told me?"

For the first time, Tim blushed. "We were just hanging out until very recently. As soon as this mess blows over, I'm taking her to England to meet my family."

Max looked around and everyone was smiling back at him, even Hank.

Chapter Ten

The alarm clock went off at five and Max moaned as she reached over to shut it off. "You don't have to come, you know," Olivier said as he slipped into wool pants, a high-vis jacket, and wool hat.

Max looked at him and laughed. "Speak for yourself." He waited while she pulled up wool pants with suspenders and slipped into a puffy down jacket.

"I would really lose face if I bowed out," he said, "especially with your father."

"No doubt about it."

Olivier felt absurd in the borrowed clothes, and more than that, he had never liked the idea of killing animals that were at a severe disadvantage, the way the boars were. Their natural predators, wolves, had been killed off, and now the boars were chased by men and dogs. The injuries to dogs when boars attacked them with their long tusks were gruesome, and often fatal, yet Olivier knew the hunters had the wounds dressed and took them back out to hunt. He and Max rushed to the kitchen to make coffee and were happy to see that Hank had beat them to it. He was in what had to be her grandfather's ancient hunting clothes—a heavy wool jacket a size or two too big, and a wool fedora-style hat, with high boots worn over his pants.

Hank grinned. "Like it?"

There was a dusting of snow on the ground when they walked to Olivier's car, but the day was supposed to grow warmer. Olivier felt overdressed. "It's not far to the club," he said. "We will be given rifles and ammunition there."

"My grandmother told me that women have their own hunt club," Max said.

"Male hunt clubs have always been exclusive," Olivier said. "I'm not sure what strings Anne pulled to get the three of us in here. Don't be upset if we're not well received."

"I'm used to it," Max said.

"What's so special about the boar?" Hank asked.

"The *sanglier,"* Olivier said, "or wild boar as you call it, is the *bête noire* that you read about in myths and fairy tales. They're considered a pest in France these days, as they wreak a lot of damage on gardens and farms, and worse, on vineyards, as they've developed a taste for the ripe grape."

"Tell me how the hunt works."

"Preparations were made last night," Olivier said. "There is a *chef de battue*, a chief of the hunt, who will lay out each person's position. You and I will be among the men who stand about fifteen meters apart from each other, approximately two hundred yards from the edge of the woods. The *rabatteurs* will have already gone deep into the forest to rout out the *sangliers*, and once they are successful, they and the dogs chase them toward us."

They arrived at a nondescript building on the outskirts of town, and Olivier led the way inside. Approximately a dozen men were seated in front of plates of cheese, *jambon persillé*, and baguettes. Two bottles of the local grappa, marc de Bourgogne, were open on the table, but the hunters gravitated to the liqueur, *du jaune*, flavored with anise and herbs. They had no qualms about swigging down a glass or two.

"They're going to hunt after this?" Hank asked, looking around the large shed-like structure that was attached to Jean-Claude's house. Jean-Claude's face was flushed as he held court from the head of the table. Alain rushed over to Olivier, and shook hands. Yvette had driven up and there she was, bright red lips curved into a big smile. "I remember you from school days,

Olivier," she said. "You were always making the rest of us look like idiots with your smart answers."

"I'm sure I was trying to impress intellectually," he said, "since I don't recall the girls falling all over me the way they did Alain."

She laughed, but he noticed sadness in her eyes. "Times change," she said.

"I hope to meet your son."

She frowned. "Perhaps later. He was out partying last night. You know how that goes." Her comment was followed by a boisterous laugh. "Alain says one of France's most eligible bachelors is marrying an American." Yvette was staring at Max. "After the girl we had at the vineyard picking grapes, I'm not so keen on American girls."

"What did you not like about her?"

"She thought of herself as a winemaker, not just a grape picker. She refused to do domestic work. And she threatened to take Roland away if Alain and I didn't stop arguing. Which was fine with Alain. He and Roland are oil and water." She looked over at Max again. "Your fiancée could stay and help me here with the dishes."

Not on your life, Olivier wanted to say. "It's a kind offer, but she is being allowed to observe the hunt."

"Who said she could do that?"

"Jean-Claude."

Her eyes narrowed. "So he compromised. I wonder what Anne held over his head this time."

Olivier decided Yvette was a pot-stirrer. He excused himself and went to join Max and Hank, who were talking to Jean-Claude. Hank took a sip of the marc, as Jean-Claude referred to it, and was told that it was the generic term for spirits distilled from the skins, pulp, and seeds of grapes after they are pressed to make wine. "The point is," he was told, "it warms the blood."

"But dulls the senses," Hank said, putting his glass down. "The ham is great, though."

Tim walked up to them, a camera slung over his shoulder,

and a smile on his face. "Don't you go anywhere without that thing?" Jean-Claude asked.

Tim held up the camera and snapped a picture of Jean-Claude in response. Olivier observed that the moment Tim swept the camera up in front of his face to take the photograph, vanity took over and Jean-Claude grinned. Olivier could barely hear over the din. Dogs barked in the distance. One of the men stepped forward, and bellowed that they would be heading out in five minutes. Max whispered to Tim, "No Lucy?"

"Don't worry, she's close by. I plan to take a few photos and pick her up."

"She's going to find herself in real trouble if she decides to run again. Do you know how old she is?"

"Twenty?"

"Seventeen."

He laughed. "The little liar. Then her uncle may have legal control of her. I'll marry her, if it means having him out of the picture."

Tim followed Max outside, but Olivier decided to have a taste of the ham and backtracked to the table. Yvette, he saw, had called Jean-Claude aside and was pointing at Max. Jean-Claude strode away from her, looking unhappy. Alain walked toward Yvette, and Olivier was surprised to see that he was weaving slightly. The couple engaged in a small verbal altercation, and Olivier noticed that Alain appeared coiled to strike. He didn't really respect Alain now.

Jean-Claude walked over and Olivier thanked him again for accommodating them. "You can thank Madame Bré," he said, "and not me. I'm catching a lot of flak from the guys." *And from Yvette,* Olivier thought. He suddenly wished they hadn't come, and wondered if there was some way they could excuse themselves and leave. He had observed the men eyeing Max warily, a few of them showing unveiled hostility. Burgundy was changing on the surface, he realized, but the old ways ran deep.

He sat with his back to the remaining people in the room. He could overhear Alain and Jean-Claude's conversation behind him. Alain complained that Roland hadn't shown up the night before. "He must have met a girl," Jean-Claude said. "*Mon Dieu*, at that age I lived for the girls."

"He's obsessed with a girl named Lucy," Alain continued. "Yvette forbade him to see her again. You can imagine how that backfired."

"Who isn't obsessed with Lucy?" said Jean-Claude. "My son Luc is crazy about her. I know from an investigator that she is being accused of killing Yves. She's good press. Young, white American girl, maybe pleading, what? Self-defense? She doesn't deserve this."

The gossip mill was alive and well. Olivier strained to listen as Alain said, "Roland had better bring his ass to this hunt, I can tell you that."

Jean-Claude said, "You've got to control your temper, Alain. What have you got against your boy?"

"You're telling me what to do with my own family?" Olivier felt a tense silence. Then, "Did my wife tell you that I had Yves following her? If she's messing around, she'll be sorry."

The *chef de battue* bellowed that it was time to leave. Olivier turned and saw Jean-Claude speaking to Yvette, who appeared frightened. *Surely*, he thought, *nothing is going on between those two*. If it is, then Alain's comment was a veiled threat.

Outside, the hunters donned orange vests and hiked out to a field less than a kilometer away, where they were assigned positions. Max took two steps up a handmade stand and was told to stay there. She said to Hank, "You think I'm put here as a target?"

Hank said firmly, "I've got you covered."

Alain said he had to go take a piss, but would be back. He set his Kimber rifle 308 down and took off. Jean-Claude, who was in position next to Hank, said, "If he doesn't kill a boar with that rifle, something's wrong with him. It's the best. He bought one for himself, one for his son, and probably one for Yvette, too."

"She's a good shot?" Max asked from her perch.

"She's won some women's competitions."

"So she's a good shot for a woman."

"*Exactement.*"

Olivier, who was more or less in the center of the line, had been handed a Winchester Model 94, an old-school lever-action gun, which felt more familiar than he had thought it would. He looked over and saw that Jean-Claude had held onto his Weatherby Mark V rifle, which he claimed was his favorite. Hank had been placed at the far end of the line, and Max was a few feet from him. He stood rigid, holding the Binelli RI rifle that had belonged to Max's grandfather. Tim moved around more than he should, Olivier thought, clicking his camera. The other hunters stood prepared.

Forty-five minutes had passed when they heard the sound of the bells around the dogs' necks, in the distance, which meant the boars were on their way. They all stood at attention, waiting, the dogs' braying coming closer. Olivier felt tension in his mind and throughout his body. He heard shouts, and saw a boar run out at one end of the field. Shots were fired as another emerged from the forest at the opposite end. While his eyes were fixed on the other end of the field, he heard Max scream, and saw her leap off the stand and run toward the woods. At that moment, a boar thrust through the brush midway down the field and was shot dead before he made it fifteen feet. The chief of the hunt shot three times into the air and silence prevailed.

Olivier chased after Max and saw that she and Hank were bending over what he assumed was a boar. Moving at a slow pace he turned to one of the hunters who said, "Something's wrong. I can't see what's happening from here." Olivier picked up speed, and as he drew closer, he saw that the form on the ground was a human. He heard Max say to Hank, "We stop the bleeding, treat for shock, and keep her warm."

"Okay, but I'm putting pressure to the wound and the bleeding won't stop."

"Let me. She began pressing hard below the armpit. "I've got to wrap my fingers around the brachial artery. There, it's better, but she's losing a lot of blood."

Hank said, "Her pulse is awful weak." He touched the girl's face, "Hey, don't leave us. Hang in there." To Olivier's annoyance, Tim had his camera up in front of his face, taking multiple photographs. When Olivier reached him to ask him to stop, Tim moved the camera away from his face and tears were coursing down his cheeks. "I will know who shot her!" he shouted in French into the air. He lifted his camera again and the click, clicking started all over again. Some of the hunters turned their faces. A group of them had gathered a few yards away and were busy lighting cigarettes. Tim had started yelling again. "Who the fuck would shoot a girl? She doesn't look like a pig!"

Hank stood with the girl in his arms, pausing for a moment to regain his balance, and started walking toward the house, breathing heavily. The girl's silvery hair made her look ethereal in the early morning light. Olivier motioned to the chief of the hunt who was calling the police and ambulance on his cell phone. Max and Tim kept pace with her father as he took long strides toward Jean-Claude's house. Tim turned frequently, continuing to take photographs.

Olivier had to stay and take charge. He went to the chief of the hunt, and told him to call everyone together, which he did. "Can anyone step forward as a witness?" he asked.

No one budged.

"We put the warning signs up," Jean-Claude said. "We did everything according to the law. What the hell was she doing running out like that?"

The other hunters clustered around closer.

"Everyone gather at Jean-Claude's house," Olivier said. "And hand your rifles over to him once you arrive there. They must each be labeled with your name and phone number. The police will take them after that."

The men began mumbling among themselves, and Olivier overheard remarks like, "Who does he think he is?" Then someone whispered, "Shut up! He's a *magistrat*." Another said, "No crime has been committed. He can't just take over."

Alain, who looked soberer than earlier, said, "We called the local police, Olivier. It's an accident. These things happen, and they know how to deal with it."

"First we must officially identify the victim," Olivier said.

"That's easy," Alain said. "It's Lucy."

Chapter Eleven

Max walked rapidly alongside Hank, her fingers pressing the artery. Tim kept taking photographs—turning to focus on the men who were slowly wending their way up, and then back to Lucy. Click. Click. The door was unlocked, and Max held it open for Hank. The room where they were gathered earlier was empty. Hank lowered the girl onto a long table, and Max removed her own coat and placed it under her to elevate her. The bleeding started again and Max ran and grabbed a scarf hanging on a hook, and made a tourniquet. The blood flow ceased.

"I'm worried about the bone being shattered," she said. "I could make a splint."

"She's already passed out," Hank said, "probably from pain. We've staunched the bleeding, that's the main thing." Tim was hovering over her, talking quietly to her. Max paced. She hadn't felt right about the hunt from the moment it was mentioned. She felt in her jacket for the pocketknife her brother Frédéric gave her years ago, and wrapped her hand around it for comfort.

Yvette entered the room wearing a coat and hat. "What happened?" she asked in French, standing mid-room, looking unsure, and not a little angry.

Hank turned to Max. "Ask her to make sure the ambulance is on the way. And ask her where she's been."

Max waited while Yvette called to make sure the ambulance was on the way. "Five minutes," she said. She walked over and looked at the girl and said, "*Mon Dieu*, it's Lucy! I step out to the boulangerie to get more bread and come back to this." She turned on Tim and his camera, and said in a strident voice, "Put that thing away." She looked again at Tim. "You were on the hunt, too?"

"I was. I wanted to capture a boar mid-air. No idea what I got, it all happened so fast."

"That film will be a big help to the police," Hank said to Max. "Make sure he keeps it."

"The ambulance is here," Yvette said, glancing out the window. Two emergency technicians rushed in and immediately began working on Lucy. "We'll hook her up to oxygen," one of them said. He looked up at Max, "You did the tourniquet? Looks good."

Olivier walked into the room, a grim look on his face. He stepped back as the attendants passed by. He whispered to Max, "Is she alive?"

"Barely." Max followed the stretcher out to the waiting ambulance, with Hank and Olivier behind her. Max turned to them, "I'm going with her."

"I'll follow in my car," Tim said.

"We'll be there soon," Hank said.

As the ambulance turned around and slowly moved down the driveway, Max looked out the window at the hunters standing in a circle, then turned her attention back to Lucy, who looked lost in the blankets the attendants had wrapped her in. "She'll need a blood transfusion for sure," the attendant said, "but we can't do that."

Max reached over and held Lucy's hand, her thoughts going back to the day her brother arrived at the hospital in Manhattan in an ambulance, full of tubes, and already dead. "She's your sister?" the attendant asked, and Max nodded.

The emergency room in Beaune was quiet, compared to the ones Max frequented for her job in New York. A woman doctor appeared, and within minutes Lucy was taken to surgery. Tim arrived, camera in hand, and sat down. "What a mistake to let Lucy leave last night," he said. "I think she went back to Anne's cabin. I was afraid if I went looking for her, she would show up at my place, so I waited. I sat up all night. I didn't know if she had decided to end our relationship, if you can call it that, or if something happened that prevented her from coming."

"She'll be able to tell you herself once she wakes up after surgery."

"She could die."

"Not likely. I've seen someone shot eight times and survive. If the bullet misses your brain, you have a good chance of pulling through."

"That's a relief. I'm going to get her through this, and I'm going to prove her innocent of everything she's been accused of. And then I'm taking her to England."

Two policemen entered and looked around, then went to the receptionist to explain that they were here on account of a foreign girl being shot in the woods. Max waited while the receptionist explained that the girl was in surgery. Both policemen sat down in chairs placed along the opposite wall.

The door opened and a woman doctor dressed in scrubs walked directly to Max and Tim. "You are family?"

"Yes," Tim lied. "We were with a hunting group..."

The doctor said, "My sister called ahead to tell me she was coming in." She looked disgusted. "These are the only gun accidents we have, of course. They are always ruled accidental. Personally, I hate the sport."

"Is your sister Yvette?" Max asked, but the doctor ignored her and continued speaking to Tim in broken English, though Tim assured her he understood French. "*Bien.* The bullet clipped the brachial artery," she said. "There is massive damage to the tissue and tendons, as well as nerves and blood vessels. And there has been dramatic blood loss. If someone hadn't been there to perform first aid, she wouldn't have made it. We have her on IV antibiotics because the danger of infection is high."

Max said, "Prognosis?"

"Recovering fully is unlikely, but we shall see. I am a good surgeon, and I hope for the best. The bone wasn't shattered, and her arm is strong. I will probably have to do another surgery before it's over."

Max persisted. "Her eyes fluttered, but then she seemed to drift into a coma."

"Well," the surgeon said, still not having introduced herself, "there was a lot of blood loss, even with the tourniquet. There is also psychological incapacitation. The person is too frightened or in too much pain to continue the fight. We will know more in a few hours after she is out of recovery. And now, I have another surgery." She walked briskly away.

Max noticed the police had waited at a respectful distance, but now they ambled over.

Max said to Tim, "You go and see her and I'll hold off these guys. Go!"

He entered the door to the recovery room and the police turned to follow, but Max said, "*Bonjour.* I was a witness at the shooting. I happen to be a detective in New York, here on vacation, but I am happy to give my report."

They motioned her to a chair. She told them all that had happened in French, using technical terms that made them keep nodding their heads. "We get a lot of gunshot wounds in New York," she said, and they didn't bother trying to hide their fascination with a woman who had so much more experience with this than they did. She said, "I want to see the girl for one moment, and I will ask her fiancé to leave. Is that acceptable?" and they nodded. She raced in and saw Tim cradling Lucy's head, and telling her over and over that he loved her. "Squeeze my finger if you hear me," he said, and when she didn't respond he said it again. He turned to Max, "The pressure was minute, but it was there."

"You need to go," Max said. "Olivier will come and find you."

"I'm going to be busy developing film," he said. He smiled, "I do it all the old-fashioned way. The door to my house will be unlocked if you need me."

He exited through a side door, and Max motioned the police in. "You really think she's going to make it?" the younger one said.

"Oh, yes. She's going to be a bridesmaid at my wedding on April twenty-eighth."

Abdel was in the waiting room, and Max excused herself to speak with him. "Monsieur Chaumont called and told me what happened. He's interviewing the hunters."

Max told him about the morning and all that had transpired. He listened carefully, then said, "She didn't go back to my cousin's after leaving Tim's. Monsieur Chaumont learned that there is a small cottage on the Bré property, and we think she may have been hiding there."

"That's what Tim thinks, too."

"He and Lucy were caught on the surveillance camera leaving Yves' building, looking like they were on the run. A hooded guy met up with them. The police are all over it, especially now that the uncle is screaming that French police are incompetent."

"Lucy is obviously unable to be interviewed now," Max said. "Can you keep them away from Tim until he gets all of his film developed?"

"I'll try."

Olivier and Hank entered the room together. "It was difficult at Jean-Claude's house," Olivier said. "There was a lot of silent resistance from the hunters. In the end, they were saying that she had no business being on private land, and it was her fault that she was shot."

"Great."

"Alain helped me collect the guns."

"He disappeared into the woods," Max said. "Just before the hunters lined up. Remember? He had to go pee."

"I don't recall," Olivier said. "Are you saying he didn't return to his station?"

"I don't think so," Max said.

Olivier said, "I overhead Alain telling Jean-Claude that he had hired Yves to follow Yvette. It could have been an empty threat."

"By the way, where was the kid, Roland?" Hank asked.

"He was supposed to show up at the hunt," Olivier said. "Yvette said he had partied late the night before. Alain is certain he can have him in my office by five. As for Lucy, we have both a victim and a suspect in the same person. The Beaune police are here to guard a comatose patient who was shot, and who allegedly had escaped from a mental hospital in Westchester County, New York, and the Lyon police want her for questioning in the case of Yves' murder."

Abdel said, "I'll let the Lyon police know that she has a guard, and that we are here."

"A dose of logic might help," said Hank. "Max?"

Max knew he was referring to their old game of connecting the dots. She started. "Lucy Kendrick arrived in Lyon on September tenth and bought a red, vintage Vespa, which she drove north to the village of Viré, where the *vignerons* had started picking grapes. She was hired by Alain Milne, and picked for ten days, after which she migrated an hour north, to the Côte de Beaune region to pick. She went to Anne Bré, who hired her. She had made friends with Roland, age eighteen, the son of Alain, and soon he was going up to Beaune to see her. While at Madame Bré's, she befriended Yves Laroche, a man who traveled each year from Lyon to pick grapes for Anne, a private investigator. Age forty."

Max turned to Olivier, who said, "After the *vendange* at Madame Bré's, Lucy Kendrick took off to pick grapes in Chablis. Madame Bré had liked the girl and invited her to spend the winter, which she did. When we arrived in Burgundy on April sixth, we learned that she had disappeared.

Hank interjected, "I bumped into her in a café and she took off like a mad hatter. She was running from an uncle named George."

Olivier continued, "Then on April seventh, Yves Laroche dies."

Max said, "Lucy is seen leaving Yves Laroche's party with Tim. Roland was caught on camera exiting the building ten minutes after them. Others exiting the building are caught on the security camera, but we believe he is the last of Yves' guests to leave. Tim and Lucy were nearby when Yves hit the pavement, and Roland joined them. Tim took photographs throughout the evening. He wanted to start developing them and sent Lucy and Roland to Anne's cabin.

"It is on the news that Yves jumped to his death. Tim takes Lucy to Paris for the night and Roland stays in the cabin and sleeps, claiming he was afraid of his father. When they return, Lucy goes to the cabin to check on Roland, and stays, as Tim is going to a hunt the next morning. During the hunt, Lucy is shot."

"Here we are," Isabelle said. The outside emergency room door had opened and Isabelle and Anne Bré, both in elegant attire, stood there. "Jean-Claude told me what happened," Anne said, "and I called your grandmother. Is Lucy alive?"

Max nodded, surprised to see her grandmother looking vulnerable and afraid.

Hank said, "She's in a coma."

The two women took the seats offered them. Ignoring them, Olivier said, "I will wait twenty-four hours before asking the prosecutor to open an investigation into Lucy's shooting. Let's see if Lucy's uncle shows up with the proper papers. He may want to move her to the United States as soon as possible. We will have to clear her name, though, before she can leave the country."

Isabelle, overhearing Hank say that his hunch was Lucy would be better off as a murder suspect in France than as a mental patient in the U.S., joined them, her face contorted. "Either alternative is wretched," she said to Olivier. "Anne and I can watch over Lucy while you go arrest whoever did this to her."

"It isn't as simple as that, Madame."

He huffed out the door, followed by Max and Hank, who said, "We don't need those two in the picture." They went to the lobby.

"Dad, technically we shouldn't have our noses in this, either. None of us are authorized."

"I'm changing that as of now," Olivier said.

"You're taking charge?" Max asked.

"It will work as before. You and Abdel and I will work as a team."

"Why don't Max and I go back to the field where Lucy was shot and see if we can pick up any information there?" Hank said.

Olivier agreed. "If anyone asks, say you are out for a walk."

Anne joined them. "They are taking Lucy to a room. Anne and I told the nurse that we are her great aunts, and were given permission to stay with her."

"I'm going to see her," Olivier said. "Come with me, Max."

They went quietly into the recovery room and peered down at the girl. She was hooked up to an IV, and was wearing an oxygen mask, which did nothing to hide her frail, child-like beauty. The tiny gold ring in her nose struck Max as a symbol of hope.

"I'm posting a policeman at the door," Olivier said to Anne when she entered silently. "Please telephone me when you are ready to leave."

Max, Hank, and Olivier walked to Olivier's car. Juliette pulled up beside them. "Isabelle said you need me to drive you somewhere?"

What innocence exists in people who don't do police work, Max thought. She and Hank climbed into the little car, and Olivier mumbled something about going to meet up with Abdel. Max knew that he was desperate to have time alone to think about all that had transpired so quickly. She knew when he said he was taking over the case that he didn't think anything that had happened was accidental. She didn't resist being sent to do fieldwork with Hank. Maybe it would help the investigation.

Chapter Twelve

Olivier decided that, instead of calling Abdel, he would drive the hour south to check in with Alain and Yvette, and while in the village he would have coffee with his parents. When he knocked on the door of Chez Milne, Yvette came to the door looking efficient and sounding cheerful. "Olivier! Here you are. *Bon*. Alain is in the vineyard to the right of the house and up the hill. Where he always is."

"Bonjour, Yvette."

She spoke rapidly and so softly that Olivier leaned in to hear. "How's the girl doing? I'm sure the police will call it an accident. The *sangliers* are dangerous, and very fast. I personally would not be caught dead in the woods without a gun." She suddenly looked alarmed, and ran over to the oven. "*Pardon,* I have a cake in the oven." She removed it and placed it on a hot plate, then turned, "You're still here?" She pointed out the window. "I can see him. He's a wreck over all that has happened. As if I'm *not*."

Olivier had barely understood her words, they were spoken so rapidly and with no thought. "Is Roland home?"

"Roland! Oh, not yet. He *is* eighteen, you know." Olivier had never seen anyone so anxiety-ridden. "He called. He may be with Alain. You didn't tell me how the girl is."

"She's in a coma."

Yvette said, "I have to make a phone call."

"*Bon*. I hope your cake turns out well." *Could a woman this fragmented follow a recipe?* he wondered.

"*Merci,* Olivier."

Olivier wandered desultorily toward the two figures he could barely make out on the slope, behind the house. The warm weather was encouraging the vines to issue tiny shoots of green. Soon the entire landscape would be transformed into a panoply of abundance and beauty.

Olivier peered into the distance and could vaguely make out Mont Blanc, over one hundred kilometers away. A rare sighting. He was near the cemetery now, looking down on the village that had changed very little since his childhood. For decades, the *vignerons* here had planted vineyards for the many co-ops, rarely making their own wines. The wine merchants, of which there were many firms, then purchased the grapes from the growers and created their own brands. It was prohibitive for individuals to purchase the extensive equipment needed to make wine, though some persevered, often with mediocre results.

Alain, who was a co-op president, elected by all the *co-opérateurs* for a couple of years running, was opposed to the changes that were manifesting as more and more young producers were moving in, wanting to follow in the footsteps of their neighbors up north, who were producing sustainable wines. According to Olivier's parents, Alain was up against the young director of the co-op, who wanted to disallow the big machinery used for cultivating the fields and return to the old-fashioned method of horses and plows.

Olivier waved to the young man who was standing a few rows over and staring at his approach. The man eventually put up a hand, and bent down again. Alain looked up as Olivier approached. "See the roots?" he said to Olivier, pointing to a hollow in the ground, exposing the ancient plant's rootstock. "I'm replacing this one after half a century." Olivier knew from the higher elevation of the vineyard and the mention of the *vieilles vignes* that a higher-end wine would be produced from these vines. "Amazing that something so old and gnarly can produce such a fabulous fruit, *d'accord?*" He studied Olivier for a moment. "Are you and your fiancée planning to have a family?"

"Eventually. Of course."

Alain laughed. "If you don't hurry, you're going to be too old and gnarly."

Olivier suddenly thought he understood women who were constantly being asked if they were still ripe enough to have a baby, though the question was phrased with a bit more discretion. Alain said with a scowl, "Stop looking so insulted. I'm just joking, Olivier. Men at sixty are producing heirs. It's just that Yvette and I started so young, then had only the one. She said she could never love another as much as she loved Roland, and so that was that."

"Farmers used to have big families," Olivier said, "to share in the workload, of course, and as many more children died then, they needed replacements."

"I wanted more children," Alain said. "Life can get pretty dull when the kid leaves home. Then you wait for the grandchildren, and these days it might never happen."

"I'm here about the girl Lucy, Alain."

"I figured. I guess whoever shot her will be a hero. She was running from the law."

"I'm trying to learn exactly what she was running from."

"Maybe a boar was chasing her."

Olivier thought he was being sarcastic, but realized he wasn't. "The boars exited at the opposite end of the field. As I recall, you went into the woods."

"I shouldn't have had anything to drink. I was a little sick to my stomach. Do they know what caliber bullet hit her?"

"Not yet."

"At least six of us were shooting .30 caliber bullets. Even your lever-action rifle had .30 ammunition. Did you shoot, by the way?"

"No."

"I saw your guest, the tall, skinny American named Hank, raise his rifle. Or at least Jean-Claude saw him." Olivier wasn't surprised to learn that the men had been talking among themselves. "A few of us were practice-shooting earlier in the morning.

Jean-Claude has a target-shooting area. It's going to be difficult to tell who shot when and where."

"Did you see anything in the forest?"

"No."

The young man Olivier assumed to be Roland was a row away; as he got closer Olivier could see from the earbuds he wore, that his beatific expression was probably due to the music he was listening to. Alain yelled over at him and the boy looked startled, then bent down to dig into the ground.

"He can't live without his music," Alain said. "I don't know what's happening to kids these days."

"I'd like to talk to him," Olivier said.

"Oh, that's not Roland. It's his cousin who helps me sometimes. My wife's sister's son. They're all good boys."

"The sister who operated on Lucy?"

Alain was caught off-guard. "*Oui.*"

"I need to know if Roland was with Lucy the night before she was shot. There's no proof, but I hope he will tell me if he was."

Alain's voice grew suddenly harsh. "Leave him be. He has a scooter and goes off and comes back, but we don't keep up with his every move. His mother forbade him from seeing Lucy, I know that."

"I assume you would rather have me ask Roland a few questions than have the police at your door, correct?"

"So you're here in an official capacity. I should have guessed. I'd rather have the local police come, to tell you the truth. I don't like having a friend spying on me."

"I'm trying to help. I don't have a son, but if I did, and if he were in trouble, I would be grateful to an old friend who tried to help. *Au revoir, Alain.*"

Olivier felt he had no choice but to leave. Making his way down the hill, he was frustrated that he had learned nothing, not even Roland's whereabouts. If Roland showed up now, the family had been warned, and they could create a story. All the guns had been turned over to the police, who were, he was certain, not on the victim's side, especially now that Lucy was named a suspect in a murder case. He slowly made his way back to his car, waving to Yvette, whose face he saw in the kitchen window. She didn't wave back. He couldn't believe that he was perceived as the enemy in the village he loved above all others.

In that moment he made a decision. It was just that sentiment, he suddenly realized, that had made him hold back from requesting a full-on investigation. He hadn't wanted to see the darkness that had started to cloud his childhood memories. He would see the local prosecutor immediately and ask to be put in charge of Lucy's shooting, and if his team could prove the link of this case to Yves Laroche's murder, then he would ask to be in charge there, too. Driving back to Max and the family, he recalled the bet he had with Max, and smiled. At least he thought about his and Max's bet, now stripped of its playfulness. Who cared about choosing an apartment in Paris when a girl's life hung in the balance?

Chapter Thirteen

The day was fleeing too rapidly, and Max was tired. The hunt. The shooting. Getting Lucy to the hospital. And now Hank wanted to return to what he was now referring to as the crime scene, a term Olivier refused to utter. It was already two o'clock, and overcast. Rain was predicted. Juliette was along because she had brought a picnic hamper and neither detective had the heart to let her down. They suggested she come with them out to the field, and they could picnic there. It had only taken her three seconds to know what they were up to, but in the end she agreed. Max suddenly saw with a new clarity how difficult Juliette's role had been, spending her life with a man who had always put his cases above everything else. Then Max had joined him at the NYPD, and learned to do the same thing.

Hank and Max stopped in at Jean-Claude's to tell him that they were going to take a walk and maybe have a picnic. He asked after Lucy, and then offered them a rifle in case they ran into a boar. "What are you looking for?" he asked.

Max decided to be honest with him. "My father and I are detectives, and we hate conjecture. We need to know why Lucy Kendrick was shot. This is unofficial, of course, but we won't stop until we have some answers."

Jean-Claude said, "Accidents happen. She was in the wrong place at the wrong time."

"Anne mentioned a cabin that her daughter used as a retreat. Can you take us there?"

He hesitated. "I guess so. But I have to take my son to an appointment now. You think Lucy was hiding out there?"

"Who else knew of the cabin?"

"It's never been a secret. Yvette accompanied me there once, when I wanted to get a few things belonging to my wife. You met Tim. The Brit. He takes guests mountain biking, and I caught him there once with a woman and ran him off. Anne took Lucy there, I'm sure. I saw she raced to the hospital to care for her. Lucy has become a replacement for Caroline."

"Even your son brightens up at the mention of Lucy's name."

"My son is like my mother-in-law. He's desperate for a mother and she for a daughter."

And what about you? Max wanted to ask but didn't.

Juliette joined them, and Jean-Claude told Max he had to leave, quickly sketching a map of the path to the cabin. "Lucy's Vespa is in my garage," Jean-Claude said, "in safekeeping."

"Was anything in it?" Max asked.

Again, there was that slight hesitation that indicated someone was probably lying. "No."

They started toward the field where Lucy was shot. "Let's do this methodically," Hank said to Max. "We'll walk through the woods while we still have a little light."

Juliette, spotting a stand ahead, said, "I'll go there and be the lookout." Max thought she was making fun of them, but she was perfectly serious. Juliette went up the three steps and pulled out a small set of binoculars, and put them around her neck. "I brought these to watch the birds," she said. "But it will work for humans, too. I have a snack if you need it," she said to her family, "but don't tell Maman. At least don't use the term snack."

Max smiled, knowing that it was a social crime in France to snack before mealtime.

"Thanks, Ma."

Max and Hank made long strides toward the tree line. "Lucy emerged from the woods at a run here," Hank said, pointing, "so let's go in that way and see if we see any tracks."

They moved rapidly. Max watched her father, impressed. "I used to do this tracking stuff in the Army," he said. They were moving too swiftly for her to answer. "We know the bullet went clean through her arm. She was in a running position when she was hit, her right arm up. The bullet had to come from our end of the line, maybe six men in. If you move to the center, where Olivier was, then it's the wrong angle. I had my gun raised to shoot, and if you hadn't yelled I might have. Just saying I understand if somebody shot her by accident. The reason I'm questioning that theory is that not one of them said he could have done it. Their reticence makes me suspicious."

He stopped. "Look, Max, a bullet hole."

Max studied the indentation in the tree trunk. "But they shoot in this field all the time. It could be old."

"Maybe. But it could also be new." He looked around, found a small branch and stuck it in the hole. "A hundred to one it's a .30 caliber bullet that hit this tree." He bent down and raked his hand through the weeds. "It's my lucky day. Here's a .30 caliber bullet, waiting for me to see it. Now we need to learn about the entry and exit of the bullet, and the distance."

"Meaning, if she was shot from two hundred yards away or closer."

"Yep. Most of our gunshot wounds are up close and personal. We have to reason that she could have been shot from behind, meaning from the woods. The shooter had to be close, I would guess fifteen yards, for the damage it did."

"The surgeon was so abrupt I couldn't get much information. You're sure the bullet passed through her arm?"

"If it was still in her, the doc would have said so."

He dropped onto one knee. "Looky here," he said. "These are fresh. Someone with big feet running. Little feet in front. Looks like he tripped here. Little feet kept going. Little feet stopped in her tracks. Fell. Then the backtrack. Big feet turned and ran back. Let's go."

Max walked rapidly behind him for a kilometer and then they were in a yard in front of a small cabin, a charming dwelling that made Max think that country living for a young girl could be magical. Hank went to the door and found it unlocked. They entered and looked around. Two single beds, a quilt pulled up on the bed on the right in a careless fashion, the other one undisturbed. "Someone was here, alright," Hank said. "My guess is that Lucy was either here alone and someone frightened her, causing her to run, or she was trying to get away from a person she was with."

They stood in stillness. Hank visibly relaxed. "We have to get back to your Ma, but we can take a one-minute breather." He looked at her. "You okay?"

"Sure. Why not?"

"Why not? You're about to change your life in a major way. A new country, clear across the ocean from your mother and me. Switch jobs. All this with a couple of crimes to solve as well." He leaned against a small, white table. "I won't go all sentimental on you, but being in this little house built for Anne's daughter, and realizing that the little girl who played here is dead, kind of chokes me up."

Max understood. He was losing her. Anne had permanently lost her daughter. And they had an orphan they were trying to protect.

"Do you look at this and wish you had grown up in a place like this?" he asked. "You could have. Maybe if you and Frédéric had grown up here, he'd still be alive. But I was adamant that it was New York City and the NYPD, no matter what. I couldn't picture myself anywhere else. But you have roots here. You'll be bringing up your kids here. It amazes me."

Max crossed the tiny, enchanting room and put her arms around her father. "I am glad I grew up where I did. With you and Maman and my little brother. They were all the roots I needed."

"Let's go disobey the French rules and have a snack," he said, suddenly grinning.

Max laughed.

He followed the same path, stopping when he saw fresh tracks. "These are new, and they lead to the field where your Ma is. Let's go."

Arriving at the edge of the woods, they noticed two figures on the hunting stand. Juliette was talking to a large, stocky young man. "This is Roland," Juliette said. "He hasn't eaten since yesterday. I explained who we are and gave him some cheese and bread and *saucisson*."

"*Bonjour*," Roland said. His rifle was propped against the railing. "My cell phone didn't work and I was scared to come out of the woods."

It took Max and Hank a second for the shock of seeing him to dissipate. "You were with Lucy," Max said. It was more of a statement than a question.

"Is she dead?" he asked, but he seemed more interested in what was going into his mouth.

"She's in a coma, but she will live. Your tracks were behind her, then she was shot and you took off running back to the cabin."

"That's how it happened."

The air had grown chilly. Hank said, "Let's go up to Anne's. We can talk there."

"Am I a suspect?" Roland asked, still leaning against the railing as though he didn't have a care in his head.

Max glanced over and saw Hank's intolerance building, though he hadn't understood what Roland was saying. "We can have you arrested, if you prefer," Max said. "Or you can answer a few questions for us."

He led the way up to the house, a broad-shouldered farm boy with big feet and a big head with hair dipping into his eyes.

"Your parents have been worried," Max said.

"They'd be relieved if I disappeared for good."

"All teens say that."

"I did disappear. Last year. And they sent the P.I. from Lyon to find me. Stupid." He had not raised his voice, and remained unperturbed.

"Where did you go?"

"I was hiding out in the suburbs of Paris with some friends. Yves Laroche found me, and my dad came and got me."

They were approaching the house and Max could see Anne shielding her eyes, curious who was coming up her road.

"Which means they do care." She turned to Hank. "I will go back for *Maman*."

Anne came rushing toward them. "You must be chilled," she said. "Come inside and I'll make a warm drink." She stopped and looked at Roland. "You are Alain's and Yvette's son, right?"

He nodded, but didn't reach out to shake her hand. Max thought of young Luc who, at age eight, had demonstrated excellent manners. They insisted to Anne that they remain in the kitchen. She began preparations for *vin chaud*, a red wine heated with spices.

"He reeks of pot," Hank said under his breath.

Anne looked from Hank to Roland, then spoke in English, "Jean-Claude has known this family a long time and says the boy has been a problem. Why is he with you?"

Max explained, and was unprepared for Anne's wrath against Roland. "That is private property. Tell me how you got in there," she demanded.

Roland gave her a surly look and said, "Lucy and I were hiding because everybody wants to blame her for what happened to Yves. I slept most of the time."

Anne could not hide her distaste and dislike of the young man yammering on and on, all the attention on him. "I don't care about all that," she said. "Why didn't you defend Lucy?"

"Lucy can take care of herself."

"Obviously, she couldn't."

Max asked Roland if he was carrying a gun, and he said he was. "You're a good shot?"

For the first time he smiled and looked boyish. "The best. My dad had me shooting at age eleven and I started hunting at sixteen."

"Why did you turn back when Lucy was shot?"

He shrugged. "I was scared, I guess."

Hank scoffed, and Max thought it was pointless to continue the interview here, as no one had any authority. She went outside when she saw her mother in the yard. She texted Olivier, who told her to bring Roland to the police station in Beaune.

Hank walked out with the boy. He put himself at the wheel of Isabelle's car, with Juliette in the front seat, and Max and Roland in the back. Hank said in English, "The boy is guilty of something. Maybe it has to do with sex, or with running away from home, or attempted murder, but guilt is written all over him."

Roland sat with his head back on the seat, eyes closed, oblivious.

Chapter Fourteen

Olivier met Max in front of the hospital, and listened as she recounted to him the events of the afternoon. He was in a foul mood after meeting with Alain, and on the drive back to Beaune, had pulled over to phone the Lyon prosecutor, Emmanuel Caron, who finally agreed to make the investigation of Yves Laroche's death official. Caron would agree to Olivier being in charge of the investigation, but with his men operating under him. Olivier didn't like the idea, as he would have to insist that Max stay removed from this one. Difficult ground to traverse, with her grandmother and Anne Bré feeling responsible for the girl. Not to mention Hank, who hadn't met a case he couldn't solve, which were his exact words two nights ago after three beers.

Olivier's cell phone rang and he stepped out of the waiting room for a moment to listen to the police inspector of Beaune tell him that the boy, Roland Milne, complained that he had been harassed by two Americans who he understood were detectives from New York. "This is not permissible," the inspector said in a firm voice. Olivier announced that he, too, was French, and knew the rules. He re-entered the hospital waiting room, and told Max about the call.

"That brat!"

"Caron is looking for any excuse to make me bow out of this investigation," Olivier said. "He would prefer to accept that Yves Laroche committed suicide, and let that be the end of it. It's going to end up being all about drugs, and I have no compassion for anyone involved."

"Let's face it, Hank and I are part of the problem. Hank is going to follow behind me, no matter what. I tell you what. I will take him to see the medieval ruins in Brancion, and we will bow out of Yves Laroche's murder case, and maybe the attempted murder of Lucy Kendrick."

"She is also a suspect in the death of Laroche."

They stood in silence. *Were they in conflict over the girl?* Olivier wondered. Her lack of response made him uneasy. She had just given him an out by agreeing to go off with her father. At the same time, he felt compelled to explain himself and set out to do that. "I have to move with extreme caution, and follow protocol. The police in Beaune are calling Lucy's case an accidental shooting. The uncle is bearing down on them, and says he is taking her to Paris tomorrow, and they are glad. It might be in her best interests, as they will do all in their power to get her name cleared of Yves' death. Saying it was self-defense on her part makes it easier."

"That makes sense," Max said in a fake conciliatory voice. "But it doesn't explain her getting shot." She looked at her watch. "I'm famished. I'm going to collect my grandmother and head home."

Max was off the case.

Olivier spoke to the gendarme on duty outside Lucy's room and entered, with Max behind him. Isabelle looked up and smiled. "We know people in comas are supposed to be stimulated. One of us is trying to read to her fairly constantly. I read a book on winemaking to her."

"No wonder she hasn't opened her eyes," Max said.

Olivier laughed in spite of himself.

"I can stay here for a while," he said. "A new gendarme will be coming on duty soon."

"Come for dinner if you like," Isabelle said to Olivier. "Progress is being made on the wedding. Lucy knows all about it, don't you, dear?"

"And what about her guardian arriving?" Olivier asked. "Has there been any word?"

"Tomorrow," Isabelle said. "We heard it from the nurses."

Isabelle picked her coat up from the chair and slipped into it. She stopped in the doorway and said to Olivier, "Another of the women from *Femmes et Vins* will be arriving soon. She is young and happy to stay the night with Lucy."

"I don't think that's necessary," Olivier said. "The care here is good, I'm sure, and I have a gendarme guarding the door, don't forget."

"But Anne and I do think it's necessary," Isabelle said. "I saw the gendarme head to the toilette, leaving no one in charge."

Olivier thought he saw a smile flit across Max's face, which he found annoying. "Very well," he said. "I won't be able to make it for dinner tonight. I have a lot of work to catch up on."

"*D'accord*," Isabelle said. "I will let Juliette know. I'll see you downstairs, Maxine." The door closed.

Olivier, knowing that he sounded grumpy, said, "Those two have taken control. Of what I'm not sure. This girl could be a murderer, and they are acting as though she's a child."

"Olivier, she's only seventeen. I simply don't see her as a murderer, or a drug addict, but more as a frightened teenager."

There was a light tap on the door, and Hank stuck his head in. Olivier looked at Max as if to ask whether she knew he was due to show up here. This time her face was a blank.

"Sorry to bother you," Hank said. "Lucy's guardian, George Wyeth, called Isabelle's house and I took the call. He was on a rant and I told him I'd come in and have a chat. We've been in the waiting room downstairs. The three of us have a meeting with him in five minutes, in a small conference room on the first floor. You may want to start your line of questioning with the fact that he had the brilliant notion, a few days ago, of offering a reward to whoever turns his niece, Lucy Kendrick, in to him. I have a hunch he didn't stress 'alive.'" He formed quotation marks with his fingers." He had already let the police know she was an escapee from a mental institution. Now he's up in arms that she got shot."

The door closed.

"I haven't had a minute to tell Hank he's off the case," Max said, embarrassed.

"Is he implying that whoever shot Lucy did it in order to receive the reward?"

"Somebody could have gotten a little too enthusiastic, maybe."

"He's probably handcuffed the poor uncle by now," Olivier grumbled.

Chapter Fifteen

The poor man looked anything but poor. George Wyeth was a sartorial wonder, and on top of that, he was a walking cliché, tall and handsome. His smile was warm, and Max smiled back reflexively when she shook hands with him. As did Olivier, she noticed. *Maybe*, she thought, *Lucy is a bit like him. Inviting you in with his openness, making it difficult not to respond.*

"Hank has filled me in a little," George said. "She's put everybody through quite a lot. I can't tell you how grateful I am to you for all you've done. I want to plan a night for all of us in Beaune before Lucy and I leave. Dinner in a fine restaurant. I hear you two are getting married. Maybe a dinner in Paris would be just the thing. I've been going back and forth."

Hank sat on a hardback chair, attentive, quiet.

"I'm thinking about moving her into Paris," George said. "All this crap about some guy being pushed off a balcony sounds made up, though, trust me, she's capable. A nice contribution to the police department in Lyon might speed things up a little."

"Before you are put officially in charge of Lucy's well-being," said Olivier, "the police need proof of your guardianship."

George waved his hand. "The hospital office already has that."

"And her mother is deceased?"

"In a nutshell, her mother died suddenly while Lucy was under my care in a little hospital I run in Westchester County. I'm a psychiatrist. Lucy blamed me for her mother's death. She pulled a big escape, and now here we are."

"You didn't call the police?"

"She wasn't hospitalized officially. Once you get the police involved, you lose all control. I found a P.I. in Lyon, or you could look at it the other way and say he found me. I paid him to keep an eye on her. He told me there was a woman here who wanted to adopt her. That's when I decided I'd better come get her."

Hank said. "This sounds like a sad story, George. Mother dies, and here she was, hoping to find her biological father. No secret to anybody here, so why'd you leave that part out?"

George laughed. "Lucy invents wild stories, just like her mother. Diane told her about the months she spent in France when she was forty and divorced. No kids. Our mother had died recently and Diane had some money, so off she went. Lucy was the result of a magical union with a Frenchman, but Diane had sworn to never reveal his name. Reads like a movie. The next man in her life was a lamebrain on Wall Street who died five years after they got together. Thank God, they didn't marry. He always claimed the baby was his, and the truth is, who cares?"

Max said, "Lucy might care."

"You gotta know, little Lucy has a devious side that goes against her Botticelli look."

He seemed to notice Max for the first time. "Who are you again?"

He smiled, and she smiled back. Involuntary.

Hank deftly jumped in. "She's the daughter I told you about who's here to get married."

Max understood immediately that she was being presented as bride, not detective. She was dismissed in his mind, Max knew, as George's attention went back to Hank. "Let's go check out my niece," he said.

Back they trooped to Lucy's room. A young woman sat reading from *Le Petit Prince*. She wore round glasses, and her dark hair was pulled back. A don't-fuck-with-me look on her face, Max noticed, which wasn't unusual in a French woman.

"*Bonjour*," she said to Olivier. "I'm a winemaker in the area. My name is Estelle, and I am a friend of Madame Bré, who asked me to come and sit with the girl."

"No change?" Olivier asked.

"No." She looked as if she was deciding whether or not to share anything more, then finally said, "I got to know Lucy a little when she was working for me and found her to be such a vibrant being. She came to observe me making wine. Everyone around here was fascinated by her. Now people are saying she brings bad luck."

"Hey, hey," George said in a quiet voice. "Mind switching to English? I know a few words of French, but not enough to get the details." He turned to Olivier, "What's this young woman doing here?"

Olivier explained that some women friends were taking turns sitting with Lucy, and immediately George said, "Tell her it's fine now. She can go."

She picked up her jacket and left before anyone told her to, and George took her place. "Lucy looks awful. She might not make it, huh?"

Max thought about Isabelle's and Anne's insistence that coma patients could hear everything, which made her feel uneasy at George's obtuse comments.

Olivier must have had the same thought, for he said, "Let's continue this discussion downstairs, shall we?"

"It doesn't matter," George said. "She's in another world. Always was, in my book. A dreamy child. Encouraged by her mother."

Olivier said, "How did you become her guardian?"

"Long story short, Diane couldn't handle a teenager. *She* was the perpetual teenager, for God's sake. Lucy was in a private school and started smoking a lot of pot, moved with the wrong crowd." Olivier wanted to give Max an I-told-you-so look, but refrained. "Diane was worried. One night Lucy got picked up with a bunch of kids for stealing soda or something stupid from a deli. I went by to see Diane and she told me she didn't know what to do."

Hank said, "How old was she?"

"She'll be eighteen on her next birthday." He laughed. "I bet she's told everybody she's twenty-one. Anyhow, I'm now her only family. I talked Diane into giving me temporary guardianship. That meant I didn't have to get her permission every time I wanted to administer a medicine. I put Lucy in my hospital for observation. She was pretty depressed."

"Her mother was okay about that?"

"No. But Diane was an enabler. I allowed Lucy to go home one weekend, and that's when I think she and her mother concocted some scheme. When I arrived to get Lucy, Diane took me aside and told me she was going to court in two days to rescind my guardianship. She had decided to take Lucy to France and would enroll her in school there. She was to meet with a lawyer in a few days. And, of course, she had told Lucy the next big plan."

"And you agreed?" Olivier asked.

He gave his fake, open smile, displaying teeth that were too white. "I'd known Diane since I was ten and our parents married. She could never make a decision and stick to it. She had enough inheritance money to be able to dabble in things. Anyhow, a week later she was dead of an aneurysm."

They sat in somber silence. "How did Lucy take the news?" Olivier asked.

"Oh, the way you would expect. She blamed me. Accused me of murdering her mother. And within a few days she was gone. Escaped."

"And Yves Laroche happened to call," said Olivier, his skepticism obvious.

"Oh, I ran a little ad in the Lyon newspaper. Looking for blahblahblah."

"And now Yves Laroche is dead."

"Which is another reason I called this meeting. I paid him a substantial sum of money, and have received nothing in return so far. He betrayed me, as a matter of fact, and told Lucy I was on my way, which is why she was running. You probably know this."

Olivier looked grim. "If she survives, Monsieur, I can assure you that because she is an underage girl, the French police will intervene. I still don't understand why you didn't notify the police in Westchester County."

Hank said, "I forgot to tell you that I'm an ex-NYPD detective, and my daughter here is still active. We will be happy to help you in any way we can."

George's eyes darted around the room and landed on Max. "I feel ganged up on."

Olivier said, "You were here in Beaune the night Yves Laroche died, correct?"

"We'd just arrived. I brought a lawyer, a man named Steve Gates, with me."

"He was waiting to grab your niece from Laroche's party, correct?" said Hank.

Max saw that George's control was slipping. "He had every right to be in a hotel there. And the police in Lyon and in Beaune had been informed of what I was doing in the area." He stood up. "I know my rights. I want the information from Yves Laroche that I paid him to find."

"It's all in the evidence pile now," Olivier said. "I will let you know when it is released. You have your niece, so there is no urgency that I can see."

"There is as far as I'm concerned. I also paid Yves to find Lucy's father, though I still don't believe there is one. But I want to know once and for all."

Max thought of the potential financial windfall for George once proof of the father emerged.

"George." George raised his eyes to look at Hank. "Who inherits your stepsister's estate if Lucy is incapacitated?"

"As guardian, I will manage all of it."

"I checked out your mental facility in Westchester County and it looks like there's a couple of lawsuits against you. Your hospital is in trouble."

"This is common with any medical facility. Especially in the States. But what instigated this investigation?"

"I decided that if the girl is on the run, as she was claiming to be, it wouldn't be any skin off my back to check out why she might be running from you."

"She's delusional, and needs help."

Max could see that Olivier was about to go apoplectic over Hank's revelation that he was actively on the case.

"I'm sure you don't mind if I keep doing my research. I'm an old retired detective with time on my hands. Do you need a lift to the hotel?"

"I have a car outside."

"The Peugeot with the two thugs sitting inside?"

George gave a nervous laugh.

Max said, "Okay if I stay with Lucy for a short time? I want to make sure the nurse comes and turns her before we go."

"Fine by me," George said.

"There are two cranky old women who've gotten attached to her," Hank said. "One of them is the woman who said she wanted to adopt her. My advice is to let them stay here with the girl, and they will be much more accommodating."

"Don't the women in this village have anything to do but nurture sick people?"

"They like to solve crimes, too."

The two American men left the room, neither of them turning to say good-bye.

"Did you know your dad was checking up on George in New York?"

"He mentioned it. Notice how he buddied up to George? That's what he does when he's about to pull the rug out from under someone. It's an old tactic, and George fell for it."

"I'm not sure he fell for anything."

The door opened and Anne entered. "Esther called me the minute she was sent home," she said. "Do you really think they will take her away tomorrow?"

"I'm going to try to prevent it," Olivier said. "But no guarantees. It's not like she's going to the moon. Paris is an hour away by TGV."

"I can spend the evening here." Anne sat and pulled out her knitting.

Olivier decided to drive to his parents'. Max spotted her father and said she'd see him later and climbed into the car with Hank. "I didn't carry that girl across a field, get her resuscitated and into an ambulance and through surgery just to have her knocked off when she doesn't have a fighting chance," he said.

"Welcome to France, where our hands are tied. I really hope Interpol hires me so I'm not constantly perceived as stepping on toes."

"The guy's clever. I think he's networking here, and he could be handing out money under the guise of donations. Of course we're talking about Lucy's money. Try to get a copy of the guardianship paper from the hospital and I'll work it on my end."

"Olivier needs you and me to butt out of this."

"You've got to be kidding. Olivier wouldn't have a clue what to do with this type of narcissistic American. It would be like dealing with a Donald Trump."

"He's a buffoon."

"A very smart buffoon."

"It's not the end of the world if Lucy goes to Paris," said Max. "The medical facilities there will be great."

"Max. Shed the fear. You've never been a man-pleaser and this isn't the time to start."

"Olivier is going to be my husband!"

"Didn't I give you enough approval to make you secure? Don't lose your autonomy. Once you do, it's hell to get it back."

Soon Hank pulled into Isabelle's driveway and they entered the house together. Isabelle and Juliette came to the door and greeted them warmly. "Anne dropped off the wedding dress," Juliette said. "It's a bit *trop petit*, but I'm sure we can make it work."

"How? By adding two yards of material?"

"Not quite that much," Juliette said.

"I was joking, Ma."

"Oh."

"On that note, I'll go for a run before you have to add a third yard."

Max stood on the path and gazed into the distance where she saw the porch light on at Anne's. Anne rarely left Burgundy, and her best friend, Isabelle, had moved to Paris where she spent most of the year, yet the two women knew each other's deepest secrets. Now that they were widows, they dined together at least twice a week when Isabelle was in the village, and Anne traveled to Paris once a month to stay with her friend. Max thought she would like to have a friend like Anne. She thought of Chloe, now living in Paris, and decided she would devote more time to the friendship once she was living there.

Jean-Claude's house was a short run away. The evening was bright enough to see where she was going, and she had the flashlight from her grandmother's kitchen, if needed. The evening air smelled delicious in the unseasonably warm weather. She decided to jog to Anne's cabin. She had a strong hunch that the cabin had something yet to reveal.

Chapter Sixteen

Olivier had known men like George. Wealthy. Often self-made, which gave them a brashness that heirs generally didn't have. And a ruthlessness that rode just beneath the surface. Heirs carried more of an insouciance, though often a smugness set in, which meant they had convinced themselves that they were more deserving than most. He guarded against these attitudes in himself, for he knew they were contagious after having spent most of his education among the elite.

He knew that Max knew he was miffed, yet he felt he could not say anything, since Hank conducting his own research on George Wyeth—and then confronting him with what he had found—was overstepping boundaries, yet not exactly wrong. He could see clearly where Max's wiliness came from. She and Hank both were interested in cracking a person's psyche before they knew what was happening. Olivier's was a more languid approach but, he thought, equally effective. This was important with George, because the man had already ensconced himself in the middle of everything, and somehow managed to have the local police on his side by convincing them that Lucy was dangerous. No one was happy that she was lying in a coma from a gun wound, including the police, for it brought too much public attention on a popular sport. The simplest solution was to allow George to take his niece to Paris, and be done with it. It shouldn't take too much to prove her innocence in the case of Yves Laroche.

Just as he arrived at his parents' house, Olivier's mother rushed to the door to tell him that a gentleman, the well-known *négociant* and winemaker, Hugo Bourgeot, was on the phone. Olivier answered and a mellifluous baritone voice told him that he hated to disturb him, but that something rather urgent had come up. He said that he had met with Monsieur and Madame Chaumont a week ago, as they had known each other for many years, and they told him that their son was arriving for a long visit. Thus the call.

"And the urgent matter?" Olivier asked.

"It's nothing I can discuss on the telephone, unfortunately," he said. "A visitor came to my office some weeks ago, and I believe his actions were illegal."

Olivier felt a headache coming on. "I'm an hour away, as you know, at my parents' house."

"I could leave Beaune now."

"*D'accord.*" Olivier related this information to his mother, who assured him the visit must be necessary for Hugo to drive an hour. "He says he knows you and Papa. What's he like?"

His mother poured an *apéritif* for each of them. "Hugo's ancestors were some of the earliest *négociants* in Burgundy," she said. "And his is the sole private firm left."

Olivier's headache disappeared as he sat listening to his mother. It was she who had instilled in him his love of Burgundy lore. "*Alors*," she continued, "Hugo's family bought the *négociant* firm in the 1880s, and expanded its operation to include vineyards situated in the best areas of the Côte d'Or. Hugo was a visionary, for he was the first to purchase vineyards in Chablis, which brought him fame, and then he bought land in the U.S., much later."

"And what is his role now?"

"He's a widower. His children have taken over the running of the business. I've heard he is frail."

It was rare for Olivier to confide in his mother, but this evening was different. He told her about the visit of Lucy's uncle, and to his surprise, he told her how everything that was going on made him have reservations about marrying. "I see what Alain and Yvette are going through, and how challenged they are by Roland. The death of Anne's daughter has left her bitter and sad. Imagine, one of the greatest winemakers in the world and she wants to fight over a tiny parcel of land. And I watch Max with her father and how he unconsciously controls her. Can she manage without him?" He got up and tuned the radio to the classical station. "*Brahms' Lullaby*?" he said, laughing, and his mother said, "What irony. Continue."

"I think Lucy's presence, absence, and then being shot, has magnified peoples' hopes and misgivings. Is it fair to say she has instigated a lot of pain?"

His mother said, "From the little I have heard, she is at the axis of the wheel, where each person affected is forced to deal with some aspect of themselves. It's interesting that she is unable to speak or move, yet there is tremendous activity around her, as well as all the energy radiating from her."

He nodded. "The surprise is Hank. Rational, reasonable Hank. Legendary NYPD detective. The girl's effect on him is far greater than I would think."

"And Max?"

"She appears to be the least affected, at least outwardly. Lucy is the same age Max was when her brother was killed in a car accident. As I think about it, the girl must conjure up all kinds of memories from that era."

In time, their conversation was interrupted by the doorbell. Olivier's mother opened the door to Hugo Bourgeot, and they exchanged the usual pleasantries. He was tall and lean with good posture, and a crop of white hair that gave an impression of arrogance. Olivier led him into the salon, where Hugo surveyed the wall of books for a moment before speaking. "I'm sorry to interrupt your family time," he said. Olivier's mother, who had meanwhile left the room, returned with an *apéritif* for Hugo, and set a tray of olives and a few chips on the table between the two men. She excused herself discreetly and pulled the door closed behind her.

"I brought you a little something," Hugo said to Olivier, "as someone told me you maintain a small collection."

Olivier accepted the bag, extracting the bottle of Chambolle Musigny Premier Cru, from Domaine de Vogüe, of the Côte de Nuits region, a quintessential Chambolle that he knew from experience had magnificent depth and weight and that, when opened, would emit aromas of blackberry and possibly a hint of wood smoke. "I'm afraid this is too much," Olivier said. "I have done nothing for you."

"But you will."

A man who is used to commanding, Olivier thought. For the first time he noticed a slight tremor in Hugo's hand. Olivier placed the bottle on the shelf.

Hugo said, smiling, "This can be consumed now, though you can give it more time if you want. The history of this wine goes back to 1450. Same family for twenty generations."

"When I think of time that way the present moment almost has no meaning."

Hugo sipped his *apéritif*, "For me, at my age, it's the opposite. Each hour overwhelms. There is so little time left." He put his glass down. "I will get on with my reason for coming. Two weeks ago a gentleman came to my office in Beaune, and told my secretary, Maryse, that he would like to meet with me. She explained that I rarely met with people these days, which is true. But I try to attend traditional wine-tasting events. In fact, there is a big event coming up in two weeks and I'll make sure you're invited. Anne Bré will attend with me."

Olivier smiled. "My fiancée and I are getting married in her home."

"Bravo! She is fabulous. My wife, Camille, was always a bit jealous of her, thinking she had overstepped boundaries by lighting out on her own to make wine."

He turned ice blue eyes to Olivier. "As much as I would like to remain on the topic of wine and women, the two greatest inventions ever manifested by God, I shall continue with my story."

"You mentioned a man calling on you at your office."

"I met him in the reception room. You know, I only live a few meters from the business."

Olivier knew the fabulous stone house on a narrow lane, one of the most beautiful places in Beaune.

"The gentleman got right to the point. He was searching for the father of an American girl named Lucy Kendrick, the one now on the news who has been shot in a hunting accident."

Olivier nodded.

"He said that a client, who I assume must be Ms. Kendrick herself, had hired him to find her biological father. He told me the girl's mother had recently died."

"Why come to you?"

"I asked him that myself, and he replied that he had been to the offices of ten other exporters already who had been working in the area in the mid-nineties. He asked if I would submit to a DNA paternity test, and I said absolutely not, that anyone in such a predicament had the right to remain anonymous. He said he understood. I poured wine for him and myself, and asked how much he was being paid. He said ten thousand euros. I told him that in support of my fervent belief that privacy be allowed any man, I would pay him fifteen thousand euros for the information he had collected, the computer files and the hard copies, and he would have to sign an agreement that he would never mention this to anyone."

"A contract of secrecy."

"If you will."

"But you don't know if you are the father, Monsieur."

"I am ninety-nine percent certain that I am. Eighteen years ago, an American woman came and asked to pick grapes at my vineyard. France didn't have such strict labor laws back then, as it does these days, that make it difficult for working people to come from abroad."

Olivier calculated the year to have been 1997, when Hugo was around sixty or so. "There she was, all eyes and curiosity, with a great mane of blond hair bunched under her cap. She was strong for her size, and her skin was burnished golden by the sun. A bit on the wild side, I think the Americans say. Just so you know, she was almost forty. I'm not one to rob the cradle."

Olivier realized this was his way of confessing to an affair with Diane Kendrick.

"Did you remain in contact?"

"No. I saw her once in New York when I went there on business two years later. She told me she had had a child. I had four by then, and was traveling constantly. I asked her if the child was mine and she said yes, but she hadn't put my name on the birth certificate. In a moment of guilt, I told her I would put aside a little parcel of land for the child, that she could inherit once I was gone, but there had to be proof. There never was."

"And that was the end of it."

"She gave me a letter that day which I put aside. I only recently opened it, after the fellow paid me a call." He pulled it from his pocket. "It's a love letter."

"You were never tempted to read it before now?"

"Of course I was. But my life was on a steady course I could not, or would not, change. She wrote that she would hold my secret until the girl was eighteen, and then she would reveal to her who her father was. She thought that was fair." His smile was sad. "She was most likely certain that I'd be dead or incapacitated by then."

"Did you set aside a parcel of land as promised?"

"No." He paused. "Do you think the girl will live?"

Olivier blurted, "This is why you're here?"

"Of course not! I realized after the private investigator left that he had stolen the glass I drank from. I was furious."

"For the DNA."

"Exactly."

"And now you want the file he had on you."

"He stole my DNA. I should think it's an illegal act."

Olivier sighed. "Your file is one among many. I can tell you that her file is missing. All that was in yours was the receipt of fifteen thousand euros. The police, of course, are curious."

He looked relieved. "I can manage the police."

"I'm sure." Olivier was certain that it was George who paid Yves to find Lucy's biological father, but it was likely that Yves had destroyed the information once he cashed Hugo's check.

"I have no idea if Monsieur Laroche told the child or not. If she's at death's door, then it doesn't matter, I suppose."

Olivier thought Hugo took dispassionate detachment to a new level. He knew from listening to his parents that Hugo had clung to the old ways of the early *vignerons* who were secretive about their methods of making wine, and who were uncooperative with neighbors. All business was conducted with a wink and a handshake. He didn't bother to bring up something Hugo already knew: a child in France did not have to be legitimate in order to inherit; in fact, all children inherited equally, as a result of the French Revolution.

"I trust that Monsieur Laroche's findings have been destroyed, as agreed upon. It would be unbearable to my children, who adored their mother. Everything is in place for them when I die. Each has their own parcel, and they are now running the company. If the girl survives, I will honor my promise to her mother and negotiate a piece of land for her. I wanted you to know that, but it will be done in secret. Anonymously."

"Perhaps if you met Lucy…"

"*Non*! Monsieur Chaumont, would you like to see an old man abandoned by his children?" Tears welled in his eyes, and Olivier looked away.

"*D'accord,*" he whispered, as he got up to let the old man out.

"You're okay to drive?" he asked him, and was rewarded with a look most indignant.

When the door closed behind Hugo, Olivier and his mother returned to the salon where he shared the story with her, knowing that threatened torture could not extract it.

"My son," she said, "you have done all you can do for now. Hugo has always acted from his brain, not his heart. He has hurt many people with his wheeling and dealing, and he may likely continue to."

"Not least of all Lucy."

"Each person has their own fate. What Hugo doesn't realize is that his deep secret in fact alienates him from his children. All secrets do that." She enfolded him in her arms, and he put his head on her shoulder. She wore Fleurissimo, the fragrance he deeply associated with her, created by Creed for Grace Kelly, when she married. When his mother soothed a wound, when she worked in the garden, when she called them to dinner, always the subtle fragrance resonated, reassuring her son that all was right with the world. His mother said softly, "The girl will be alright. Wait and see."

Chapter Seventeen

It was dusk, and Max had no trouble finding the cabin again that was so storybook-charming. The first image that came to mind as she entered the neat room was of Hank leaning against the little white table, opening up enough to make her want to weep at the memory. She wished she had told him in that moment how much he meant to her, but she had been too surprised to speak. She glanced around at the two small beds, and at the shelves above, holding two dolls and a few propped up books. A sofa was placed across the room, and a child's drawing had been taped to the wall. *So this is what it's like for a girl growing up in the country*, Max thought. How easy it must have been to float into a world of imagination and remain there. How wonderful that Anne provided such a place of wonder for her daughter.

A noise from outside made her jump, and she realized she didn't even have a stick. The door opened and Jean-Claude entered, a frown on his face. "What are you doing here?" he asked, and she explained that she was due at dinner at her grandmother's soon, but had wanted to see if Lucy might have left any clues.

"Madame Bré doesn't like anyone coming here, not even me. She's sentimental about this place."

"I apologize. Also, I've wanted to tell you that I'm sorry for your and Luc's loss." He nodded. "I'd hoped the house would speak to me and tell me who had frightened Lucy and Roland."

"They were stupid to come here. Roland had a rifle, for God's sake. He could have shot whoever showed up instead of running. That's what I would have done."

"Maybe he knew the person?" Max offered.

"One of the *rabatteurs* could have passed this way." He stopped. "Madame Bré told me you are with the NYPD in New York." His smile was charming. "We don't have crime in Burgundy. Maybe a theft once in a while."

"I have to be honest and say I can't believe a place exists that is completely free of crime, but I'm open to being convinced. Lucy is an American, and unconscious in a hospital. If I were a detective, I would try to find out what happened to her, and to the man she worked with in your mother-in-law's vineyard."

"Her injury was accidental, and I was under the impression that Yves' death was ruled a suicide."

"The authorities have officially switched the cause of death to homicide."

"For them to change their minds, calling it a murder makes it easier for them to make drug raids on peoples' homes," Jean-Claude said. "As for Lucy, who would have a motive?"

"Anybody wanting the money that her Uncle George offered?"

"It's not like he put a bounty on her, but he let it be known that she was mentally ill, and possibly dangerous."

"You've met him, I take it."

"The police chief sent him to me when he was demanding to know how she got shot. He's better about it now that he knows it was an accidental shooting."

"I wonder if it was he who walked up to the cabin, causing Lucy and Roland to run. But of course he had to have been told about this place."

Jean-Claude's face remained passive.

She suddenly had a hunch. "Did you know the kids were at the cabin?"

"I saw Roland here the day before the incident. I never saw Lucy."

Max recalled that that was the day she was in Paris with Tim. "You didn't tell his parents?"

"I told Yvette and she pleaded with me not to tell Alain. He and Roland fight a lot, and Alain has knocked him to the ground a couple of times."

"Aren't you in a precarious position there?"

He laughed. "You're being discreet. I am. I've told her no way."

"But Alain…"

"He told me he paid Yves to follow Yvette. He didn't point his finger directly at me."

"Did you go to the party hoping to find out if it was true?"

"Yes. Yves hinted that night that he had some information I might want, and when I asked what it was, he suggested we meet up the next day. 'I'm looking for the highest bidder,' he'd said, and I told him my cash flow was low."

"You have already explained how Yves played one friend against another."

"He was obsessed with Lucy. He was at his worst that night at the party when he saw her come in with Tim. I knew that was going to cause trouble. But she was desperate for the information about her father that Yves had promised her. I left before the inevitable blowup."

"Lucy babysat your son some while she was living with your mother-in-law. Did you two get along?"

"She was great with Luc. But some of the people in the community thought she was using Anne. And I haven't hidden my feelings about Anne's crazy notion of adopting her."

They heard a high-pitched voice calling and Jean-Claude dashed out to the porch. "Papa!" Jean-Claude picked Luc up and brought him inside. "You said you were coming right back," Luc said, trying to hold back tears.

"You were afraid?" Jean-Claude asked, and the boy stoutly shook his head. He hopped down and ran over to his mother's books. "Here's Maman's Babar!" he cried, extracting it from the shelf, and eyeing Max at the same time.

"Let's take it to the house," Jean-Claude said. "Did you say *bonsoir* to Mlle. Maguire?"

He gave her a quick smile. "She taught me jiu-jitsu."

"Oh, so she's the one!" He was at the door. "Let's go home," he said. They waited for Max to walk out, and together they went up the path. It was dark now and drizzling. "Follow me. I know the way blindfolded," he said.

She thanked him, and he said, "I have the feeling that I've been through an interrogation. I never believed that detectives in real life were as pretty as the ones on American TV, but you've proven me wrong."

Rushing up the path, Max realized she was blushing and was grateful for the darkness.

Chapter Eighteen

The waiting room at the hospital was full and the staff overtaxed. Olivier displayed his ID and was given a nod. He spoke briefly with the guard at the door. Olivier and Max entered Lucy's room. Her face had flushed slightly, but she remained immobile, eyes closed. Anne sat in the only chair, her head drooped over her chest. Slowly, as though sensing that someone was in the room, she lifted her head. "*Bonjour,*" she said. "I must have dozed off. Juliette will be here soon to relieve me."

"The Society of Nurturing Mothers," Max said to Olivier.

"We are more accustomed to nurturing our vines," Anne said. "But everyone in our organization wants to help Lucy."

"Has the doctor been in?" Olivier asked.

"Yes, but he says he can't speak to us about her condition."

Olivier said, "Lucy's step-uncle is staying in a hotel in Beaune and will be here later today."

"Has anyone checked his credentials?" Anne asked. "He could be a fraud." She looked annoyed. "This is where Yves could have been a big help."

"Hank is doing research in the states," Max said. "Yves was hired by the uncle, so he must have thought he was legit. Or not."

"Which, then?" Anne asked. "Now you're questioning Yves, who is dead and can't defend himself. I suppose it's my right to ask if I am a suspect?"

Olivier smiled at her. "In the beginning everyone is a suspect.

But in your case, no, you are not suspected of anything but kind nurturance."

Taking her coat from the hook, she said to Max, "Your grandmother told me that you had a conversation with Jean-Claude down at the cabin."

"I was on a run. I hope you don't mind that I went in. Jean-Claude came to check out who was trespassing."

"I'll bet he did."

Olivier was surprised that Max blushed. When her eyes skittered over to him, he tried to give her warning with his. Max laughed, "Anne, did you ever consider becoming a prosecutor?"

She smiled suddenly. "I did, but I don't have the patience to pursue justice. I would have an opinion about who committed the crime, and that would be that. I don't change my mind easily."

Olivier said, "Don't make a quick judgment on this case, please."

Anne stopped in the doorway. "I'll tell you who I would question. That weird boy, Roland. Lucy felt sorry for him, and refused to think he could be dangerous, but he's in a walking coma. I never liked his attachment to Lucy, I have to say."

It was clear to Olivier that she didn't condone many attachments. He was relieved to see Juliette enter the room with a cheerful smile. Anne said she had to continue with errands, and Olivier and Max waited as Juliette took the chair by the bed. "I am knitting a hat for Lucy," she said. "What is the latest?"

Olivier explained that the uncle was due later in the day and that a decision would be made then, but he felt certain she would be taken to Paris. Juliette said, "When Lucy wakes up she will either find herself in the hands of that monster, or accused of murder. She has no reason to wake up." Looking up at Max, she said, "I thought you and Olivier could stand an hour off-duty. Maman and I are planning to talk to the wedding caterer about last-minute details and would like to have you along."

Max made a face, and looked over at Olivier who thought, *thus begins a new life of compromise.* "Of course," he said.

Juliette looked at her watch, "I forgot to call your grand-mother. I will step out and do that now. Max, will you come with me for a quick café? Do you mind, Olivier?"

He wanted to say, I am always happy to have a few minutes alone, and nodded. He watched mother and daughter exit the room and thought, *today I am sitting here in a hospital room; soon Max and I will marry, and in the meantime we are solving a crime that I wanted nothing to do with. This is going to be the rhythm of our life together.* He sat in the chair, and the stillness made him feel how tired he truly was. He closed his eyes for a moment. A shadow had descended over his beloved Burgundy. Was he naïve to think that people who farmed the earth, who were one with the land, creating wines year after year, a process that had started thousands of years ago, could err to the point of murder? Had people given up on the notion of roots, and the importance of history in their own lives?

Some of the problem in Burgundy, he knew, had to do with the absurd inheritance laws, including the taxes that caused many to sell out. Look at Hugo, who was willing to dole out large sums to protect his name and his relationship with his children. What had not been stated when they had spoken, was that Lucy had the right to the same inheritance as his four children. Perhaps that was why he was going to such great lengths, and expense, to maintain his secret. But maybe more disturbing than the land issues were the family behaviors. Alain and Yvette's marriage was at risk of crumbling over their son's antics and in fact, Olivier thought, they might have a bigger problem than they imagined. Yet he must not listen blindly to Anne, for she had become so embittered over her lifetime that she was too quick to point a finger.

Suddenly, he had the eerie sensation that he was being watched. He slowly fluttered his eyes open and looked at the girl who lay there peacefully. *Why*, he wondered, *did she have an obsession to find her father?* She was the result of a fling, nothing more. Many children went through life with no father, why was this one so determined to discover her roots and force the issue?

He was glad she had Tim, who seemed like a good guy; she could finish growing up under him—unless George somehow managed to maintain guardianship of her, for which he knew he would be blamed by the women around him. Lucy would be eighteen in a few days, officially an adult. And then, of course, there was his beloved Max, who had also only just tapped into her French roots when she brazenly introduced herself to her estranged grandmother. She was starting to accept the reality that she would be leaving her parents behind in New York. Only two nights ago she had said that Hank could not be uprooted from New York, which is when she explained that he went to his son's gravesite, on average, four times a week.

The door opened, and Isabelle entered quietly. "Max is waiting for you downstairs," she said softly. "I will sit with Lucy."

"I must be called immediately if her uncle shows up."

"Of course. I have your mobile number here, and my phone is charged, for once. Max made sure of that. It should only take an hour or so for you two to plan the menu and select the wines." Olivier knew instinctively that it would take much longer than that.

He smiled at her. "Thank you for all you are doing."

"*Pas de quoi.*" She picked up the copy of *Le Petit Prince* that had been collectively read to Lucy. "She could do with some of Saint-Exupéry's wisdom."

Olivier stood. "I felt overcome with sadness sitting here, realizing that there is so much instability right now for so many people."

"I think that's an interesting way of saying there is an unnamed murderer in our midst."

"Indeed."

Chapter Nineteen

Max was surprised to bump into Anne in the parking lot. "All the women are congregating?"

"*Mais, non*!" Anne said. "It's by chance."

"Olivier and I are going to decide on food and wine for the wedding," Max said. "Join us if you like."

"I have ten minutes before my hair appointment, but thanks." She looked at Max. "I was feeling a bit off in that hospital room," she said. "It brings back too many memories."

"Olivier feels certain that George will move Lucy to Paris."

Anne's lips formed a horizontal line. Max thought of the expression "my lips are sealed."

"Oh, here comes Olivier now," exclaimed Anne, with a wink. "Time for you to be off. Isabelle and I are going to shop for proper wedding attire after my appointment."

With a nod to Anne, Olivier took Max's hand and they started off in the opposite direction. "They all seem in a tizzy," he said, "behaving as though the wedding is days away instead of two weeks. I imagine your father is hiding out somewhere."

"He was on the phone when I left the house, talking to a detective about Diane Kendrick. The medical examiner had listed her cause of death as aneurysm and she was cremated immediately, the day after she passed. The funeral home said very few people showed up."

"Did she own her apartment?"

"I think it was a co-op, and the answer is yes."

He stopped, his hand in hers. "I meant to tell you, I had the strangest sensation in the hospital room that someone was watching me. I suppose I mean Lucy."

"I've had that too. Maybe Diane is hovering over us. Guiding us."

"Now we can assume to have Diane and Caroline both directing us from above. We can't fail."

Max laughed and Olivier squeezed her hand, and said, "I also realized in that room that I'm grateful to you and Hank for working behind the scenes."

"Now I know some angels were hovering."

He rang the doorbell of an eighteenth-century building and they waited calmly. A beautifully dressed and coiffured woman opened the door, her red lips curving into a smile. After an hour Max felt that the dissection of food and wine options had dragged on for far too long. Olivier on the other hand, was in his element as they tasted wines and pored over the list. At the end of the meeting they had settled on twenty-five guests. The day following the wedding, they would take Hank and Juliette in to Paris to catch their plane, and they would stay in the city for a few days before flying to Melbourne to see Olivier's brother and family.

Just as they were wrapping up the meeting, Olivier's cell phone rang. It was the prosecutor in Lyon saying that the investigation of Yves Laroche's death was underway, and that Olivier was to be part of it. Immediately after that call, Lucy's uncle George telephoned, and they set up a meeting at his hotel in forty-five minutes.

Once out on the street, Max said they needed to set aside a day to look at apartments in Paris. Olivier agreed, but reminded her that his friends had offered them their apartment on rue de Meslay in the Third Arrondissement—which made sense, as they had decided to sell it and Olivier had first option to purchase.

"But we'll still look around," Max said. "I sure hope Lucy wakes up."

"Well, we all do, but what brought that up?" Then he laughed.

"Oh, you're thinking about our bet! You want to have the final word on the apartment."

"Maybe I'll go pour cold water on her," Max said.

"How kind."

Hank called Olivier's cell and said he was in Beaune, as he was bored stiff out in Auxey-Duresses. He had more information about Lucy's mother and uncle, which he thought Olivier should know. Olivier glanced at his watch. "Max and I have time for a café and then we have a meeting with George." Hank was there within ten minutes, which made Olivier think he had been lurking nearby. Olivier ordered a café for Max and himself and Hank ordered a *bière blanche.*

It was another unseasonably warm day, and they sat facing the famous Hospices de Beaune, an extraordinary building designed by Flemish architect Jacques Wiscrère, which served as the heart of the small city. Olivier explained its origins: Founded in 1443, it had served as a free hospital for the poor until the late 1970s. Founder Nicolas Rolin had hoped charity would relieve him of his sins—one of which was his habit of collecting wives. Today the original hospital building, the Hotel-Dieu, was a museum, displaying superior examples of Gothic architecture and a veritable treasure trove of panel paintings, including intricately detailed portraits of Rolin and his wife.

Hank got right down to business. "I mentioned that one of George's patients died a year ago. The autopsy revealed that he had an abnormal amount of an antidepressant in his system. The family is suing. I would say George's ship is sinking. He's also engaged to a woman who has now moved into Diane's co-op. Keeping it in the family, you know."

"This is depressing news," Max said. "Is Lucy more of an advantage to him dead or alive, I wonder?"

"Dead, as far as the apartment, her inheritance, which I'm sure he's spending like crazy, and her being a pain in the ass is concerned, but alive if there's another cache somewhere. He told me on the day that I had a little time alone with him that he paid the P.I. ten thousand euros to check into Lucy's biological father. The ten-thousand-dollar question then is, does George know who that might be? He will cling to that guardianship rule, I know that."

Olivier sat silently, and Max knew that Hank didn't have a clue about the identity of Lucy's father.

They finished their drinks, and walked to the hotel. "This city reeks of money," Hank said. "I wonder what they're hiding behind the high stone walls in front of their houses."

Olivier said, "Burgundians like their privacy. The city is built within ramparts. Don't forget Beaune was first ruled by a Gallic tribe, and built as a fortress by the Romans. The Dukes of Burgundy were here until 1477."

Hank said, "That's when they lost the Battle of Nancy to King Louis XI, after which it became a French province."

"*Exactement*," Olivier said, obviously surprised by his knowledge. "And you are right. Many secrets are harbored here. What you might not know is these cobblestoned streets conceal a labyrinth of subterranean caves holding millions of bottles."

They had arrived at the hotel when Hank said, "I think you two are better off than I am talking with this guy George. He gets edgy around me. I'll say hello, then I'm going to butt out. I'll see you outside."

George was on his cell phone when they arrived. He swung the hotel room door open and beckoned them in, then stood on the balcony talking loudly to someone about an investment. He was swigging from a liter water bottle and pacing. *An active volcano*, thought Olivier. Hank began to nose around, picking up an empty bottle of champagne, looking at it, putting it back down, then glancing down at a notepad. Olivier cleared his throat loudly when he noticed that George had hung up and was moving toward Hank.

Hank turned around and gave an insouciant grin. "How're you doing, George?"

Olivier said, "Shall we sit down for a few minutes?"

George looked non-plussed. "So read me my rights." He laughed, but not getting a response, he muttered, "You don't get it. Never mind."

"A murder suspect cannot leave the country. Both you and your niece are suspects in the murder of Yves Laroche. We can have your name cleared within the next few days, I'm certain, but an officer will be interviewing you in the meantime."

George stared hard at Olivier in disbelief. "Come on and confess. Not one witness saw me there. You know why?" He was yelling now. "I wasn't there!"

Hank headed out the door as Olivier continued. "We have witness confirmation of a certain Steve Gates who was there at the end of the evening. Someone saw a stranger get off the elevator…"

George laughed. "My attorney got off the elevator, ran and pushed a man off the balcony and left. That's what you're saying?"

Max could see that Olivier was unsure how to be with this man, who was garrulous one minute, and snide the next. "George…" she said.

He stopped. "What?"

"You're a suspect. Answer the questions."

He fixed his gaze on her. "Who are you again?"

"I'm a detective with the NYPD. I want to know about your moving into your stepsister's apartment before her body was cold, and I…we…the French magistrate and I…want to know what you're doing here."

He seemed to grow contrite. "I came for Lucy. She is in my charge, and I have the papers to prove it."

"And don't deny it. She is your source of income."

"I happen to be a psychiatrist."

"Who is losing his hospital and being sued. If you lose, you lose guardianship, but you know that, right? Anyhow, I'm not impressed with your credentials. And just so you know, the French are rarely impressed by anything."

"What do *you* want?"

"I'll tell you what we want. We want you to release Lucy from your guardianship, as her mother wished."

"No!"

Olivier spoke quietly. "Then I can keep you in France for a long time. You can think about it."

"I'll report you."

"Please do," Olivier said. "Now. I know you paid the P.I., Yves Laroche, ten thousand euros to find Lucy's biological father. Do you know his identity?"

Silence. "No. Not yet. Somebody else says he thinks he knows the identity."

"Who?"

"This has nothing to do with Laroche's death, and I won't answer." George poured himself a drink of Scotch and downed it, then marched out the door.

Olivier and Max walked out, and once in the parking lot looked around for Hank. "I don't know what to do," Olivier said, and then they saw him, bobbing up and down among the cars. Then, "What the hell…?"

As though they were watching a film being made, they saw George make a beeline for his car, cell phone in hand. Hank was lying in wait. Didn't George know? He continued on, then stopped at his car, gesticulating.

Olivier started to laugh. "My God, he's insane!"

"Who, George or my dad?"

Olivier looked at her as though the answer were obvious. "Your dad."

"That's not nice…"

Olivier answered his mobile. He listened and said, "I'll be right there." Turning to Max, he said, "Lucy's disappeared."

"Kidnapped?"

Hank opened the back door and jumped in. "I overheard George talking to Jean-Claude. You must forbid Jean-Claude from revealing the name of Lucy's biological father."

Max wondered if Anne had told him, or if he was just leading George Wyeth on. We can't deal with that right now," Olivier said. "Lucy is gone."

"She died?"

"Hardly."

Chapter Twenty

As they boarded the elevator to Lucy's hospital room, Olivier did a quick rundown of possibilities. Lucy was an escape artist, according to her uncle. She could have been feigning the coma, and waiting for the right moment. Someone could have kidnapped her, in which case her life was in danger.

A police officer escorted them to Lucy's room. The bed covers were pulled back, revealing two pillows that had been stuck under the comforter, vaguely resembling the shape of a body. *Amateurs*, Olivier thought. He went to the open window and looked out. The room was on the back side of the building and overlooked a small park. A couple of pedestrians were walking briskly along the sidewalk. The room was on the second floor, called the first floor in France. She wouldn't have jumped, he thought, unless she had been under attack.

Two more gendarmes arrived, with the director of the hospital behind them, who introduced himself curtly. Hank sat calmly in the chair by the bed, the one usually filled by Anne or Isabelle, or some other woman, completely lost in thought, his fingers creating a steeple. *A skinny meditating Buddha*, Olivier thought. He called Abdel, and told him to come quickly. The room was filling up.

Another gendarme entered, this one the *capitaine.* Olivier told him the prosecutor was on his way, and that the staff needed to be questioned. "Monsieur," the captain said, "the patient may have left of her own volition. Did anyone check to see if she signed herself out?"

"Of course," Olivier said. He turned to Max. "I have to call George and tell him what has happened."

A slight disturbance outside the door and all eyes went in that direction. Olivier watched Max go to her grandmother, who looked indignant. The last person he wanted to see. She peered around the gendarme, and said to the young man, "This is no way to treat an old woman." He knew Isabelle would never refer to herself in that way unless circumstances were dire. A voice behind her grew louder, "Olivier, it's us."

Olivier, ever polite, went to the door and told the gendarmes that no one had to guard the room at the moment, that the guard had been put there to keep the patient from leaving, not for keeping others from entering. The gendarme looked baffled. Was the magistrate being sarcastic?

Anne entered. *"Alors,"* she said, her lips pursed. "This is what everyone feared, *n'est-ce pas?"*

Everyone turned to the door when they heard a loud voice exclaiming in English. "This is outrageous. She could be dangerous, either to herself or to others. I told you that. I want someone to explain to me what is going on." George's entrance was dramatic. A much shorter man walked beside him, and was introduced as Steve Gates. George said to Olivier, "This was going on under our noses." He turned to the women, "What are you doing here?"

They couldn't hide their indignation at being spoken to in that way. Isabelle collected herself first, and spoke slowly in English. "I hate to disturb you, Monsieur, but this is not about you. We came by to see Lucy to deliver some of her things that were left at Anne's house. And to say good-bye."

"What things?" George asked, his eyes narrowing.

Anne spoke up. "Some papers, and a few articles of clothing. She lived with me during my *vendange*."

"Whatever that is. I will take them."

Olivier was surprised to see Anne hand them over. "I'm glad to be rid of her, to tell the truth," Anne said. "She told me stories that had me worrying too much. Things like her mother being murdered and no way to prove it. And everyone knew she was looking for her father, the poor darling, and what father wants to be found at this stage of the game I'd like to ask?" All this said in a strong French accent. "If he is alive, of course. It was always rumored that your stepsister slept with an old man. She told one villager he couldn't get it up."

Olivier shifted his gaze from Anne to Hank who looked slightly amused, to Isabelle, who was nodding as though she were listening to a song, then to Max, who was obviously flummoxed. He regained his authority. "Everyone leave, please." Turning to George, he said, "We have already issued an alarm for your niece, Monsieur Wyeth. She can't have gone far."

"I'm going to my hotel. Call me with any updates." He stalked out.

Isabelle and Anne said they had to get going. "What were the papers you gave him?" Olivier asked.

Anne said, "Scribblings in Lucy's journal. A photograph of her mother. A sweatshirt. Nothing of consequence."

"You sure had a change of tune about the girl," Hank said to them.

"George is a boor," said Anne. "We didn't want him accusing us."

"Had nothing visibly changed when you were here with Lucy earlier today?" Olivier asked.

They shook their heads vigorously.

"Did anyone come in?"

"The handsome Brit came in, but for no longer than five minutes. Tim. He declared his love for her, held her hand. He said there was nothing to worry about as far as her being a suspect of anything."

Isabelle spoke up. "The nurses came in after Tim left and said it was time for us to say good-bye. They expected the ambulance transport to Paris within the next hour. We went to the hairdresser's and decided to stop by once more to drop off Lucy's few things and heard from the nurses that Lucy had disappeared."

Olivier said, "Because of your attachment to her, officers will be searching your homes and all around the premises. If she is conscious, it seems likely that she would head to your house, Anne."

"We hope that's the case," Isabelle said. She turned to her granddaughter. "Max, will you drive us home? We're worn out."

Officers entered and announced they had rounded up the hospital staff. Everyone filed out, and Olivier found himself alone in the room. He felt he had never been so relieved to see someone as when Abdel walked in.

Chapter Twenty-one

Abdel had been busy in Lyon. He had a list of everyone who had been at Yves' apartment on the night of his death, which Olivier quickly scanned. "I see your cousin's name is on here."

"There's an explanation."

"We'll deal with this later. We have to find Lucy Kendrick. You spoke to the guard who was supposed to be stationed at the door?"

"Yes. The guard explained that the two grandmothers had gone out before lunch. He heard on his scanner that a car had been broken into in the parking lot, and ran to see if he could help. When he arrived, the young woman who sometimes came to sit with Lucy, Estelle, was standing outside her car. She claimed that her laptop was missing from her car, which she was sure she had left there. Another gendarme arrived at the parking lot, and said he would handle it. The guard returned to his post in the chair outside Lucy's door."

"He didn't check in on her?"

"*Non, Monsieur*. He explained that he had not realized until the nurse came by to check an hour later, that Lucy was gone, and he called his boss immediately."

Olivier went back to Lucy's room, where Hank sat as still as stone. Olivier surveyed the room, then rested his eyes on Hank, who said, "I don't think she was in a coma."

"You mean the entire time?"

He nodded. "Which means she heard everything," Olivier said. "If she's alive, my hunch is she's in the area.

"We call that hiding in plain sight. But if she didn't escape on her own, it wouldn't surprise me if someone wants her dead. There you have a real problem."

"Like who?"

"Anne may not be too far off about Roland. I personally can't stand him. His parents have no control over him. Even his mother's crocodile tears don't faze him."

"If somebody wanted Lucy dead," Olivier said, "It would be easier to kill her in the hospital. A pillow over her face or a drug inserted into her vein would not have made anyone suspicious, if you get my gist."

"I do," Hank said. "On the other hand, let's just say she was removed while still in a coma. That means lifting her, putting her on a gurney or stretcher, and somehow getting her into a vehicle. We're talking dead weight in broad daylight."

"That would be a good way of getting her out, even if she was strong as a boxer." Hank laughed, and Olivier looked over, startled. "I hope that's the case," Hank added.

Olivier wasn't so sure. "Abdel will interview the ambulance drivers. Having a doctor or a nurse pushing a gurney wouldn't draw much attention."

"Neither would an ambulance."

Abdel knocked and entered. "We're not making much progress," he said. "No one noticed anything that unusual. One nurse said she noticed an ambulance driver she hadn't seen before. Dark-skinned. She thought a Muslim. Translate, jihadist."

Olivier winced inwardly. "Did you ask around to see if he could be identified?"

"I'm about to do that."

Olivier said that he would wrap up the staff interrogation, and after, they would meet to go over Abdel's notes from Yves' party. Abdel nodded and left, but not without delivering a parting shot, "Those two women, Max's grandmother and the other one, were mentioned twice by staff as hovering and interruptive.

One of them questioned everything the nurse tried to do. I put it all in the report."

"Yes, we know," said Olivier. He knew he should have kept them at bay, but how?

Once in the parking lot Hank said to Olivier, "Your assistant has a chip on his shoulder?" When Olivier looked puzzled, he mentioned the reference to jihadist.

"We're all feeling a bit sensitive these days. I agree there is prejudice, but here it is more about class than color. His cousin Ali was at Yves' party solely because Lucy invited him. I have the impression that she doesn't comprehend class differences."

"Americans don't give a rat's ass about class, but we're more racist, if you get my meaning."

"Interesting."

"If I were to make a guess about the one element that brings the party-goers together," Hank said, "it would be secrets. The Brit seems pretty clean."

"We all have one or two stowed away, don't we? But I agree. Yves Laroche knew how to extract them, and then sell the information for cash."

• • ● • •

Max sat having a cup of tea with her grandmother and Anne. Abdel had called and was to come by for her in half an hour, and they would meet up with Olivier to discuss his report about Yves Laroche.

"Tonight is our monthly *Femmes et Vins* meeting," Isabelle said.

"I thought you were tired," said Max, glancing up from the laptop on the table in front of her.

"A cup of tea gives new perspective."

"What is the plan for finding Lucy?" asked Anne.

"I don't know." Max wished they would leave her to her funk.

"You sound discouraged."

"I'm worried sick that she's dead. I don't know if I can handle it. But if she's off running around, I'm ready to throw her to the wolves. Turn her in."

"That's what motherhood is like."

"You two were supposed to call Olivier when you left the room. She was unattended long enough to escape."

Their silence made Max look up. Anne said, "There was a gendarme, remember? And we thought Estelle was going right in. Her car alarm went off and there was quite a to-do about that."

"And who do you consider the wolves?" Juliette asked from her chair in the corner, where she sat knitting.

Max shrugged. "I was referring to the uncle."

"The wolf in fairy tales is usually disguised," Juliette said.

A knock on the door brought Abdel into the room. The women fussed over him and he accepted a cup of tea. Anne said, "Was the staff cooperative?"

"No one saw anything," Abdel said. "Which makes me suspicious. There are always one or two things that stand out."

"You think they know what happened to her?"

"Lucy has been in the news enough…as the poor waif, the orphan, the unfairly accused, the victim…that she now has the public on her side. It's one of those situations where the fugitive…and Lucy is a fugitive now…becomes the hero in peoples' eyes. It's all projection."

"Sometimes the people are right," Juliette said.

"It's illusion," Abdel said, patiently. "Someone thought they saw her on her red Vespa driving through Lyon. A nurse saw a dark-skinned man pull up in an ambulance. This is people's imaginations gone haywire."

Anne looked serious. "What is your opinion, Abdel?"

Abdel took a deep breath. "The last anyone knew, Lucy was in a coma. If she was kidnapped, she could be dead; if she escaped, she and everyone involved could be in big trouble."

Max sat half-listening. She was relieved when she heard a car drive in. Olivier had arrived. Isabelle glanced at the clock. "Oh, we must be going," she said. "Juliette, are you coming with us?"

"Okay, Maman." She picked up her coat and within seconds they were gone.

"Was it something I said? Or didn't say?" Olivier asked, and Max smiled. "Be grateful. We have a comfortable place to meet and they are out for two hours."

Abdel looked up from his phone. "The news of Lucy's disappearance has leaked. We'll see it on television tonight."

"I hope George is not going to offer up a reward again," Max said.

"We made sure he won't, and he's not allowed to be interviewed." Olivier turned to Abdel, "Shall we start?"

Abdel explained that the police had gone through all of Yves' records, and that the results revealed that he was a thorough researcher. Abdel said that he had copies of all the reports in his files, but he would try to sum it up for them now. Max whispered to Hank that she would explain everything in English when he was done, and he nodded.

"We will start with the party Monsieur Laroche hosted on the night of his death, April seventh, because it brought together a disparate group of people, most of whom had connections in this area. From what we have pieced together, Lucy Kendrick met Yves Laroche during the harvest at Madame Anne Bré's. I shall refer to people by their first names from now on. Yves had been coming to Anne's harvest parties for over a decade, for the pleasure of it. He was single, turning forty, and the son of a successful private investigator who started a firm in Lyon with his wife as partner. They retired, and handed it all over to Yves. He was an extrovert, and made friends easily. His failing was that he talked too much, quite unusual for an investigator. Some considered it a pathology that he played people against each other. I have brought copies of the files of people that I thought would be of interest in this case. There is one on Anne Bré, and her husband, Gervais Bré."

"She hired him?" Olivier asked.

"It appears so. But it was so long ago that she actually hired Yves' father. She suspected her husband of philandering twenty years ago and, indeed, that was the case. He had an affair with an American woman who was in Burgundy for some reason or other, and when Anne learned this news, she confronted Gervais, who asked for her forgiveness. Her file remained dormant until this year, when she went to Yves to have him research a small plot of land that her husband had left to their daughter, Caroline, when he died. It turns out that it wasn't legally his to give away, as the land had been in Anne's family."

Olivier said, "No doubt, if Caroline had lived, Anne would not have contested the deed."

Abdel nodded and said, "There is an even darker side to Yves Laroche. He enjoyed smoking pot for years, and was a small-time dealer, but two years ago he got hooked on opioids after shoulder surgery. He started to become desperate. He had lost a large sum of money, and according to one witness, it was as though the many cases he handled had started to weigh too heavily on him. When he met Lucy Kendrick she became a messianic figure, a savior, which is completely irrational. He is said to have wanted to marry her."

"The drugs caused this obsession?" Olivier asked.

"It has more to do with his character, perhaps enhanced by the drug use. Anyhow, the police were watching Yves at this point. I have those reports, too." Abdel continued, "There is another file with the name Hugo Bourgeot attached to it. There is a receipt of a check for fifteen thousand euros. I don't know what it's for."

Olivier said quietly, "It seems that Yves was attempting to establish this gentleman's patrimony in the case of Lucy Kendrick. Bourgeot was purchasing his file."

Max translated quickly for Hank, who asked, "Was proof established?"

Abdel said, "Lucy Kendrick's file, which we assume has that information in it, is missing."

Max said, "Hugo would have wanted that file."

"Anybody who wanted to blackmail Hugo would want that file," said Olivier.

Max told them about Hank eavesdropping on George in the parking lot of the hospital, and quoted him as saying there was a potential new source of income. "If Lucy's uncle knew of a wealthy French father, he would go after him, for sure. Threaten to blackmail him, or at the very least demand money for her health care."

Olivier said, "Because Lucy went into hiding, I am going to assume, as does George, that Yves told her of her uncle's pending arrival."

Abdel went on to explain that, as corroborated by neighbors and other guests, he could safely say that attendees at the party included Lucy, Jean-Claude with a girlfriend, and Tim Lowell. Neighbors had seen a young man wearing a hooded sweatshirt leaning against a doorway smoking a cigarette.

"Roland?" Max said.

Abdel said, "He arrived with Lucy and Tim. A dark-skinned, curly-haired man was seen entering the building at nine o'clock. That was my cousin Ali, but he explained that one of the neighbors called him a hoodlum, and he decided to leave. He has an alibi. He looked at his notes. "An apartment camera shows that Lucy arrived at nine as well, with Roland and Tim in tow, Tim with his perpetual camera slung over his shoulder."

Max was relieved, for Abdel's sake, that Ali was not a suspect.

"At what time did Yves Laroche die?" Olivier asked.

"Time of death is eleven. By the time the police arrived ten minutes later, the apartment door was wide open and neighbors had gathered around in the hallway, all of them speculating. The guests had disappeared."

"What do the Lyon police think?"

"My cousin was interrogated. He deals in small amounts of marijuana, and it turns out the boy wearing the hooded sweatshirt, is in, fact Roland Milne, who also is a known dealer. I forgot to mention that Yves also had a file on him. Roland's father, Alain, paid Yves last year to locate his son, who had taken off. He turned up in a suburb of Paris out of his mind on prescription painkillers, but they put him in rehab for a month, and he returned home and continued with his school activities, and no further problems were mentioned."

"Do you assume these boys were buying drugs from Yves?" Max asked.

"Absolutely. Yves apparently had a healthy stash of cocaine and opioids hidden in his kitchen."

"Did the apartment video pick up people leaving the building during the party?" Olivier asked.

"The police are still studying the video, which is quite blurred, in an attempt to verify everyone who entered or exited the building. Don't forget, there are eighty tenants in the building as well. One does stand out, though: Lucy. She left the building just before eleven, with Tim in tow. Roland appeared a few minutes later, and someone grabbed him, but we can't yet identify that person."

Olivier said, "I want to see the full-length video. The police are searching for Lucy, and will continue throughout the night. Abdel, Tim Lowell is very close by. Please head there. I'm going to meet with the prosecutor, and will return here for dinner, Max."

"So my role is to make dinner?" Max asked, her tone sarcastic.

Olivier looked from her to Hank. "I'm sorry. You know why you can't be perceived as helping with the investigation." When neither of them replied, he hurried to the front door, and was gone.

Hank turned to Max. "Go with Abdel."

Max looked from Abdel to Hank. "No."

Hank looked at her for a long moment. "I'm going in the kitchen for a beer. Do what you need to do."

Abdel said, "What's going on?"

Max shrugged. "We can't have the prosecutor issuing a complaint, as my application for Interpol could be put into jeopardy. And I don't want Olivier mad at me."

"A visit to a B&B doesn't sound very complicated."

She looked up at him, brightening. "Where I don't want to be is in this house when my mother and grandmother return. I find them so irritating right now, and I'm not sure why."

Abdel gave his toothy grin. "They're domesticating you?"

"They're always whispering, and when I come around, they talk about the wedding. It's weird. The real problem is I don't know where I belong. On second thought, I do." She picked up her jacket, and followed Abdel outside.

"This is a convoluted case," Abdel said.

"When have we ever had a simple case? It's time to ask, did Lucy push Yves?"

"My instinct is to say no." He grew thoughtful. "We must be careful not to focus entirely on Monsieur Laroche's friends. There were others at the party, many of them low-lifes, small-time dealers, people like that. He stopped. "Any reason you know of, before I walk in, why Tim might want Yves Laroche or Lucy, or both, dead?"

"You mean some motive other than the seven deadly sins? Nope."

Abdel laughed and knocked on the door. Max felt happy to be with him.

Chapter Twenty-two

Olivier had felt a calm descend over him as Abdel recounted as many details as he knew from the party. The police were looking for Lucy, and though he had entertained the notion of joining the search for her, reason had prevailed, as he knew that he wouldn't be much of an asset. Her fate was out of his hands. His phone rang, and he saw that the prosecutor, Emmanuel Caron, was calling. Olivier had just entered the city of Beaune, and was looking around for a quiet bar to sit in, but now he pulled over to listen. "You must come to headquarters immediately," Caron said. "A young man has shown up and confessed to the murder of Yves Laroche and to shooting the American girl."

"I'm on my way."

Roland Milne was a mess. Obviously drunk and reeking of pot, he sat with his head in his hands as though trying to make sure it didn't fly off. He was mostly incoherent, Olivier soon realized, but what could be understood went like this: "I saw Yves Laroche's body on the pavement. The thing is, I wanted to push him off the balcony because he hurt my friend Lucy's feelings. I saw on the news that she has disappeared again. We are in a video game, she and I, and she is always running and I am always pursuing." He laughed obscenely. Then, "I should be with her. I'm the only one who can take care of her. Did I shoot her? Maybe. Maybe not. Everybody was shooting. I tripped over a root and my gun went off. She was running ahead of me, like a gazelle. Then BAM! She turned to me with frightened eyes. I had slipped. Did I shoot her? His eyes brightened. "I did it all!"

"Put him in a cell," Olivier said. Monsieur Caron nodded, and two officers helped Roland to stand up and led him away.

"This is the son of Alain Milne, a reputable wine producer in the south?" the prosecutor asked, and Olivier nodded.

"An old friend from high school," Olivier said, not caring at all that his despondency showed.

"I feel for him with this kid. Drugs are a bigger problem than even just a few years ago. Kids are drinking too much, and smoking rates are up among the young. They should have come down harder on this boy." He looked up at Olivier, "You think he killed Monsieur Laroche, or shot the girl?"

"He is certainly capable, though I can't imagine a motive. But people high on drugs sometimes don't have a motive. He is obviously operating under some delusion that he is Lucy's savior. This could be mental illness."

The door swept open and Alain entered with Yvette behind him, dressed inappropriately in a too-short skirt and low-cut blouse. Alain was barely recognizable. He hadn't shaved in a few days, it appeared, and his face was rigid with apprehension. "Where is he?" he demanded.

"Calm down, Alain," Olivier said. "He's drunk, and they took him into the back to let him sober up."

Emmanuel said, "He has confessed to the murder of Monsieur Yves Laroche and to the shooting of the young American, Lucy Kendrick."

"*NON*!" Yvette shrieked. "He is incapable of such a thing, Monsieur Caron. The girl Lucy is the devil incarnate. She seduced him and threw him away. She's a slut!"

Alain spoke, sounding like the voice of reason. "Our son is on a medication, which he has probably neglected to take. I would like him to be put on bail and we will keep him at our house until tomorrow morning."

The prosecutor hesitated, but then said no. "The girl has gone missing from the hospital," he said.

"At least you can't blame Roland for that," said Yvette.

"I'm going to insist on putting him in rehab, even if he is declared innocent," Olivier said. "That is my prerogative."

Alain said, "Yvette and I have been having problems, and even split up for a few months. This has affected Roland, of course, but I think we can pull together again as a family, and he will be okay."

"It won't hurt for him to spend the night in jail. A confession, no matter the circumstances under which it is delivered, is not to be dismissed."

"What a shame," Monsieur Caron said as he watched them outside the door in conversation with their son, who had been brought to them. Yvette reached out to embrace her son, and he jerked away. "I worry that we are going to fall into a drug crisis with our youth the way the United States has. The number of overdoses there is appalling."

"I feel seismic tremors happening here," Olivier said. "Not underground, but in our people. Am I imagining a new layer of general anxiety?"

Monsieur Caron sighed. "*Non.* Sometimes I think it's my age. I retire in four years, and I can't wait."

They bid each other good-bye, and Olivier felt relieved by the thought that this was a man he could work with. Maybe he could speak with him over the next couple of days about incorporating Max into the investigation. He could feel her frustration, and besides, he needed her. He decided to give up the notion of a quiet hour of contemplation in a bar, and instead to return to Max's grandmother's house. He would try to get a few hours of sleep, and awake fresh, hopefully to the news that Lucy had been found...alive. It was nine when he pulled into Isabelle's driveway, and he felt comfortable enough to knock and enter.

The housemaid, Jeannette, greeted him, said the family was relaxing in front of the fire, and took his coat.

Entering the room, he noticed that Max wasn't there.

Jeannette brought him a glass of wine, and Isabelle said that dinner would be served in half an hour. "Max should be returning soon."

"Oh, where is she?" Olivier asked.

Hank said, "I sent her off with Abdel."

Olivier felt his body stiffen. He watched Isabelle scurry to the kitchen. "She's not currently allowed on the case. She and I have discussed this and I thought she understood."

"Her going with Abdel doesn't mean she's on the case," Hank said. "She might pick up something on the interview that Abdel wouldn't. This is why in the U.S. we work in pairs."

"Abdel and I manage pretty well as partners."

"I can see that, but better to have her think she's contributing."

Olivier sipped his scotch and closed his eyes, allowing the flavor to mingle on his tongue before swallowing. "I think you are more keen on working the case, as it were, than Max is. I wonder if you were smart to retire when you did?"

"I didn't have much of a choice. I was thinking earlier about the P.I. who died. He had a good business, and I can't help but wonder if it was the secrets of others that drove him to drugs, and if taking drugs led him to destroy his business."

"I agree that these questions, often unanswerable, are what keep us interested. Monsieur Laroche, lost in love or obsession, or whatever you want to call it…that can cause collapse."

"Collapse is a good word for it."

The door flung open and Max entered alone, her cheeks flushed. "Where is Abdel?" Olivier asked.

"He had a long drive ahead, to meet up with his cousin, and decided to carry on. Tim is, naturally, deeply worried about Lucy, and is working double-time to clear her name."

"He didn't happen to tell you where she is, did he?" Hank asked. "It wouldn't surprise me if he didn't stash her somewhere until he could prove her innocence."

"That crossed my mind, too."

"What was his friendship like with Yves?" Olivier asked.

"He knew him slightly, but their paths didn't cross after Tim started seeing Lucy. Yves was a bit of a high-roller, it turns out. He went from cocaine to opioids, and grew nastier by the week." Max smiled. "Tim claims to have negatives in his possession that will provide proof of who pushed Yves and who shot Lucy. I invited him for dinner tonight, but he declined as he wants to finish. He said for us to come by after dinner and he should be done."

Olivier said, "Text him and tell him we'll be there." Max nodded. "He hasn't been absolved of guilt, either," Olivier added. "He's protective of Lucy, as any man in love would be, and if he thought Yves meant to hurt her, he might have shoved him."

"He sounds like the best witness you have," Hank said.

"I found him immensely earnest and entertaining," Max said.

Olivier felt a tinge of jealousy, for he had already seen that Tim was a pleasing extrovert. Max scooched in beside him on the sofa and whispered, "If these photographs from the party and from the hunt are what he claims they are, we won't have all this hanging over us at our wedding."

"He could have told Abdel who he caught on camera."

"He said one photo is grainy and another one from the hunt is blurred, and he wanted to be sure."

"I hope he hasn't shared this information with anyone else."

Juliette called them to dinner, and they promptly entered the dining room. Olivier was happy to see sorrel soup, bread, and cheese—a simple country supper, shared with family. Isabelle had brought out a red wine from a local winery, nothing out of the ordinary, yet still satisfying.

"I feel on solid ground now with Monsieur Caron, by the way," he told Max. "I will call someone in the justice department to see what your pending status is with Interpol. Perhaps we can rush the application."

She leaned over and kissed him. "You weren't upset that I went with Abdel?"

"I was, but your father helped me to see it differently."

Max laughed, and glancing at her watch, said, "Don't be jealous of Tim. You'll find out why I like him so much. Even Abdel declared him a good guy."

Chapter Twenty-three

It was after eleven when Max and Olivier strolled over to Tim's for a Vieux Marc de Bourgogne and a look at the photographs. Olivier carried a flashlight. "I think Yves Laroche's murder may have nothing to do with Lucy and everything to do with drugs."

Max agreed. "It was a party crowd, and men as disparate as Tim, Jean-Claude, and Yves were a part of it. Men who were attractive, unattached, well-to-do by most people's standards. Tim had pulled out. He and Lucy were talking about traveling."

The porch light was on. Olivier knocked, and they waited.

"He's probably still in the darkroom. He didn't text me back." Max opened the door and called out his name.

"He likes Schumann," Olivier said.

Max listened as piano notes rippled around the room. "I don't like this," she said. "Something's wrong."

"He may have gone into Beaune."

"The lights are on and he was expecting us." The darkroom door was ajar and Max looked in. Tim lay on the floor, his head in a pool of blood. "Oh God, NO! Tim!" She knelt and took his pulse. Olivier had squeezed into the room. He pulled out his phone and called Abdel, who answered immediately. "The police will come from Beaune," he relayed to Max. "Abdel is on his way from Lyon."

Max swore and looked around. "A .22 to the back of the head. He never knew." She glanced around. "All the photographs and negatives are gone." She looked at Olivier, "I despise whoever did this, and trust me, I will nail him."

A man's voice hallooed from the front door. Max and Olivier looked at each other, then she followed him into the living room, both of them relaxing when they saw Jean-Claude, who looked from one to the other, a smile on his face. "I wasn't alone in wanting a cognac, I see," he said. "Is Tim still serving?"

"He's dead," Olivier said dryly. "Assassinated."

"*C'est pas possible!*" Jean-Claude put his hands over his face, and sat down. "I spoke to him only a few hours ago." He went to the cabinet, poured a snifter of cognac and sat down heavily, obviously shaken. Max knew that Olivier wanted to get to work, but he was also operating under his theory that five minutes of patience often produced positive results, and so he leaned wearily against the counter. Max donned some plastic gloves and saw that her hands were shaking. *If only we had come back immediately*, she thought. *If only. If only.* "If fucking only we had not left him," she yelled, startling the two men into silence. "I wanted to stay, but I was expected for another family dinner! I should have stayed and helped him." She began to sob. She looked at Jean-Claude, "You called him a friend. Did you know about the pictures he was developing? He must have told you."

"He was always taking photographs. Why are you asking this?"

"Because he knew who killed Yves Laroche, and he knew who shot Lucy!"

"I would tell you if I knew. I could be next."

"What do you mean?" Olivier asked.

"Yves is dead. Now Tim. Alain and I are left, and we are barely speaking."

"Why?"

Jean-Claude hesitated. "He and Yvette are quarreling, and Alain blames me." He sighed. "Since Caroline died, my life has taken a terrible turn downhill. I began drinking too much, and when Yvette started showing up to help me, we started having sex."

Oh please, Max thought, picking up a Mont Blanc fountain pen from the counter, and trying not to think about the dead body of a recently healthy young man a few metres away. If she were Jean-Claude's friend, she would have advised him to "man up" if he was having an affair, and for God's sake, to own it.

Olivier said, "Whether victim or aggressor, you cheated on your friend."

"Yes, and it was a mistake. I have tried to call it off for several months, but Yvette shows up and cleans my house, and does her best to make herself indispensable. Anyhow, Yves managed to take some photos of us having sex in a field."

"Where was the photo taken?"

"In a meadow near here. I arrived early at Yves' party with a date, and Yves told me that I could buy the photographs, but the price was exorbitant. He then told me that I ought to give up on the parcel of land I inherited from my wife, that the *notaire* was on Anne's side. I felt like the world was crashing on my head, then Yves said, "I am close to having proof that Lucy is Gervais' daughter, and if so, I think Anne will make sure she gets it."

"I was in shock at what my mother-in-law was up to. Then Yves said, 'Maybe Lucy will let you get in her pants if you haven't already, and I suspect you have.' I told him that was a ridiculous assumption, and he said that my mother-in-law was complaining about Lucy working in my vineyard. I told him I wasn't a pervert like him."

"Any idea why he had turned so vindictive?"

"Lucy. The kid is okay, but she has caused a lot of problems. Yves turned on me because she worked with me, and he was enraged when he learned Lucy had chosen Tim. I believe he was insanely jealous. That night at the party he was crazed. I had to get out of there…"

"Or what?"

"I threatened him. I told him I would like to kill him. This after he said he'd give Yvette a bargain price on the photos of us. Ten thousand."

Max was all attention now. "You called her."

"Of course. She unraveled, especially when I said Yves threatened to put them on the Internet. She demanded that I put up half the money and I said no. She said she was going to confess to Alain if I didn't."

"What did you do then?" Olivier asked.

"I went home, got drunk, and passed out."

Or went back to Yves' at the end of the party and pushed him off the balcony, Max thought. Exactly what I would have wanted to do.

"It's normal for you to drop in at this hour?" Olivier asked.

"I stop by often when Tim's lights are on. He had no enemies that I knew of. He was always boosting me, telling me not to worry, things always turned out alright. That was his philosophy."

"Someone wanted the negatives from the party and from the hunt."

Jean-Claude shrugged. "He was determined to prove Lucy innocent of Yves' death. He must have caught something because he told me to be prepared to be shocked. The same with the hunt, he said."

"But he gave you no indication?"

"None."

Flashing lights in the driveway diverted their attention, and Olivier went to the door. A gendarme entered and, recognizing Jean-Claude, shook hands. "You can go," Olivier said to Jean-Claude, leading the gendarme to the darkroom. "We will talk tomorrow."

Max thumbed through photographs that were piled up, wiping tears away with the back of her hand. She couldn't imagine Lucy's heartbreak, learning the news of Tim's death. Wherever she was. If she was anywhere. The photos were of Tim on a beach with friends, and skiing and mountain biking. She assumed the attractive couple with the towhead in an earlier photograph were his parents holding him, and the grand house in the background his home in England. She stopped when she came to a photo of Lucy wearing mud boots that were too big, looking up at Tim and smiling. He had his arm around her and gazed directly into the camera. They were an unusually attractive couple. She recognized that it was taken at the picnic table in his backyard. It must have been a warm day in September, for she was wearing a tank top and shorts, and he was also in shorts.

The girl on the red Vespa, Max thought. Arriving with a patched-together story. The little orphan. Anne to the rescue, creating a new story for Lucy. 'Why not let my dead husband be the missing father?' It would give Anne a new lease on life, and she would be able to defeat Jean-Claude at the same time. Max wondered if Anne knew that Hugo had gone to Olivier privately to talk about his concerns. She doubted it.

An ambulance arrived. The police began the process of securing the premises, putting red-and-white tape around the scene. A doctor arrived to determine the hour of death. A forensics team wearing white began various tasks. It was the same routine everywhere. Max thought she'd be inured to this by now, but it was always a shock.

Olivier went to find Max. "I feel horrible about Tim Lowell," Olivier said. "Deeply sad. And sorry. You are right. We should have come back immediately."

• • ● • •

A tap on the door and Hank entered. "I had a hunch something was going on," he said. "I couldn't sleep, and then I saw the ambulance go by."

Max went to him and he put his arm around her. "It's Tim. We found him dead. Shot."

"I'm sorry."

"Everything is under control here, Dad. I have to get a few hours of sleep."

"Okay," he said. "I'll walk back with you."

They stepped out into the night. Max switched on a small flashlight. "I wish I had felt this one coming," Hank said. "Knowing that he was developing controversial photographs maybe should have rung an alarm bell."

Somehow it was comforting to have Hank express what she and Olivier were feeling.

"I've been in this position at least a hundred times. I sometimes think the person is going to die, no matter what I do. It's their time. One of the most lame-ass expressions of all time. If somebody said that to me about someone I loved I'd hit them, and hard. Tim knew he was sitting on a land mine."

"Jean-Claude arrived right after us. He is a member of the 'club of misfits', which is how I'm labeling them." She told him about Jean-Claude's confession of his affair with Yvette, and his confrontation with Yves.

"Yvette," he said, shaking his head. "Now there's a piece of work. In the shadow of her surgeon sister. Depressed husband. Messed-up son. Obsessive affair."

Max told him about the compromising photographs Yves had of Yvette and Jean-Claude.

"That could be her undoing. She would be shunned by her community if those photos were leaked. And we don't know what Alain would do. He doesn't know what he'd do."

"What would you do?"

"Shoot the son of a bitch who messed with my wife, and maybe her, too. How many cases do we have on file like that?"

The rays of the moon filtered through the trees bordering their path.

"I've been accepted by Interpol. The call came through."

"Good job, Max. Really. I think Olivier and Abdel would be a little lost without you at this point."

"And I'd be lost without you." She put her arm through his. "I've never been on a case you weren't a part of."

"Sure you have. The Champagne case."

"You were the remote detective on the job."

"I hope you never told Olivier that."

"I think he figured it out. You're hard on him."

"He needs to grow a thicker skin. I'll bet you he's in Tim's house right now, blaming himself."

"That's just what he's doing."

"I got better about that as I got older. Sometimes there's just nothing you can do."

"I don't know how I'll do Interpol and raise kids all at once."

"You're not pregnant, are you?"

"No. But I want to be one day."

"I'm glad to hear it. You'll manage, like all those women out there working and running a family, including a lot of detectives."

They entered the house and went to the kitchen. "I know it's late, but do you want a cup of tea?"

"You have the tea. I'll have a beer."

"I've been thinking about the three of us," Hank said. She knew he was trying to distract her. "You and your Ma do have roots here. My roots are where you and your Ma are, Max."

"Are you saying you might want to spend more time here?"

"I think you and Olivier may be needing a little help...for the next few years, anyhow."

"He reminded me again that you have to stay in the background."

"That's my favorite place to be. But he won't find Lucy without me."

"Why do you say that?"

"Because he doesn't know people well enough yet. He might never know people the way I do. I have Irish intuition."

Max eyed him suspiciously. "You know something I don't?"

"What gave you that idea?"

Chapter Twenty-four

Olivier watched Max and her father leave, then turned to the local prosecutor who stood surveying the crime scene.

"We meet at last," the prosecutor said. "My name is Charles Dubois. I'm based in Beaune. Do you have any suspects?"

"No suspects yet." He explained about the missing photographs. "Let's wait until forensics is done. My assistant will come up with a full report."

Dubois frowned. "Why your assistant? I have my own."

Olivier was in no mood for this. The man before him was typical of the many legal functionaries he had known over the years who were well-bred, well-educated, and smug as hell. Dubois, he figured, was about his own age. Trim, hair cut just so, round glasses, pride oozed from him.

Just then Abdel approached and introduced himself while proffering his hand, but Dubois turned quickly to a forensics officer rushing by and delivered an order, which Olivier saw as a slight. Abdel slowly brought his hand down. "No sign of a murder weapon?" the prosecutor asked, turning back to him.

"Nothing so far."

Dubois said, "I know the girl who escaped our hospital and this guy were together. Any chance she could have offed him? She could be on a rampage. Her uncle…"

Olivier interrupted, unable to listen another minute to this kind of rhetoric. "We can update you on our findings."

Dubois persisted. "The uncle, George Wyeth, is gaining public sympathy. If she turns up dead, I think we'll all be fired. Between her getting shot in a hunting accident, then disappearing from the Beaune hospital, and now this poor guy…"

"This investigation isn't about you, and if you expect any cooperation from me, you need to stop promoting newsbytes from television."

Olivier watched the blood creep up in Dubois' face. "I'll send my assistant over in a few minutes." He whirled away from them, calling to an officer.

Olivier and Abdel went to the kitchen, and were soon joined by Dubois, who had evidently changed his mind. "I want to know about the shooting," he said.

Olivier deferred to Abdel, who began talking in a calming voice. "The girl was shot with a .30 caliber rifle, but the issue is, at least five of the hunters carried a .30 caliber. A bullet was retrieved from a tree trunk, it was bagged, and is now being tested by ballistics experts. The surgeon said the bullet entered from the field, going through the the girl's arm while upraised. However, a gun expert is convinced that the bullet was shot from the interior of the forest. The police will be questioning Alain Milne, Jean-Claude Villemaire, and Hank Maguire…"

Olivier said, "Monsieur Maguire was there as my guest, Monsieur Dubois."

"You must be questioned as well, Monsieur Chaumont."

"Which is a waste of time. Obviously, I didn't shoot the girl."

"The police report states that it was an accidental shooting. You are the one who wants to turn it into an attempted murder case, Monsieur. You must not be the exception."

Olivier could imagine the newspaper headline: "Magistrate Held for Questioning in Shooting of American Girl."

Dubois had a self-satisfied look. "The American female detective was not carrying a gun, but she was there on the scene, the first to notice that a human had been shot, correct?"

Olivier knew where this was going. "She was there as an observer."

"Against the wishes of several club members, I understand."

Who the hell had he been talking to? Olivier wondered.

The prosecutor glanced down at his notes. "It has occurred to my assistant and me that Detective Hank Maguire, now retired, might have been hired by the uncle of the girl, George Wyeth, to locate her. It's all supposition, of course..."

Olivier stood in stony silence, with Abdel standing beside him, glancing from one to the other.

"Tonight's victim, Monsieur Timothy Lowell, was at the hunt, was he not?"

Olivier nodded, as a wave of doubt crawled over him. It had been so chaotic with everyone shooting, that it was hard to place people during those few moments. He couldn't recall seeing Tim during the fusillade, but remembered him emerging from the woods behind Alain Milne, a look of panic on his face. What had he seen in the woods? "He was taking photographs."

"Did you notice any antagonism between Monsieur Lowell and the other hunters?"

"No more than is normal among xenophobic people. I'm sure they had strong opinions about him refusing to shoot an animal, and obviously somebody didn't like him taking pictures."

"*You* seem to have some antagonism toward the hunters."

Olivier bored in on him with his eyes. "If you try to use your psychological crap on me again, Monsieur, I will call our respective bosses in Paris and, trust me, you don't want me to do that. Now, back to tonight's shooting. I think Tim Lowell is dead because of photos he took at a small party hosted by the private investigator, Yves Laroche, and at the hunt. That is all you will learn from me."

The threat was effective. In a more modulated voice, Dubois said, "Monsieur Laroche was indiscreet with his business affairs, as you probably know. The Lyon police had their eye on him because of his heroin purchases, and were about to intervene. But that's not my territory."

"I must call it a night," Olivier said, looking around and seeing that everyone else was already gone.

"Very well, I'm off," Dubois said, and with that he walked out the door.

Olivier said to Abdel, "It's people like that who make me want to leave this profession." He looked around and felt he was seeing the B&B for the first time. The decor was somewhat eccentric and eclectic with ancestral paintings dating back at least to the seventeenth century, mixed in with folk art. Antique furniture that could have come from a grand estate was casually placed with "found" pieces. Tim was a bachelor with a degree of success with his B&B, and perhaps some family money to keep him going. Olivier recalled Max's instant rapport with him, how she had found him amusing and intelligent.

He wandered through the rooms, looking for…what? The three guest rooms were orderly. A half bottle of wine, an Auxey-Duresses from Domaine Michel Prunier et fille, was open on a kitchen counter. To Olivier's mind, it showed the discerning taste of the consumer. Tim had to be an oenophile. This bottle, more than anything, told Olivier that he would have enjoyed a repast with this man who also listed cooking classes in his brochure, and who had the volume turned up on a Schumann piece.

The police had taken quite a few items with them, but would return in daylight to analyze others. They had Tim's laptop, iPad, and phone which, these days, had much more credibility than anything jotted on the slips of paper that were scattered about. LUCY was written in caps on a post-it. Tim had doodled a heart next to her name, and beneath it he had written the date he took her to Paris. Olivier suddenly longed to be with Max. He asked Abdel if he would care to stay at Isabelle's, but he said he preferred driving back to Lyon.

Olivier reflexively thrust the note into his pocket and, locking the door behind him, walked to Isabelle's house, going over in his mind the awful exchange with Dubois. He hadn't been forced to take the case, but Dubois and also Caron, in his way, were making it clear that he was an outsider, something he had rarely experienced. He knew why he lobbied for the case. He felt responsible. And now that Tim was dead, he felt that he had failed in a big way. If he and Max had gone immediately to Tim's instead of first enjoying a wonderful dinner, he might still be alive. Olivier had experienced a moment of jealousy for the man, not because he was worried about Max being attracted to him, but because he himself would love to be more like Tim. Someone so comfortable in his life, and in his environment, that he exuded a rare positivity.

On my behalf, he thought as he neared the porch of the great house, *I have no doubt that were I not in charge, the murder of Yves Laroche and the shooting of Lucy Kendrick would have been ruled accidents by the authorities and justice would not be served.*

This would be his last investigation before joining the Anti-Terrorism Division. This coming on top of his and Max's engagement wasn't fair to either of them. Their wedding loomed large. Would they cancel if Lucy couldn't be found? He suddenly had a horrible and vivid image of her lying dead in the forest, covered with leaves. It left him gasping. The front door was unlocked, and he quietly stepped in and removed his shoes, trying not to wake anyone.

Max whispered *hi* when he entered her bedroom. He stripped off his clothes. "I almost decided to go check on you, you were gone so long," she said in a soft voice, "but I was feeling too emotional about Tim to go back. Are you okay?"

"I'm going to take a quick shower," he said. "Don't go anywhere."

She laughed softly.

Once in the shower, with hot water pouring over him, helping to ease the tension in his body, tears mixing with water, he couldn't believe how beautiful and soothing the sound of Max's voice was to him. Perhaps this was what a good marriage was, a partner waiting up for you, and desiring you. He toweled off, and went immediately to her, speaking her name, kissing her over and over, caressing her strong body, inhaling her essence. She responded with equal passion, until the moment arrived when he felt as though they were one.

Chapter Twenty-five

Max sat at *petit déjeuner* at her grandmother's, sipping *café au lait*, and listening to her grandmother expostulate about Tim's death. "No one in the village can feel safe anymore," she said, setting a plate of bread purchased at the local *boulangerie* early this morning on the table.

Isabelle was drawn and on edge.

Juliette said, "Maman, sit down and let me do this."

"I'm better off being busy. I barely slept last night."

Max, too, had lain awake most of the night waiting for Olivier. When she awoke he was gone. "Off to the prosecutor's," his note said. "You are a goddess." She was barely listening to her grandmother and mother, clinging as she was to those sweet, fleeting moments.

Juliette fretted. "You have to get some rest. Maybe we should go to Paris for a few days until this murder news isn't on every headline."

Isabelle said firmly, "I can't leave. I have responsibilities here."

"What responsibilities?" Hank asked.

"What do you mean by that, Henry?" Isabelle snapped. "Are you implying that I don't have responsibilities?"

"I think you are weighed down with responsibility, which is why your daughter is worried about you."

"There is the wedding to think of..." Her voice trailed off.

"And there is Lucy."

Max felt a shift in energy, and wondered what she had missed. Her glance swept from her father to her grandmother, who had stopped mid-step. Quickly regaining her composure, Isabelle said, "Of course there is Lucy. Everyone has so quickly forgotten about her."

Hank had not shifted position. "Her photograph is on the news every twenty minutes, it seems, reminding the world of her disappearance. The beautiful orphan haunting their lives the way missing children's photos do."

"I don't know where they got that photograph. She looks like a little bird with its feathers gone."

"I thought maybe you or Anne gave it to them."

Juliette sent Hank a warning look.

Nice little family moment we have here, Max thought.

"At least we're not looking at the face of Uncle George," Isabelle said, scowling.

"I agree," Hank said. "But until he is proven to be an unreliable guardian, he is legally in charge of his niece. It doesn't look good for the justice system that she has disappeared into thin air. There are sightings everywhere, all false of course. On the news this morning there was speculation that she snuck in and killed her own boyfriend, Tim Lowell."

Isabelle's eyes widened, and she put her hand over her heart. "*Mon Dieu*, the world is crazy. Our Lucy is the last thing from a murderer."

Max had had it. She stood up. "I'm going for a run."

Hank said, "Have a seat, Max. This is the only chance we have had as family to be together." He turned to Isabelle, "You're going to have to turn her in."

Max sat back down, aghast. "Dad…"

Isabelle looked at him, "I…I…don't know where she is."

"Is she conscious?"

Isabelle sat stoically for a minute, then nodded.

"I thought so. Is she under a doctor's care?"

"One of us is a retired doctor."

Juliette had led her mother to a chair and sat with her arm around her. Max's thoughts churned around as though they were in a blender. "I'll call Olivier."

"Give your grandmother a minute," Hank said.

"I need longer than a minute," Isabelle said. "I am clear that I won't make a decision for the group."

"What group?" Max asked, still in amazement.

"*Femmes et Vins de Bourgogne*. We are in solidarity on this, and are willing to go to prison for our actions. We planned Lucy's escape from the hospital, and now we are like the Underground Railroad in America, moving her from one home to another."

Max said, "I'm a member of the investigation and should not be listening to this."

"Lucy is preparing to step forward as soon as George Wyeth relinquishes his right to control her life. He must give up his guardianship."

Max said, "There can be no negotiation until Lucy is brought in." She hesitated, "Does she know about Tim?"

"Yes. And she's devastated. He helped with the escape. They had planned to meet up tomorrow morning at her new destination."

Hank said, "I want you to take Max and me to her."

Isabelle looked at him. "I have to make a phone call."

"Tell Anne that we will be there in ten minutes."

She got up and briskly walked out of the room.

"How did you know, Dad?"

"Your grandmother hasn't been herself lately. She has been questioning her own actions, worried about the repercussions for you and Olivier. Anne, I am sure, is the ringleader."

Isabelle returned and said, "Anne will be ready." She fixed her stern eyes on Hank. "If this gets botched up, I will never speak to you again."

He nodded somberly and Max was proud of him for not pointing out that she hadn't spoken to him for thirty years, so why would this be different?

• • ● • •

Anne smiled calmly as they entered, not in the least contrite. "We should probably leave right away," Anne said. "She's tucked away in a remote area."

"I should let Olivier know where I am," Max said.

"I didn't agree to Olivier being involved," Anne said. "Neither you nor Hank can make an arrest. Lucy can talk to you and you can advise her."

Max didn't mention her new position with Interpol. She remained silent and climbed into the backseat of Anne's car. She didn't know when, if ever, she had felt her loyalty so torn. Olivier would not understand them leaving him out of this, and at the same time she couldn't imagine herself sitting at Isabelle's twiddling her thumbs while Hank was meeting with Lucy.

Anne said, "I hope you understand why we did what we did. Thirty of the women in our group met, and we were all in agreement that we had to keep Lucy safe until she could speak out for herself."

"She was never in a full coma, was she?" Hank said.

"She was extremely weak and drifting in and out of consciousness. One day, when Isabelle and I were with her she opened her eyes, and said in a tiny voice, "Someone tried to strangle me. I have to leave."

Isabelle said, "We leaned over her bed and offered to take her to a safe place, but that she had to give herself time to heal. She began to improve from then on. We were certain the aggressor was her Uncle George."

Max deliberated about bringing up Anne's deviousness around Lucy's father, and decided to confront her, though not without trepidation. "Anne," she said, "I've learned that you're promoting as fact the assumption that your husband Gervais is Lucy's biological father. You even went to Yves to see if he could help, and of course, for a ridiculous sum of money, he could switch the DNA report, and give you what you wanted."

"This is awfully presumptuous of you, Maxine."

"Yves told Jean-Claude to forget winning the land deal, that a lot more was involved than just land."

"Max, this isn't your business. It has nothing to do with the murders."

Max glanced over at her grandmother. "Yves was holding onto a lot of secrets. Dangerous secrets. Olivier and Abdel are currently sorting through the contents of his files. He had no scruples."

"I'm doing this for Lucy's good." Anne's voice was strident. "Hugo is going to a great deal of trouble, and enormous expense, to help this girl he has never met. She could just as easily have been Gervais' daughter."

"That's not fair. Diane Kendrick never met your husband. He was in California at the time of conception. There are photographs of him on the Internet accepting a winemaking award on your behalf. Lucy could easily read the same article."

Anne's lips were pursed. She adjusted her sunglasses. "You Americans have no idea how important discretion is. It's how the French operate."

"I agree with Max," Hank said. "In this case, discretion is used to camouflage the truth."

"And what about the parcel of land you and Jean-Claude are in contention over?" Max asked.

Anne nodded. "I think it's a good solution all around. If Jean-Claude acquiesces, I will hire him to manage the parcel until Lucy knows what she is doing."

"If Lucy is all that you say she is," Max said, "then she won't accept it under the circumstances it's being given to her."

Anne pulled the car over and turned around to face Max. "And why would you say that, Miss High and Mighty?"

Max's heart was racing. She waited for Hank to jump in, but he didn't even turn his head. "Because you aren't honoring your own daughter's wishes."

"My daughter isn't here, in case you haven't noticed. She's in the ground."

Max couldn't believe her eyes were welling up. "She's irreplaceable, Anne. Lucy could never fill those shoes. You could still have Lucy come and live with you. Think about her. Her whole life has been a lie. Her mother tried to create a fairy-tale life for her. The princess can return to her roots and find her magical father. Maybe she will even find true love. The poor woman loved her daughter, no doubt about that, but she couldn't face the music either. She allowed her stepbrother, whom she didn't even like, to take and incarcerate Lucy when she was struggling with depression."

"Her mother was right to honor Hugo's request that she not reveal his name until…"

"His death. I think Uncle George was right about Diane. Somewhere along the way she gave up all her power. Was Hugo right to demand secrecy from Diane? He took no responsibility for his part in creating a child. And now he's wheeling and dealing to keep his kids from finding out. Ever. Do you really think they would abandon him if he told them the truth?"

"I don't know." Anne lit a cigarette. Max couldn't believe she was smoking.

After taking another drag, and exhaling slowly, Anne said. "Before you bring it up and try to become a peacemaker…a role that doesn't suit you, by the way…I think Jean-Claude has been having an affair with Alain's wife, Yvette. I see her entering his house when he isn't there, and to tell you the truth, I don't think she's stable."

"He knows it's been a big mistake."

"I don't want to hear about that. I'm deeply worried that he's somehow involved in Yves' murder, though I can't imagine his motive." Max thought of the incriminating photos of Jean-Claude with Yvette, but she didn't consider that as a motive for him to murder; in fact, she thought he had enough ego to feel a wash of pride rather than dismay.

"None of us should have trusted Yves, I realize that now. I'm sure now that he told Jean-Claude about my attempt to have that piece of land go to Lucy. What I'm saying is, don't be surprised if you find me murdered next."

Max had worked enough crimes to know that in families and among friends, there often came a moment when no one trusted anyone. Max understood because, as a detective, she went through it more than she liked to admit, blaming everyone. "So far he has come across as innocent."

"Sadly, none of us is innocent, when you come down to it." She started the car. "We'll be there in fifteen minutes." Max saw a sign for Bouzeron, an area twenty minutes west of Beaune that was known for the Aligoté grape, considered a poor cousin to the richer wines of the Côte de Beaune or Côte de Nuits. They were on a winding road, and had only passed one other car. "There is a woman here in this village who is a great producer of Aligoté wine, and a good friend of mine. Her name is Sarah and she is practically a recluse, working her two hectares of vines, and creating wines that are *pas mal du tout.* Her husband left her when she insisted on making her own wine."

They turned onto another winding road that turned out to be a driveway, and climbed steadily upward for half a kilometer before Anne stopped at a small house. A village steeple was visible in the distance. The wind had picked up, though the day remained sunny. A woman of around fifty opened the door and walked out, a smile on her face. "Ah, Anne," she said, "don't tell me you're moving Lucy again."

"Meet Hank," Anne said, "and his daughter, Max. I've told you about them."

"Yes, of course." She exchanged a firm handshake with each of them.

Behind them a girl walked out onto the small lawn, her arm in a sling. "Anne!" she cried. "I'm glad to see you." They exchanged cheek kisses. "I can't stop crying over Tim." Tears coursed down her cheeks.

Anne pulled a tissue from her pocket. "Of course you can't."

"She hasn't been eating," Sarah said.

Max's mind went to work summing up the girl. Lucy's voice was raspy, her figure lithe and strong. Easily, she could be the aggressor or the meek. Again, Max thought of herself at that age, and compassion arose in her. She could recall exactly how it was after her brother died, the well of depression that seemed to last forever, the self-destructive actions that had Hank threatening to "lock her up."

She felt Lucy's eyes on her. They were a deep blue and, to her surprise, hostile. Anne introduced them. "I know all about you," Lucy said, and without even glancing at Hank, went inside.

Sarah brought out a bottle of her own wine and opened it, pouring it into short, stubby café glasses. Hank, ignoring the glass meant for him, said to Lucy, "You know you have to come back with us."

"I'm not ready."

Max spoke, "You don't have a choice. You'll have plenty of protection."

"Like Tim had?"

It felt like a gut kick.

Hank stepped in. "You've put two old women through a lot. I'm worried about Isabelle. She's had a stroke, you know."

Lucy grew pensive. "Someone tried to kill me at the hospital. Probably the same person who killed Tim. I wish he'd succeeded with me, then maybe he'd be free."

"What happened?" Hank asked.

"I heard the door open and closed my eyes. I heard light footsteps come to the bed. I felt danger. The nurses made noise when they entered. The next moment a pillow was pushed over my face, and the person pressed hard on both ends of it. He was trying to suffocate me. I used my good arm to thwack whoever it was on the side of his face. I'd been exercising, and I know I hurt him."

"He didn't cry out?"

"No. He left the pillow on my face and ran quickly out the door. I got up as fast as I could and went to the door and looked out but didn't see anyone."

"Good work," Hank said. "We need you if we're going to find Tim's killer."

That did it. "I'll get my things," said Lucy.

"Max will go with you. No more escapes."

"I don't need a nursemaid." Lucy stomped off.

"You need Max," he said to her retreating back.

"I hate teenagers," Max said, following her.

"So do I."

Max stopped at the doorway of the bedroom. "I'll wait out here." Lucy shut the door in her face, and Max heard her throwing stuff around. After fifteen minutes, Max said through the door, "What's wrong?"

The door opened, and Lucy said, "I can't get my backpack zipped."

Max entered. A simple room with twin beds. Max went to the bed and zipped the backpack and handed it to Lucy. "My laptop's over there. It needs to be charged."

"I got it."

"I get to be in your wedding, right?"

"How'd you know about that?"

"You told your mother and she told your grandmother, who told me when she thought I was in a coma. Anne talked to me a lot. I feel so sad about her losing her Caroline. She wants to adopt me. She told me her husband, Gervais, had an affair with my mother, and I was the result. I'm dubious because Yves laughed when I told him. He said he had the real facts and he was selling them to my Uncle George. Who, I hear, is being a total pain."

"He's a pain, alright. But I don't think he'll be bothering you too much longer. Anyone being investigated cannot be a guardian. Period." She hesitated. "About the wedding. Olivier may change his mind when he hears what's gone on here." Max couldn't believe she was confiding in the girl.

Lucy said, "Am I your doppelgänger?"

Max laughed. "No one would think you are my twin, but you are a lot like me when I was your age. Angry. Scared. Sad. I lost my brother when I was your age."

"But now you have Olivier. I think he has too much soul to be doing police work."

"But he feels that this is how he can best serve," Max said. "He believes in justice."

"I don't expect to get any justice," Lucy said matter-of-factly. "They need a scapegoat. The only reason I'm going in with no fight is that I just don't care anymore."

"But we care."

Chapter Twenty-six

Olivier left Max's grandmother's house with a mere two hours of sleep under his belt, but he felt full of vitality. He left quietly, without disturbing anyone, and was driving through the village of Auxey-Duresses when he saw Jean-Claude waving to flag him down. He stopped the car, but not without hesitation. "What is it, Jean-Claude?"

"Do you have a minute?"

"Just. I'm on my way to headquarters in Lyon."

Jean-Claude lit a cigarette. "Alain was walking across the field behind my house this morning. He said he had come to check on his nearby vineyard, and mentioned that he had seen on the news that Tim had been shot and killed. I told him I was busy but he lingered, and finally he said to me, 'Do you worry about being next?'"

Olivier waited. "And?"

"I don't want him on my property."

"You should post the land, then, I suppose."

"I don't mind about others. Just him."

"It's not a legal matter, Jean-Claude. Just tell him."

"I also wanted to speak about the Muslim cop."

"Monsieur Zeroual."

"He led me on with his questions. Especially about the argument I'd had with Yves at his party. I want to see his report."

"You don't remember what you told Monsieur Zeroual?"

"Not exactly. He showed me a copy of a lurid photograph that Yves had taken of Yvette and me, from his file. He practically accused me of killing Yves because of it."

Olivier almost chuckled at the exaggeration. He had concluded that everybody Yves had gathered information on, or for, now wanted Olivier to set things right. Now he understood Jean-Claude's obvious distress. Not only was he worried about what his old friend might do to him if he had indeed seen the evidence of his infidelity, but he also realized that he was a suspect in the murder of Yves Laroche. Olivier liked it that he was nervous. Jean-Claude took a long drag off his cigarette and threw it to the ground. "Yves threatened to show the photograph to the boy, Roland."

This got Olivier's attention, as he was beginning to realize just how sadistic Yves could have been. It seemed likely that once he'd realized he could never have Lucy for himself, he had turned on everybody around him in jealous frustration.

"This has been horrible for Yvette. Horrible for me, too. I think Alain's question was a veiled threat."

"When fearful, everything feels like a threat, *n'est-ce pas*? I'm sorry, Jean-Claude, but now I'm running late. Are you lodging an official complaint against my assistant?"

"*Non.* But I want that photograph destroyed."

"I worry about there being multiple copies, but I'll see what I can do."

"Everybody's taking Tim's death hard, including me. If someone suspicious comes near my house, I'll shoot."

Olivier thought how each person's life who was in the circle of friends belonging to Tim had changed overnight. It was only a few short weeks ago that Tim's house had been the gathering place for an assembly of men, and a couple of women, too, who were each floundering in their own way, or perhaps teetering was the word. Yves' reason was being taken over by drugs and an unhealthy obsession with the unattainable Lucy; Alain was growing suspicious of his wife and close friend; Jean-Claude had entered into a dead-end affair that, even at the time, he knew spelled trouble, and was in a land dispute with his mother-in-law; Roland, surely aware of his parents' stormy relationship, was on his way to a major addiction problem as a means of escape. Tim was the only one who had seemed to be on stable ground, but who knew for sure? As for Yvette, his hunch was Jean-Claude was an obsession, never healthy; and Lucy had connected to everyone, and yet was a firefly, darting in and out.

Abdel was waiting in the courtroom. Olivier mentioned the conversation with Jean-Claude. Abdel said, "I didn't get the impression that he was mortified in the least. Maybe a little afraid of Monsieur Milne."

"Alain might turn out to be more like me. You recall that my first wife cheated on me," Olivier said in a rare moment of candid personal reflection. "But I never had the urge to kill the horse trainer she had been with; in fact, I can't even recall his name." Ignoring Abdel's skeptical gaze, he continued in a rational voice, "I was hurt, of course, but her indiscretion helped me to realize that we had married mainly because it was expected of us. In the end, I was relieved."

"That sounds a little passive, Monsieur. I'm afraid I might be the revenge type myself."

The comment made Olivier pause. "I find the word passive to be distasteful, but compared to killing someone in a fit of jealousy, I suppose that better describes me."

"There doesn't seem to be an in-between reaction."

Olivier said, "I predict Jean-Claude will reject Yvette, if he hasn't already, and she will be miserable. We should be considering the temperaments of the two men. Both Jean-Claude and Alain paid Yves Laroche to do sleuthing work for them, and both could have had a motive for stealing those negatives from Tim Lowell."

"You're saying that either one of them could have fired at Lucy, and either of them could have pushed Yves off the balcony. I agree. But so could have Roland."

"We're interviewing him next, but mainly because I want to assign him to rehab. By the way, Jean-Claude thinks it possible that Yves showed Roland the compromising photograph of his mother with Jean-Claude."

"That's sick. I hope it didn't happen, but if it did, Roland will never admit to seeing it. What young man would?"

A voice behind them caused them both to startle. "Where do you want me to sit?"

It was Roland.

"Take that seat," Abdel said, pointing to a chair across the room. "We'll join you in a few minutes." Olivier turned his attention to Roland, who was dressed in a suit, his hair slicked down, then back to Abdel, who said, "Where's Max?"

"Running late, I guess."

"Nothing on the girl?"

He shook his head. "Lots of breaking news on television, with the uncle ranting. He reminds me of one of those reality TV people who crave attention of any sort, whether positive or negative. Added to that, reporters have learned of her romance with Tim Lowell, and now with him dead and her missing, it's a media feeding frenzy."

"I fear she's dead, Abdel."

Abdel, avoiding eye contact at this grim statement, glanced at his iPad and said, "I have a lot of notes from the hospital staff. All were cooperative except the woman surgeon who operated on Lucy. She said she had given strict orders that there was to be only one person in the room at a time, and sometimes when she went to check on her patient the room was full. I tried to ask about the entry and exit wounds and she nearly bit my head off. I had the hunch she couldn't recall and didn't want to let on."

"Collect the scans that were taken of her arm the day she was brought in."

"Monsieur Maguire is firm that the bullet came from the interior of the woods, not from the field."

"The prosecutor will be far more interested in the surgeon's analysis than a retired American detective's, if you get my gist."

Olivier had all but forgotten that Roland was in the room until Alain entered and rushed over to shake hands. Yvette followed, her face looking bloated and distorted by heavy makeup.

"What happened to you?" Olivier asked Alain, noticing the bandage on his face. "A little skin cancer," Alain said. "Let's hope they got it all this time."

Prosecutor Caron entered and shook hands first with Olivier and Abdel. He next approached Alain and shook his hand, then took a seat, and the three family members also sat.

"I want to understand, Roland," Olivier asked gently, "why you felt compelled to confess to pushing Yves Laroche off the balcony, and to shooting your friend, Lucy Kendrick. Granted, we understand you were under the influence of alcohol and drugs, but I must ask you now if you were telling the truth."

Roland tapped his fingers on the table, and Abdel asked him to stop. He fidgeted in his seat and finally stood up, and Abdel told him he had to remain seated. At first glance Roland appeared to be a strapping, sanguine young man, with broad shoulders and expressive hands. *But there was something indolent about him*, Olivier thought. He had his father's pale, icy blue eyes, lacking in amiable expression. His lips curved up on the left side, in a sneer.

Olivier allowed himself a moment to ponder what had gone wrong with this boy, and why. Surely at Luc's age Roland had been an animated boy, curious about the world. Roland replied coolly, "You're right. I was high and so I don't remember why I confessed."

"We are going to help remedy that. You will be ordered to go to rehab until you are deemed sober, but first we must prove you innocent of any wrongdoing. We will start with Yves Laroche, and how you happened to be in his apartment on the night of his death."

"I met him through Lucy Kendrick, at Madame Bré's vineyard, when we were working together in the fields."

"And Madame Bré was okay with that?"

"She never liked me, but she knew Lucy did, and so she said I could be there."

"Was Lucy your girlfriend?"

Roland glanced sidelong at his mother. "No. She was with Tim."

"Are you aware that Tim Lowell is dead?"

"I saw it on television." His face had a flat affect, no expression. His mouth was slightly agape, a mouth-breather. *"Quel dommage,"* he finally said. What a pity, said with no pity.

"Tell me about the night of Yves Laroche's party."

Roland leaned forward, hands clasped, evoking Alain. "It's all a blur. Lucy took me into Yves' office because she wanted to find a folder. I looked up my mother's, and found photos Yves had taken of her with her lover, Jean-Claude."

Alain, furious and unable to control himself, stood up and shouted, "Roland!"

Roland turned to glare at his father and said, "It's all your fault. You were the one who paid Yves to stalk them and take that picture."

Abdel stood and walked over to Alain, and Olivier noticed him directing Alain gently to "sit, please." Olivier didn't have to look at her to know the loud sniffling was coming from Yvette.

"Did you stay at the party?" Olivier asked.

"Yes."

Monsieur Emmanuel Caron looked transfixed. Roland was sitting up straight now, but refusing to look in the direction of his parents. "And you left with Lucy and Tim?"

"I was out of it, but yes. I was with them. The other thing I remember was my father attacking me as I left the apartment. He stepped out of the shadows and grabbed my arm, demanding to know if I got my drugs from Monsieur Laroche. I yelled at him and left."

For the first time, Olivier looked at Alain as if hidden beneath his persona was the potential for a murderer.

"Did you see Yves fall off the balcony?"

"No."

"You and Lucy went into hiding. Normally people don't run and hide unless they have done something wrong."

"I was hiding from my father. Tim had work to do. He was taking Lucy into Paris the next day. Lucy stayed with me because she knew I had nowhere to go."

"And the next day she left to go with Tim. You stayed there?"

"I didn't want to go home. Lucy came back that night and told me that the police thought somebody had pushed Yves. She heard it on the news."

"Did she accuse you?"

"Me? No. She was worried that they were blaming her."

"What did you think?"

"I told her I bet my father had gone up and pushed him. The apartment door was open when I left."

"Tim and Lucy didn't tell you that he had photographs of Yves falling, and of Lucy getting shot?"

This time he was shocked. "No."

"You and Lucy stayed in the cabin again that night? No Tim?"

"He came over and brought food, then said he was going to shoot photos of a hunt at Jean-Claude's early the next morning. I said I was supposed to meet my father there, and he said I should show up and face the music. And Lucy said things had gotten out of control and she would go to Anne's."

"Why didn't that happen?"

"I opened the door of the cabin in the morning when I woke up, and somebody fired at the door. I thought it was meant to scare me. But Lucy was freaking out and said we had to run."

"Were you pursued?"

He shrugged. "Yes. I slipped and then I saw Lucy go down."

"Do you think whoever was chasing the two of you shot her?"

"Maybe I did by accident."

"Where did you get the rifle?"

"I took it from Jean-Claude's shed a few days ago. My dad and I kept two rifles there."

"Did you see anyone after Lucy was shot?"

"I saw Tim with his camera up in the air."

"You had no clue who was chasing you?"

"I thought it was a boar."

Chapter Twenty-seven

Max telephoned Olivier as soon as she had cell service, and was relieved when he didn't pick up. Better to bring Lucy in herself rather than try to explain circumstances over the phone. Glancing in the rearview mirror, she saw that Lucy's head was tilted over, and her eyes closed.

"How did you know my grandmother and Anne had kidnapped…excuse me, rescued…Lucy?" Max asked Hank, who was at the wheel.

"Don't leave out your mother." He paused while making a left turn. "Observation. They're all terrible actors. They would have been inconsolable if they had thought the girl was dead. Instead, they were alluding to the great escape constantly. They were quite proud of themselves."

"Olivier won't be amused."

"He's French. He'll be mad as hell and then grow rational. Stand by him and he'll be okay."

"You'll be with me."

"Nope. I'm stopping at the café."

"I've got your back, Max," Lucy said from the backseat.

Hank chuckled. "I didn't know you wanted to be a bridesmaid that bad."

"I've never been in a wedding."

"Oh, for God's sake, we have more serious stuff to deal with than a wedding," Max said, jealous that they were bantering in the same casual way that she and Hank usually did.

"Like my boyfriend's murder?" She began to sob uncontrollably.

"Pull over," Max said. Hank obeyed and Max got out, opened the back door, climbed in with Lucy and wrapped her arms around her quaking shoulders. "I'm so sorry you have to go through this."

"Everyone I care about is gone." She put her head against the door and closed her eyes, making small, wet, gasping sounds.

Hank turned around. "You got handed the joker, Lucy. The school of hard knocks. Some people get the queen of hearts and die with barely a scraped knee. It's what my wife calls karma. I can tell you this, which would make me feel better if I were in your shoes—and I have been—Tim never knew what hit him."

Silence prevailed in the backseat, then a muffled voice said, "Okay." Max dug in her pocket and pulled out a wadded tissue, shaking it out and handing it to Lucy. Hank started the car and continued toward Anne's.

"You'll probably be a target again before this is all over."

"Tim told me that the photos show that I was shot from behind, but the shooter's face was blurred. The guy wore a hat with a visor pulled down low, but Tim thought, once enlarged, he would be able to see who it was."

"Did Tim know that you were conscious when he came to visit you in the hospital?"

She smiled, tears sparkling in her eyes. "Yes. We talked about where we were going to travel. He wanted me to get my high school diploma before we took off." Lucy blew her nose. "After that, we decided that I would come back to France with him, we'd marry and I'd work with Anne."

Hank said, "You do know this whole thing about her husband being your father is more than likely a fairy tale."

"Anne wouldn't lie to me. She's going to adopt me. End of story."

"She also doesn't want Jean-Claude to have a certain parcel of land."

"You're hard to like, Hank."

"I'm a realist. You're not used to that. And Tim was right, the reality is that you need to finish your high school education at the very least. You can to come live with Juliette and me until you've accomplished that."

Max turned to look directly at her father, stunned. "Who're *you* replacing, Frédéric or me?"

"Whoa. Where is *that* coming from? Replace Frédéric? Not on your life. And don't even think of quickstepping into the notion that we're replacing you. We're going to jumpstart Lucy, and send her on her way."

"Ma agreed to all this?"

Hank grinned. "She doesn't know yet. I was just testing the waters."

"Geez, Dad."

"What about Uncle George?" Lucy asked.

"He'll be legally relieved of guardianship. To set the record straight once and for all, he didn't kill your mother. She died of an aneurysm. By the way, how did you escape from the mental hospital?"

"It was easy. I'd played poker every night with the guys who picked up the linens. They rolled me out in a cart covered with sheets."

"Ha! Like Annie's escape from Ms. Hannigan!" exclaimed Max, clearly impressed, and referencing the 1982 movie starring Aileen Quinn as an orphan escaping from an abusive guardian.

"I'm surprised George didn't report your escape to the police, or the media."

"He actually tried to keep the scandal from leaking because he was already in trouble with the hospital board. He contacted Yves instead."

"He must have suspected that there was a French father somewhere in the mix."

"Sure. My mother's dream was to return to France, and find him."

"If that had happened, then I don't think Anne would have been adopting you."

"Dad!"

"Here we are," Hank said, pulling up to the house. "And here they come."

Isabelle and Anne made a beeline for the car. "Your color is improving," Isabelle said, peering at Lucy. "Come inside. Juliette made cookies."

"I'm going to check on my barrels," Anne said. "Please excuse me."

Max asked if she could come along.

"If you're still speaking to me."

"I'll be right there," Max said. She turned and entered her grandmother's house. "Is Anne alright?" she asked aloud.

Isabelle lagged behind the others and whispered to Max. "No. Hugo came by and they had a long talk. He feels that he cannot go through with the land deal. He has decided to tell his children about Lucy. 'I can only hope for the best,' is the way he put it. The *notaire* also called, and the land rightfully belongs to Anne."

"That must have made her day."

"*Au contraire*. She's quite devastated about Tim's murder, actually. We all are, but she is taking it particularly hard. She says it is a blight on our collective land, which will endure for a long time. I'm afraid she's right." She turned to Max. "And you, my dear? Are we in terrible trouble with your fiancé?"

"I would think so. You behaved like the *haut monde* that you are, taking matters into your own hands, assuming that you have enough influence to avoid any repercussions."

"There was no assuming. I've already spoken with the office in Paris." Max knew that she meant the office of Philippe, who, until recently, was Olivier's boss, and who was still Isabelle's son-in-law. "Olivier will understand, once we explain."

The house phone rang. Juliette answered and handed the phone to Max.

"Philippe Douvier called me," Olivier said. "And I know what happened. It will be on the news tonight." He sighed. "I can't believe you didn't let me in on this little secret. I, too, was worried sick about the girl, and so was Abdel. I thought we were a team."

As Max anticipated, the blame was all falling on her.

"Olivier…"

"Please, let's not waste time with what has passed. I hate this legal system that allows these two insufferably pigheaded women to buy their way out of having to take responsibility for their actions. I'll need Lucy here first thing tomorrow morning."

"I'll have her there."

"I'll see you this evening, Max."

He's trying to understand me, she thought.

• • ● • •

She walked the short distance behind Anne's house to the elegant building that had served as wine cellar for generations, and was immediately thrust into an intuitively sacred space. The 2015 wine was fermenting in vast stainless-steel tanks, and wines from the 2014 vintage, in burnished French oak barrels, were standing in perfectly aligned rows, each marked with the name of the wine and the degree of roasting the barrels had undergone. It had all been lovingly nurtured by Anne, whose taste in the wine world was now infallible. Every drop of her wine was spoken for before the grapes were even picked from their vines. The vaulted room had an aura comparable to that of a library, Max thought, or of a sanctuary; mysterious places where the soul recognized home.

Mozart's *Symphony in C Major* echoed around the spacious room. Max knew from previous conversations that Anne fervently believed that only Mozart could properly season the wine aurally. Anne's philosophy permeated every drop of the wine, including tenets borrowed from Rudolf Steiner, who believed in planting according to the phases of the moon. Max continued down the aisle and again paused as she caught sight of Anne, who was at the far end of the room that contained fifty to sixty barrels, all in various stages of production. Max knew that the new chardonnay aged for about eighteen months before it was bottled. She had overheard Anne telling Hank that the wood barrels infused the wine with the circular energy of the cosmos. To her father's credit, he had nodded in comprehension.

Max realized as she drew closer that Anne was in distress. "Anne?"

"I'm sure Isabelle told you that Hugo has abandoned our agreement."

"She did."

"He doesn't want to die a coward." She said it with a cringing sense of irony.

"It doesn't sound cowardly to risk the opprobrium of one's children."

"Take his side. You've already presented your moral stance on this."

Max didn't like the cynicism, but she also didn't want to fight with Anne. "I'm sorry if I've hurt you. I've overstepped some boundaries."

"We all do at one time or another." She leaned against a barrel. "I want what I want, Max. That was my mantra for many years. I wanted Gervais, even though I knew he would wander. I wanted a child, and my adorable Caroline arrived. I was furious with my family for banishing me from the company, and so I created one of the most famous wines in the world. The name Bré resonates for millions of oenophiles worldwide."

Max nodded dutifully.

"And then it started slipping away. My husband. Caroline. The emptiness I feel now is appalling." With that, she began to cry. She was slighter than Lucy, and Max thought of glass shattering. A fine glass, like Murano glass. She didn't know whether to touch her or not. "Lucy's presence and jubilant energy began helping me to feel that my glass was half full again...oh, you Americans and your clichés! Glass half-empty. Glass half-full. And here I am in full imitation."

Max thought she would make a conciliatory attempt. "You fill Lucy's glass, too, you know. The first person she wanted to see when we picked her up was you."

"Really?"

"She will really need you now when she discovers her father's identity. He can't be everything she has conjured him up to be.

Her mother created a man who is, in clichéd American terms, a Prince Charming. That was the fantasy that Diane had clung to for most of her life, and she passed that image on to her daughter."

"Hugo is anything but that!"

Max smiled. "And Jean-Claude is not just a villain, either. Caroline loved him very much. She wanted to bestow something special on him. Give him a chance to be who he is."

"Which could be a murderer." She stared hard at Max. "I know he's a suspect. He came and told me. He's also scared to death that Alain is going to shoot him."

"At least he's confessed to the affair."

"Men are stupid. It's the classic story. Man's wife dies. Woman rushes in to nurture said devastated man. Sex ensues. Big problems are created. Woman's husband finds out. Alain might, in fact, shoot him. I would, were I in his shoes. And then, if I had that good-for-nothing son to bear, I'd probably shoot myself as well."

Max could see she was serious despite her snarky tone, and suddenly felt a well of unreasonable laughter bubbling up. It exploded out of her.

"What has happened to you?" Anne demanded.

Max was doubled over. "I think I must agree with you."

Anne smiled, and then gave a slight laugh, but it was obvious that she didn't entirely grasp what was so funny.

"You Americans," she said, but it was said with amused fondness. Then: "The one to watch in all this fracas is Yvette. Mark my words."

Max grew serious. "Why do you say that?"

"Humiliation does terrible things to people. It's the emotion most difficult to overcome. People will tend to recall ancient humiliations upon their deathbeds. People are already shunning her, I'm told. As the insidious story of the photograph gets out, the barrage of subtle insults will be painfully like the stoning of shamed Arab women. I told Jean-Claude this. He has ended it. He said he was trying to be kind; he doesn't love her. Of *course* he doesn't love her. He wanted sex and comfort. Pure and simple."

Max thought her statement a little harsh, but said nothing aloud.

But then Anne surprised her. "And who doesn't want sex? I would adore having sex these days. I am in the most sensuous business in the world. All our senses stay alert all the time. Even in the middle of the night, I am thinking of the moon, and my darling vines, and the way they wind themselves down deep into the soil for sustenance. Of how they become entangled with each other, like lovers. I adore the fecund, wet soil in my hands, and watching the clouds to see what is coming. Who doesn't fantasize when looking at clouds? And the first sip of a new vintage when it ready. After waiting, and waiting…it's positively orgasmic."

Max thought back to Olivier rhapsodizing over the bottle they'd drunk together in Bordeaux. "Olivier said practically the same thing when we sipped a 1945 Mouton Rothschild."

"Of course he did. You're lucky to have a man who has his senses open, especially a *magistrat*. They're generally the most closed group of people I've ever met."

Max wanted to see him, and tell him what Anne had said about Yvette. Her name hadn't come up once. Yet she was there on the periphery as Max recalibrated various scenes in her mind: friends with Tim, Alain's wife, Jean-Claude's mistress, mother of Roland, cook for the hunt, hater of Lucy.

Chapter Twenty-eight

Olivier hung up and looked to Abdel. "I'm more tolerant than I expected to be. I suddenly saw how I encourage Max to choose between her father and me."

"You wait for the whole story before jumping to conclusions now. You used to lecture us about that."

Olivier realized how his philosophy had changed. He now believed that all stories were inherently incomplete, that there was no such thing as a whole story. Each life was comprised of fragments that people pieced together over time. Inwardly, he went back over the story that Ali had just recounted in his interview, as he confessed to his part in liberating (as he called it) Lucy Kendrick from the hospital.

He'd said that an old lady had phoned him and told him to come immediately to the hospital, then gave him explicit directions. All she'd said about the truth of the mission was that it was in relation to Lucy Kendrick. From this comment, he'd known that Lucy was okay. He left his shop immediately, and upon arriving at the hospital, had been told by two grandmotherly types that he was to drive the getaway ambulance that would carry Lucy to a house far in the country where the girl would be safe. He had started to explain that he could not take such a risk, that he had been arrested before, and that his dark skin would make him stand out.

The older of the pair of ladies, (and Olivier knew that he meant Maxine's grandmother, Madame de Laval) had said that he had no choice, and that she would pay a lawyer whatever it took to free him if he was caught. He had looked at her askance, he said (he had used that word, which had impressed Olivier) and Madame de Laval had said, "You want her to *live,* don't you?"

Ali had shortly found himself behind the wheel of an ambulance, which he backed up to the hospital entrance and, next thing he knew, the two genteel women were wheeling Lucy out in a wheelchair. She was unrecognizable in a long coat and a woman's hat pulled down over her ears. She had looked like one of them, slumped as she was in her wheelchair. He had lifted her out of the chair and put her in the back of the ambulance, and then driven to the house quite a distance away, in Bouzeron, up a long driveway to a smaller house, hidden away and surrounded by vineyards. A stocky woman had come out and greeted Lucy warmly, and then she had turned to him and invited him in for a glass of wine. He'd told her that he didn't drink, as it was against his religion, and she'd said that she understood, but that she could smell pot on him, and if he could do that he could make an exception this once, and sip what Nature provided to her people for stress relief. He recalled that it had been, in fact, an extremely pleasant experience. Afterward, he had driven back to the hospital parking lot and returned the ambulance, with no questions asked. He was certain that the women had paid someone off, but he didn't ask.

Olivier dismissed him and, watching him exit, saw Yvette standing in the doorway. He felt that sense of dread stirring in his belly.

"Olivier, may I speak to you for a moment?" she asked.

"Of course."

She was wearing a dark pantsuit and ill-applied makeup. Her hair bounced around her shoulders like it had when she was a teenager. "I wanted to speak to you about Alain. He considers you a friend and I think perhaps you can help him."

"Is something wrong?" Olivier felt shame rise in him, as of course everything was wrong in that little household. "I mean, is Alain okay?"

She started to sniffle, reached in her bag for a tissue and began wiping the errant tears away. Her eyelashes were caked with mascara and now her cheeks were blackened. She touched her right cheek. "Alain has taken to violence and that is why I'm here. He hit me. Here." Her hand continued to rest on her cheek.

Olivier felt chastised, and deservedly so, though something in him wondered if he was being manipulated. He recalled the hostile look he had glimpsed on her face through the window when he had gone to see Alain, and realized he carried a distinct resentment toward her for that. "Yvette," he said. The first-name basis didn't come off well in these professional circumstances, he realized, and besides, he barely knew her. "I am expecting someone to arrive at any moment to discuss the deaths of Yves Laroche and Timothy Lowell. I want to hear what you have to say, but we will have to schedule this discussion for another time. I am deeply sorry to hear about Alain. Would you mind if I spoke to him about this?"

"First, Olivier, I will not publicly speak about how I am abused by my husband. This is nothing new." Her laugh was bitter, sardonic. "Can you imagine how the neighbors would take that news? They will say I'm making it up to compensate for my guilt over having an affair with Jean-Claude. Besides, here in France, to report abuse is to ask for more. Our laws are horrible protection. The police, in fact, would go talk to Alain, and they would be in sympathy."

Olivier felt she was starting to unravel. Her voice had gone up and her hands were shaking.

"I can recommend a good attorney in the region."

"Thanks for nothing, Olivier. Slough me off!"

Olivier thought that next she'd be accusing him of abuse. Abdel stuck his head in the door and looked surprised. Olivier willed him to enter with his eyes.

"Pardon," Abdel said. "I didn't know we had another interview quite so soon. I took my cousin for coffee."

"Please join us," Olivier said formally. Abdel practically tip-toed across the floor, and Olivier reminded himself to mention to him that he should walk boldly, no matter where he was.

Yvette's voice was now so low it was barely audible. Olivier found himself leaning in to hear her. "You will be more interested in what I have to say about murder than you were with my own abuse. Alain told me he went to talk to Tim about the photos he was developing, on the evening he was murdered."

Olivier felt his hair stand on end.

"Also," she said, "my son told you that Alain was at Yves' party. He didn't tell you that Alain was there to confront Yves because he had paid him to stalk me, and he wanted the incriminating photographs. He had learned through a mutual friend that Jean-Claude was also trying to buy the photographs, to prevent me from being humiliated."

Her rage was palpable, and won Olivier completely over to her side.

"Do you have proof of any of this....?" He still didn't know how to address her and so let his voice trail off.

"Of what? The fact that he hit me? Come get a closer look at my face. And the fact that he went to see Tim because Tim had caught on camera Alain shooting Lucy? I have proof, alright."

She reached beneath her chair and indicated a large envelope poking from a sizable green tote bag. "In the entrance to our house, we keep an old trunk that is full of family mementoes. I opened it yesterday, searching for a photo of Roland, and found some negatives and photographs that hadn't been before, along with a .22 that I thought Alain had given away years ago. The photographs were from the night of Yves' party, and from the day of the hunt."

"Where are they now?"

"Here." She reached under her chair and pulled out the envelope, stood up and handed it to Olivier.

"Where is Alain now?"

"Probably lying in wait for me."

Olivier caught the shocked expression on Abdel's face out of the corner of his eye. "We can find a safe place for you."

"Oh, I'm staying at my sister's," Yvette said. "If Alain comes on the premises, I will shoot him in self-defense."

"That would be an insane thing to do at this juncture," Olivier heard himself saying, and then worried for a moment that she would accuse him of calling her insane. Olivier had handed the large envelope to Abdel, who pulled the photographs from the envelope and walked them to Olivier.

He skimmed through them, but there were none of Alain holding a gun. "Are there more prints?"

"Ask Alain." She was standing now. "By the way, has Lucy been found?"

Olivier decided to lie. "No. We suspect she's dead."

"*Quel dommage.*"

The same words as her son, *what a pity*, Olivier thought, *yet not a whiff of pity.*

Olivier called the prosecutor to explain the situation and ask him what his advice would be. Monsieur Caron listened patiently and then said, "What else? Arrest Alain Milne. We can hold him for twenty-four hours with no explanation." Olivier said "*d'accord,*" and the prosecutor added, "Or longer, if need be."

He hung up, and his cell immediately rang. Max. "*Bonjour,*" he said.

"Are you okay?"

"Yvette Milne just brought in photos from Tim's and a .22. She's accusing Alain, but these photos don't prove anything." He explained where they had been found, but forgot about Yvette's accusation of domestic abuse.

"Maybe it's time she's put on the suspect list. Anne got me to thinking about that. Hank said it looks as though she's been moving into Jean-Claude's house, but he's told Anne he's ending it at once. Hank wants to search Jean-Claude's house."

"Whatever for? I'd have to get a warrant."

"I know. You just said that the photographs didn't target the killer. If she got her hands on those, where are the others?"

"This is far-fetched, Max."

She was quiet a moment. "Did Yvette look okay? No facial markings?"

Olivier hesitated. "She accused Alain of hitting her on the cheek."

"I'm leaning toward believing Lucy, who said someone came in and tried to suffocate her with a pillow, but she smacked him with her fist. She'd thought it was a him, and I did too, but I'm not so sure now."

"Are you thinking Yvette might have killed those men?"

"Maybe she and Jean-Claude together. If Alain gets locked up, they get to live happily ever after. This scenario is on Fox News every night in the States."

"I have to stay here and get Alain locked up. I'll speak to Caron here and send Abdel out with a warrant."

"What about the Beaune prosecutor Dubois? Does he have to be called?"

"I don't know who you're talking about."

She chuckled. "Thanks, Olivier."

"*Sois sage*, Max."

"I'll be careful."

He looked up to see Alain in the hall, wearing handcuffs.

Chapter Twenty-nine

Max found Hank down on his knees in the yard, fixing outdoor furniture. "I could get used to this country life," he said, smiling up at her. "My father used to do this kind of stuff."

"I wish I had known your dad. Your mom, too, for that matter."

"My father was too unpredictable to allow you to get too comfortable around him. He retired at forty-five from the NYPD and didn't know what to do with himself, so he drank. My mother died when I was eight. Cancer. We were never allowed to talk about her."

"I guess people can survive without family. Or maybe I mean love."

"Some do." He glanced at her. "What's up?"

She reported her conversation with Olivier. He was on his feet in seconds. "Well, let's go then. He's getting better at trusting, not asking so many questions." He wiped his hands on his pants, and they began walking toward Jean-Claude's.

"Maybe we should take the car," Max said.

"Abdel can give us a ride home. We don't want Jean-Claude to drive up and see your grandmother's car there, then come in and find us snooping around."

"Let's wait for Abdel."

"We know he's already on his way with a search warrant. We can start."

"We don't have a clue what we're looking for."

"Yvette came up with enough evidence to put her husband in the bin. She might turn out to be as smart as her sister, the surgeon."

"What do you mean?"

"Nice woman, Catherine. I stopped by the hospital and we had a friendly chat. She at least laughs at my jokes."

"Is she like Yvette?"

"Faint resemblance. Great surgeon, evidently. Accomplished kids. Good husband. Worries a lot about Yvette."

"What about the bullet wound?"

"I think she's lying about the bullet entry to protect her sister. She didn't want to give up the scans. She also was pissed that we were hiring another expert."

"So who is everyone protecting?"

Hank was moving at a rapid clip and talking fast, too. "Roland is a good bet. Jean-Claude hasn't been cleared, either, but he was too upset about Tim to make me suspect him. He was at Yves' party, though, and it's a damned good possibility he shot Lucy, drunk as he was."

"I was worried he'd shoot me because I'm a woman. I think he only approves of women when they're in his bed."

"You can't arrest him for being a misogynist. He succumbed to Yvette. Very different from being seduced by a woman. That means you want it. Succumbing is more like giving in, then you hate yourself for it."

"I'm not sure about that. Yves told him Anne had bested him on the land deal. If he knew Anne was planning to adopt Lucy in order for her to get the parcel, he might have been mad enough to shoot her."

"That would give him motive for shooting Lucy. I stick with my original analysis, though. The bullet was shot from behind Lucy. Jean-Claude was in the field, near me."

"Now that we've proved him innocent per the Hank Maguire Sleuth Code, where does that leave Alain?"

"Wondering what hit him. He's wound up tight, and it's possible he methodically went after Yves and Tim. We know he was in the woods, supposedly taking a piss, when Lucy was shot. If he didn't shoot her himself, I'll bet he has a pretty good idea who did."

They arrived at Jean-Claude's house. Hank said, "You remember how to pick a lock?"

"With a hairpin, and I don't happen to have one."

Hank tried a window and it opened. "I'll hoist you in." Seeing her hesitate he said, "The more officers who enter and nose around, the less chance of actual discovery. I'll boost you up. Twenty minutes and Abdel should be here. We won't touch anything."

Once inside, Max opened the front door for Hank. The entry room had knobs for hanging jackets, and Max noticed that the boots and shoes were lined up in an orderly fashion. The kitchen was in some disarray, with a sink full of dishes, and papers in disheveled stacks on the table. It was a modest house, but well maintained. She walked into the family room, and allowed her eyes to roam slowly around the room, landing on two shelves of framed photographs. Jean-Claude holding a baby. He and the woman she assumed to be Caroline smiling into the camera. Her in an elaborate wedding gown—the very gown Max would be wearing on her wedding day—holding a huge bouquet of flowers, her arms around her mother and father.

Hank entered the room, "I was thinking about Yvette. Taking a few photographs and a pistol to Olivier, and claiming the pistol is the murder weapon, is either a bold move or a desperate move. I'm sure the police are ransacking Yvette's and Alain's house as we speak." He looked under the couch in the den, and then went upstairs. "Of course she will say there were no others. I also doubt that the gun she turned in is the murder weapon."

"If we find them, it might mean she's framing Jean-Claude."

"I keep mentioning Roland, but nobody bats an eye." He opened a final door and their dialogue stopped. Max entered a walk-in closet and after surveying the small space, she thought it contained the essence of Caroline. A small bureau against the wall. An array of beautiful perfume bottles arranged on top, mingled with framed photographs of Caroline and her husband.

Clothes hung in rows in the closet to the right and a pale blue nightgown was draped over a hook. It was like a shrine.

"Look behind the dresses there." He pulled open a drawer. His hands rifled through panties and bras, then he went back into the bedroom and opened the armoire.

"I hear voices," she whispered.

"Stay calm." He stalked off like a cat.

Someone unlocked the front door and entered. Max heard footsteps on the stairs, and wanted to scream. She had always hated hiding games as a child. Her heartbeat thrumming in her ears threatened to drown out all other sound. Through a vertical crack in the door she watched Yvette enter the bedroom, and study herself in a mirror. She took out her phone and pushed a button, and the haunting sounds of Miles Davis' saxophone began a slow, haunting melody. Yvette slowly began removing her clothes. Max began to panic. She thought back to other predicaments she'd been in: face-to-face with a killer in the cellars of Champagne, locked in a freight box in a warehouse in New York City, ready to be loaded onto a container ship to France, in a shootout in Bordeaux. Yet, she thought, *this was the wors*t. She simply could not stand here and witness Yvette and Jean-Claude in a state of sexual fervor.

She peered out again and thought Yvette's lingerie must have cost the equivalent of two weeks of her salary. Still, it didn't cover what needed covering in Max's appraisal. The sound of tires crunching on gravel increased Max's anxiety. *Please, please, let it be Abdel*, she thought.

The front door opened, and she heard Luc run in. "Papa, may I watch cartoons?"

"Half an hour is all you get." The television drowned out the jazz.

Max peered through the crack in the door and almost gasped. Yvette was in an inviting pose on the bed, propped up against pillows. Jean-Claude whistled distractedly as he came up the stairs. Max couldn't see him as he entered the room, but the seductive smile on Yvette's face told her he had arrived.

"What are you doing here?" he demanded in a low voice, almost a snarl.

"What do you think I'm doing here?"

"Get dressed and leave, Yvette. My son is here. I told you not to come back."

"You bastard!" She kept her voice low. "You told me I could move in."

"That was a month ago. When Tim was alive, and Yves was okay. And Lucy hadn't been shot."

She started pulling on her clothes. "Alain has been arrested."

"Alain? For what?"

"The murder of Yves Laroche. And for this bruise on my cheek."

"You told me you fell."

"I lied."

The silence that followed seemed interminable to Max.

"We've reached the tipping point, Jean-Claude. "We can start fresh."

"You're sounding crazy, Yvette. I need you to leave." He stepped into the hallway and turned back. "They found Lucy and she's okay."

Her voice was barely audible. "I thought she had been reported dead."

"With luck she can tell them who shot her."

Luc called up the stairs to his father. "Coming!" Jean-Claude yelled back. He said, "I'll take him out to the backyard. I don't want him to see you leaving."

"You're going to regret this."

Max heard Luc start bounding up the stairs, but Jean-Claude warded him off, and then she heard a door slam. Yvette soon followed, exiting the front door.

Hank entered the room, and said, "I couldn't hear much."

"I told you we should wait for Abdel. Jean-Claude rejected her and she was humiliated."

"'Heaven has no rage like love to hatred turned, nor hell a fury like a woman scorned.' Congreve."

"Why do you know that?"

"I used it once in court when I was a witness. It worked. Let's get out of here."

Abdel was driving in and they went out to meet him. They told him briefly what had happened. Jean-Claude came around the corner and demanded to know why they were congregating in his yard. Abdel said, "Madame Yvette Milne said she was with you on the eve Tim Lowell was killed. I need you to verify that."

Jean-Claude frowned. "No. As Max knows, I came to Tim's right after he had been shot."

"I know."

"Were you with Madame Milne earlier in the evening?"

He hesitated before answering. "Yes. But surely you don't think..."

"What time did she leave your house?"

"I don't know. Nine, I think."

Just as we sat down to dinner, Max thought.

"Was there anything unusual about her behavior?"

"Are you thinking she shot Tim?"

"She is one of several suspects. We are seeking motive, and the main motive we have come up with is that Monsieur Lowell had some photographs that someone wanted."

"The photographs from the party, and from the hunt. Tim told me about them."

"Did he reveal who might have pushed Yves Laroche off his balcony, or who might have shot Lucy Kendrick?"

"No."

"Did you tell Madame Milne about the photographs?"

His answer was a whisper, "Yes."

Chapter Thirty

"Find Yvette Milne and make the arrest," Olivier said resignedly to Abdel over the phone after he told him about his interview with Jean-Claude. "We still have no proof. Only motive."

"And where will you be, Monsieur, in case I need you?"

"I'm going to try to get the truth out of Lucy Kendrick, then take her to say good-bye to her Uncle George. Anne will meet her in Beaune for a glass of champagne to celebrate her birthday, and I'll join you."

Olivier watched as Anne pulled up to the café across from the Hospices de Beaune and waited for Lucy to climb out. He returned Anne's wave, but his attention was riveted on Lucy, who bore a surprising resemblance to Hugo. Had no one else seen it? She had the same facial structure, and there was a hint of arrogance in her posture. He was glad to see that she possessed a strong vitality. Her arm was tucked into a sling. He figured her to be a metre and a half in height. Her hair was tousled; she was makeup-free, dressed in jeans and a long-sleeved shirt. He stood as she approached. "Happy birthday."

Her look was direct. "I hate having a birthday without Tim. The only reason I'm here is because I don't want to face Uncle George alone. And Anne wanted nothing to do with it."

"Very well. Shall we go?" He left money for his coffee, and started walking to the hotel, regretting that he had listened to Anne's plea for him to take the girl to say good-bye to her uncle.

"I still hold George responsible for the death of my mother

because he caused so much stress in her life. My mother knew he was a criminal, but it's hard to lock up rich criminals in New York. They buy their way out."

"I'm sorry about your mother."

"I've got some bad karma going on. All my focus right now is on Tim. The local cops aren't going to work hard to solve that one. Max told me she had just spent an hour with him before he was shot."

"She was looking forward to a friendship with him."

"He told too many people he had photographs to prove my innocence. The images were blurred and he was working on that. He told me Yvette was captured in one of the photos in the woods the day of the hunt. But he knew she might have just been looking for Roland."

"Do you know who shot at the cabin door?"

"Roland said it was his dad, because he recognized his hat. He grabbed his rifle, but I told him we should run to Tim's. We stopped for a minute for Roland to get his breath. He turned on me and called me a traitor for going to Paris with Tim and leaving him in the cabin. He said it was my fault Yves died. I took off running again, hoping to get away from him."

"That's when you were shot."

"Soon after."

"You were sober at Yves' party?"

She nodded. "It was stupid that we went. I told Tim I planned to sneak into Yves' office and find the information about me he had on his computer. He gave me his password months ago when I was helping him some."

"But he turned on you."

"He couldn't hide his jealousy, but he was up and down. He called to invite me to his party. And Tim, too."

"What happened after you got there?"

"I couldn't find my file. Then Roland came in and he said he wanted the file on his mom he knew his dad had paid Yves for. We found that one. Lots of nude photos of his mom with Jean-Claude. I shut down the computer, and we went out."

"Roland seemed okay?"

"I didn't see him for a long time, then he found me, and I knew he was high. Tim said we needed to leave. Everybody was starting to leave anyhow. I told Roland to meet us downstairs at the car. Tim and I went around a curve where the car was, and heard Yves up on the balcony yelling good-bye to everybody. He was leaning against the railing. Tim aimed the camera and started snapping pictures. I said I'd run up and get Roland. We met on the second set of stairs. We walked out together and his father came from the bushes and gave him a lot of shit, and asked if this was where he got his drugs."

"Was his mother there?"

"I didn't see her. Roland told his father to go to hell, and we went to the car. Tim was a wreck when we got there. 'Yves fell,' he said. We saw neighbors running toward the body, and people were calling the police. I went close enough to see the body, but Tim said I shouldn't get involved."

"Did Roland say anything?"

"Nothing. He said he was tired, and got in the backseat."

"You didn't think Roland had anything to do with Yves falling?"

"Tim wondered, but I told him not to go there. The next day we saw it was ruled an accident, and that was when Tim said he was taking me into Paris. When it came up on the news that Yves was pushed, Tim said he might have some kind of proof with the photos."

"He didn't actually see anyone push Yves?"

"No. He said it happened so fast, but sometimes the camera sees what the naked eye can't."

"Somebody wanted those photos enough to kill for them."

"I don't think the negatives were with the photos."

"What do you mean?"

"Tim was a little worried that someone would want the photos. Not bad enough to kill him, but enough to break in and steal them. He kept his negatives in separate places."

"I should have gone immediately to Tim's when Max told me about the photos he was developing."

"Tim didn't believe in regrets. He will end up being the one to solve this case if we can find the negatives."

They had arrived at the hotel. "You sure you're up for this?"

Lucy nodded. "I don't really have a choice. Uncle George said he had some information for me that he knew I'd want. I don't ever have to see him again after today."

George was standing in the parking lot yammering on his cell phone, waving a hand in the air for unnecessary emphasis. "About time you got here," he said to Lucy, muting the call and the tinny voice squawking back through the phone. "Listen, kiddo, I wanted to wish you a happy birthday. I didn't chase you all the way across the ocean to kill you, so let that one go."

She gave him a skeptical look. "What do you want?"

"You need to learn about gratitude. I paid Yves Laroche a lot of money to prove or disprove your father's identity."

"Oh, I already know who my father is, and he's dead."

Olivier knew she was talking about Anne's husband, Gervais.

George's eyes were fixated on Lucy. "Wrong. Your father's alive. The bastard outbid me, and Yves turned over his folder to him. But I can be a wily fox, and I had other methods of tracking him down. This man will never claim you. But I can help you go after him to get some financial reward."

"You're full of it."

"It's Hugo Bourgeot," George said. "A famous exporter right here in Beaune. I thought we might swing by there, and announce ourselves."

Lucy was out the door before Olivier could even extend his arm to stop her. He ran after her, but she was fast. When he got to the sidewalk, he saw her in full run, then stop and throw an object into the trash can. He chased her and at least was keeping her in sight. Then he saw her approach a policeman and point in his direction. The policeman loped up to Olivier, asking why he was following the girl. Furious now, Olivier pulled his ID from this pocket and within moments had the officer apologizing to him. They said a civil good-bye. He retrieved the cell phone Anne had given Lucy from the trash, and walked on.

Anne was eagerly waiting at a glass-topped wrought iron table, a bubbling glass already at hand. "Where's Lucy?" she asked.

He explained what had happened and Anne said, her eyes fierce, "Hank gave me the responsibility of taking Lucy into town to make sure no one would be stalking her around my house. We have to find her."

"Give her a few minutes. She might come back." Olivier ordered a Scotch on the rocks for himself when the waiter appeared, then looked at Anne. "The same," she said. They drank in silence. Half an hour later, Olivier, calmer, said, "I have no choice but to call the police."

His cell phone rang, as if on command. "Monsieur Chaumont, this is Hugo Bourgeot. A young woman has appeared at my door just now, and demands that I admit to being her father. I thought I had your word on this!'

"I take umbrage at your attack, as I did not reveal your identity to her. But I will be there momentarily. Don't let her escape."

"How do I do that?"

"Give her a drink. She's eighteen today."

"Let's go!" Anne said.

"I want to finish my drink. They may have to get to know each other."

An hour later Anne parked outside the elegant eighteenth-century brick building that housed the Bourgeot Company that had been in the family for centuries—the inner sanctum of the wine kingdom. Until the modern era, most wine growers sold their grapes to the company, where they were turned into wines of character. But today, Olivier knew, the young upstarts, as Alain had referred to them, were insistent on creating their own wine. Bourgeot still sold wine made from grapes purchased from local vineyards, but they also excelled in wines that they produced from their own grapes.

The receptionist looked up and said, "Monsieur Bourgeot is expecting you, upstairs in the conference room."

A door to the left of the reception desk opened, and Anne greeted a man who appeared to be in his forties. He greeted Anne and shook hands with Olivier. "My sister is on her way over. Our father has locked the door to the conference room and refuses to allow anyone else to enter. We know that a young woman bullied her way into his office, where he happened to be, and confronted him. We were about to call the police when he told us to wait and slammed the door."

"He invited us here," Anne said. She led Olivier up a short flight of stairs to a carved wooden door, took a deep breath, and knocked.

"*Qui est la*?" a baritone voice asked from the other side of the door.

"Anne. Et Olivier. *Ouvrez la porte,* Hugo!"

The door swung open and they found themselves in a high-ceilinged room with a massive, and highly polished wooden table occupying the center. Lucy was sitting at the head of the conference table with five glasses in front of her, and as many bottles. They were tasting.

"She's not bad," Hugo said, raising a glass. "She has discovered the fragrance perfectly in the Clos de Reine."

Lucy looked at them and gave a smile of accomplishment. Hugo poured wine into two more glasses and handed them to Olivier and Anne. They sipped, surprised to have entered a scene of calm celebration, and smiled mawkishly at each other. "Lucy explained that everyone around her is dropping like flies, and she thought she'd better meet me before I die." He looked amused.

An insistent rapping at the door made Hugo get up. "My poor children," he said. He picked up his cane and made his way to the door. Three adults—two men and a woman—entered, their eyes going uncertainly from their father to the strange girl sitting at the head of the great table, surrounded by uncorked wines.

"I was intending, in due time, to sit down with each of you and explain," he said to them with a ragged sigh. "But here we are. This is Lucy Kendrick. Your half-sister."

Olivier thought he had never seen more shocked faces. The eldest son turned on his heel and left the room. The daughter, Vanessa, went to Lucy, who stood up, and said, "Forgive us, we are in shock. Please come to lunch tomorrow at our father's house, and we will get acquainted." The younger son shook Lucy's hand, but said nothing, his face a drawn mask. Vanessa went to her father and kissed his cheek, "Lunch tomorrow, then." She shook hands weakly with Olivier and Anne, and departed.

Olivier turned to Hugo. "We, too, must leave."

"Vanessa has invited Lucy for lunch. I insist that you and Anne come as well. And bring your fiancée, of course. I don't want Lucy feeling ganged up on."

Anne exchanged cheek kisses with her old friend.

Hugo turned to Lucy and said, "It took courage for you to come here. I am glad to be found. And I will be sure to tell my children that your mother was a remarkable woman."

She smiled up at him.

Once outside, Olivier asked Lucy to ride with him. He explained the police were searching for Yvette Milne, and that until she was caught, Lucy was not to be alone even for a minute.

"I'm done running, Olivier."

"In the end I guess we could say your Uncle George did you a favor."

"But it wasn't his intention. Hugo is okay. It's weird, today, for the first time, I saw myself in someone other than my mother. I thought it might be like how someone feels after receiving a lifesaving organ from a dead stranger. They feel the stranger inside them. Share some of the same feelings, maybe. That's how I feel. Like I just had a heart transplant."

"I see," said Olivier, with slightly raised eyebrows.

"You don't, really, but that's okay."

They were entering the village. Olivier said, "I wonder where you will go once this is all over."

"Oh, it's decided. I'll go back to New York to live with Hank and Juliette and get my diploma, then come back to help Anne."

"Does Max know?"

"She was annoyed with Hank when he told her, but we're working it out."

They passed the turn to Tim's B&B, and Lucy said, "I want to go into Tim's house now."

"But we're expected for dinner."

"Please? I'll only stay a few minutes."

Olivier turned the car around. The police tape still surrounded the house, but Olivier knew where the key was, and retrieved it from beneath a stone, and unlocked the front door. Lucy turned on a few lamps, and looked around. "It's as if he's still here, waiting for me. I haven't really said good-bye."

Olivier wished Max would come. He thought about texting her, but decided not to. Lucy disappeared into the bedroom, and he heard her crying. He went to the doorway. "Can I be of assistance?"

She was sitting on the side of the bed. "May I take this photograph of us?" and Olivier nodded. He thought of the post-it note had seen the night forensics showed up, the one with the word L U C Y printed out and a heart beneath, and another word or two. He had pocketed it. Reaching into his jacket pocket, he felt it, a small piece of folded paper. "This was on the counter the night we discovered his body," he said.

She opened it and looked at it. "Oh, Olivier, this means a lot to me. He was always leaving little notes around for me. I wonder why he put Uncle Jeremy on it. Look." Olivier looked at it. U N C L E J E R E M Y! He shrugged and handed it back to her.

"The ancestral paintings are unusual in a B&B," Olivier said. "There are three or four. He must have felt pride in his family."

"A brief tour," she said, going from one to another. "Grandfather James, Aunt Rosalind, mother Matilda, and in the kitchen, Great Uncle Jeremy, who was a bigwig in government, I think. Huh. Uncle Jeremy, why did he write your name under mine?" She turned to Olivier, "I have a thought. Remember I told you Tim kept negatives, and often hid them? Can you get that portrait off the wall? And don't look at me like I'm crazy."

It was heavier than Olivier had imagined, but they got it down, and turned it around, and saw a big envelope taped to the back. He called to tell Abdel to send someone out for them. They could be developed in a day.

Isabelle's house was aglow when they pulled in. Lucy said, "I told Max Tim would solve this crime. All in one day I'm no longer an orphan, and we know who shot me. And who pushed Yves."

"It's a lot for one day. I agree."

She smiled at him, and all he saw was Hugo.

Chapter Thirty-one

Max glanced at her watch. She had played outside with Luc until the temperature dropped. Jean-Claude said he needed to get home, but then he accepted a drink, and Hank got him engaged in a discussion on hunting rifles. A small, cozy fire was crackling in the fireplace. Isabelle came in from the kitchen. "I wonder what's going on in Beaune. I haven't heard a word from Anne."

"Olivier hasn't checked in either. Let's enjoy the temporary quiet." She had been in constant touch via text with Abdel, but so far they were having no luck finding Yvette. When she heard a knock at the back door, her restlessness had an outlet. She jumped up to open it, and Yvette Milne stood there. "*Bonsoir*," she said in a low voice. "May I come in?"

Max opened the door and allowed her to step in. Had she come to turn herself in?

Juliette turned from the stove, and said innocently, "Oh, *bonsoir*, Yvette. May I offer you a glass of champagne?"

"*Non, merci.*"

"I'm looking for Lucy," Yvette said.

"They should be along soon," Max said. "It's her birthday and Olivier and Anne took her for an official glass of champagne."

Jean-Claude came into the kitchen, and stopped short. "Yvette."

She smiled wryly at him. "I wondered if you were hiding out here." He flushed. "Everything I did, I did for you, Jean-Claude."

Her voice was eerily calm. Max tried to prevent her thoughts from returning to the bedroom where Yvette had waited in her finery for her lover. Only to have him vaporize the dream.

Jean-Claude said, "Yvette, the police are looking for you."

"That's all you have to say to me?"

She opened the door, her eyes still on Jean-Claude. Max thought, *No way*. She suddenly knew Yvette had come to shoot Jean-Claude. Max yelled as she darted across the room and pushed Jean-Claude hard. But she was too far away to stop Yvette from lifting the gun from her coat pocket and shooting herself in the heart. She fell onto the steps, landing in a heap on the dirt. Max reached her in seconds, with Hank right behind her. Juliette came to the door and Hank told her to call the ambulance. "She's not going to make it," Hank said to Max in a low voice. He ran inside for a pillow and blanket, and Max stayed with her, constantly checking her vitals.

Jean-Claude came out, carrying a drink. "I don't know why she did this. She went crazy." He lit a cigarette, standing away from Yvette's body.

Hank went in and returned with a coat for Max. "She's gone. I told everybody to stay inside." He looked at Jean-Claude, "Your son needs you." Jean-Claude tossed his cigarette on the ground and stomped it out, and went back inside. The door opened quietly and Olivier stepped out and took a seat beside Max. "I heard the shot just as I was entering the house," he said. She reached for his hand.

Abdel arrived half an hour later with the local police, who removed Yvette's body. Max didn't want to go inside just yet. "We still don't know if she killed Yves, though it's pretty certain she killed Tim."

"We know," Olivier said. "Lucy found the negatives attached to an ancestor's painting. Here's the way it will go down: Roland pushed Yves off the balcony, and Yvette shot Lucy and Tim.

Abdel said they'd have the photos by tomorrow. He bid them good night. They went into the salon and Olivier stirred the few embers left in the fireplace, then poured them each a glass of cognac.

Max sighed. "She must have learned the morning of the hunt that Roland and Lucy were in the cabin, and walked over with her rifle to scare them. The chase wasn't planned but her rage drove her to pursue Lucy."

"But her rage was over Jean-Claude's rejection of her, don't you agree?"

Max nodded. "And rage at men. We know Alain was verbally abusive, and her only son was a drug addict, and his attachment to Lucy felt like betrayal. She probably blamed Lucy for Roland spontaneously pushing Yves off the balcony, though my hunch is it was seeing the photographs of his mother and Jean-Claude that incited him to violence."

"I think it is all a blur to him, considering the drugs he was on."

Max put her head in Olivier's lap. He told her about the afternoon with Lucy, and she laughed. "I'm not going to lunch with Hugo's family. We have a wedding in four days. Walt O'Shaughnessy and Carlos will be here in two days."

"And Lucy is still to be a bridesmaid?"

"If she agrees to wear a dress. Otherwise, I'll never hear the end of it from Anne and my grandmother."

"She said you two were working things out when I asked her if you were okay with her going to live with Hank and Juliette."

"'Working it out.' That takes the prize. I'm glad she found Hugo. She has a dad now." Max yawned. "She would either be dead or in a mental institution again if we hadn't intervened."

"I was wishing her back in a mental hospital earlier today."

"They sat a long time, staring into the fire. The image of Yvette holding the gun to her heart and shooting was still painfully vivid, but Max knew that it would fade, as so many other terrible scenes she had witnessed had. It made her feel jaded, yet she preferred this to the crushing blows every death had delivered when she had been new on the police force. Tomorrow she and Hank would talk it through.

Chapter Thirty-two

Hank was looking up directions to the train station in Beaune when they went down in the morning. Isabelle had found a local B&B for the newly arriving Americans, and arranged lodging for Max's friend, Chloe, from Champagne, and her new fiancé, Ted Clay. The suicide of last night wasn't mentioned, nor was the case. *Classic French behavior*, Olivier thought, what Anne referred to as discretion. Olivier took his coffee outside and sat on the terrace, looking out onto vast fields of vineyards, where delicate shoots of green jutted from the old stalks, and surrounding hilltops had turned yellow overnight from the flowers of the rapeseed. Further proof of spring was the pile of asparagus he had seen in the kitchen.

He went in an hour later and announced he was off to release Alain. He leaned down and kissed Max, and they agreed to meet up later. Anne and Lucy were drinking coffee, and Anne said she and Lucy would see him at one at Hugo's.

"If I go," Lucy said.

Olivier asked her why she would consider not going.

"Why put myself in such a negative situation? The way his son looked at me made me shudder."

"People have a funny way of turning things around, though. They must first overcome judging their father for cheating on their mother, of course. And they might be worrying about you cutting into their inheritance. By law, every child inherits equally in France."

"Oh, you mean they'll think I'm a gold digger, in other words."

"Hugo's children will either accept you or not. The best you can hope for is the chance to find out. And the same goes for their father. Don't forget, the children have to explain to their children, some of them probably your age." He hesitated, "You went to Hugo and declared yourself, and he praised you for your courage. It isn't fair to run now."

"Okay, okay."

On the drive to Lyon Olivier thought about how differently, one from another, children were raised, depending on lottery of birth, and the persona of their parents. Obviously, Lucy's mother lived in her imagination, and taught Lucy to do the same. His mother had been the opposite, leaving little room to explore the imagination as he migrated through the French education system. He had taken up oil painting after he became a magistrate, and couldn't have been more surprised to discover that dreams could be painted. His thoughts reverting back to Lucy, he admired her resilience as much as anything else. He thought her magical manner of thinking had protected her in some way; on the other hand, she was as tough as any street kid he'd ever seen. Her going to her father and demanding acceptance was a life or death move for her.

Entering the city of Lyon, he wondered what he would say to Alain who sat in a cell, depressed, waiting for either sentencing or release. Olivier thought he wouldn't object either way. He decided to visit Roland first, for surely Alain would want to know how his son was doing. Roland was in a central room watching television. "Roland?"

The boy glanced up, then his eyes went back to the screen.

"I need a few moments of your time."

Roland got up and shuffled begrudgingly into a small visiting room that Olivier led him to. "Unfortunately, you may have already seen it on television. I'm sorry to tell you, that your mother died last night."

"I know." He looked up. "Why are you sorry?"

"Her death is a tragedy." He wanted to yell, *She killed Tim trying to protect you, you bastard!*

"If you say so."

Olivier cleared his throat. "I'm going next to see your father. You can visit him if you want before you are taken to rehab."

"I don't want to see him."

The interview was turning out to be as awful as Olivier had worried it might be. "May I ask why?"

"He drove my mother crazy. Not speaking to her for weeks at a time. Calling her a slut all the time. That's all I care to say."

"Very well. May I ask why you pushed Yves?"

Just when Olivier thought he wasn't going to answer, he said, "I don't remember much. He was on the balcony waving and calling to his guests, and he turned and saw me and said, 'It's the son of the whore,' and I pushed.

"Do you know why she shot Lucy?"

He shrugged. "She thought she betrayed me when she started going out with Tim. She said she was making a fool of me."

"You had told your mother you were in love with Lucy?"

He nodded.

• ● ● ● •

"Alain," he said, once Alain was led out, "I come with sad news."

"Yvette?" he asked, his eyes wide.

"I'm sorry. She committed suicide last night."

"*Mon Dieu*," he whispered. "Does Roland know?"

"Yes. We know that Roland pushed Yves off the balcony. I doubt that he remembers doing it."

"I figured he was back on hard drugs. Not a big loss, Yves, but someone has to pay, right?"

"Yvette chased Lucy and Roland, and shot Lucy. You knew that, didn't you?"

"What was I going to do, turn in my own wife? I saw her stop and aim her rifle at me. She either changed her mind, or Lucy got in the way."

"Were you with Yvette when she killed Tim?"

"*Non.*"

"You will need to have concrete alibis, someone to vouch for you."

"That won't be easy."

"What the courts can't prove, as you know, is the degree of bullying that went on in your household."

"Oh, stop patronizing me, Olivier. You're getting married in a few days. I haven't forgotten. Wait until your wife becomes obsessed with another man. It's a new world these days. Women go after what they want."

"I won't see you again," Olivier said. "I'm off to a new assignment. I wish you well, Alain, for whatever that's worth."

"I want to see my son."

"These are painful words to utter, but he refuses to see you. *Au revoir,* Alain." Olivier turned away from his old friend.

• • ● • •

The days leading up to the wedding were all that Olivier had imagined they would be. He was deeply saddened by the recent fatalities, but he realized that he wasn't as full of self-blame this time as he had been in the past, nor did he lie in bed wishing that the fates of all those involved had been different, as he used to do. Evil existed, he could accept that now, and sometimes people became troubled enough to do great harm to others. Nothing, he realized, on the day before his wedding, could erase the joy he was feeling over his imminent marriage.

The lunch at Hugo's was painful to sit through because of the tension, but Olivier wasn't sorry he was there as advocate for Lucy. She had held her own pretty well with her siblings, and by the end they all seemed more tolerant of the situation. Vanessa offered to help get her enrolled in a wine school when she returned. Lucy said she would like that, but mostly she wanted to follow in Anne's footsteps, learning through hands-on experience. It helped to have Anne by her side at the luncheon. Olivier had a moment of wondering if she and Hugo weren't a little cozier than one would expect, but then attributed it to his own state of being in love. Max used the word projection. He continued to look around at the mélange of faces, gathered together by chance. Lucy was...well, Lucy. She wore skinny jeans and a jean jacket, and Olivier was reminded of Max when he first met her. Her uniform had been denim and cowboy boots, and it took him a while to see that she was dressing like her father.

The lunch ended at last. Hugo said that he needed to rest, but he first walked them out to the car. Anne said to him, "You're coming to the wedding, aren't you?"

"I would be pleased to come, of course, but I wonder if Maxine wasn't just being polite when she invited me." Olivier assured him that she was sincere.

Anne and Lucy stopped at the shop for Lucy's wedding attire, and insisted that Olivier come in with them. "I tried to talk her out of red," the saleswoman said, "but she was determined." They went back to Isabelle's, and Max was there in the yard with Carlos and Walt. Olivier shook hands vigorously with each of them, and they were introduced to Lucy.

"Lucy, do you mind if I drive your Vespa around to see the sights?" Carlos asked, lighting a cigarette.

"You have to take me. It doesn't like strangers."

"You can hang on with one arm?" It was obvious. He was instantly charmed.

They watched him enter the garage and return with the Vespa. Lucy went inside to fetch two helmets, and they climbed onto the Vespa. With a wave they were gone.

"That's a dangerous combo," Max said.

"With Walt and me here, he'll think twice before he messes up," Hank said.

"I'm more worried about her."

Chapter Thirty-three

Max joined Hank, who was sipping his morning coffee while observing the staff putting bottles of champagne in great containers for chilling and arranging trays of oysters on the half shell lined up. "Come with me for a walk?" She glanced around. "You would think this was a wedding for two hundred the way my grandmother is behaving."

"I love seeing them so excited," he said. "Isabelle is about the biggest pain-in-the-ass I've ever known, but I have to admit I admire her. And how is the bride they're making all this fuss over?

"I adore Olivier," Max said. "My worry is that I won't be mysterious enough. I'm the kind of woman who wears her heart on her sleeve. I hate to admit it."

"Women are mysterious, whether they intend to be or not." He put his arm around her shoulder. "Just be you." They walked along a path leading to the vineyards and, hearing Juliette hallooing in the distance, stopped to wait. She caught up with them and said, a little breathlessly, "I saw you walking off together, and I left my atelier right where I was making my special *foie gras* with fresh figs. It can wait."

Hank took her hand. "Our last time as a family. A pretty small family, if you ask me. We now have a son-in-law, which helps to round things out, and perhaps there will be some little rug rats coming along soon."

"Dad!"

"I don't know this expression, rug rats," Juliette said. "Explain."

Hank laughed. "Babies."

"I don't think I like babies and rats in the same sentence."

Max and Hank shared a chuckle. Max asked Juliette what she thought of the idea of Lucy coming to live with them while getting her high school diploma?

"I think it will be good for us. She will be a challenge, but if Hank can keep her focused she'll be fine. Anne told me not to be shocked when I see her outfit today. Did you see it?"

"All I know is that it's red."

"*Rouge*?"

"That's the challenge part of her."

They looked across the rows of vineyards and saw Carlos madly pedaling a bicycle, with Lucy sitting crossways on the bar in front. Hank flailed his hand back and forth, but they never noticed. "If she falls off that bike, that's the end of her arm healing," he said. Juliette and Max exchanged smiles, and walked arm in arm back to the house.

Olivier ran up. "You're not dressed, Maxine?"

"On my way," she said. She heard her name being called and turned to see her old friend Chloe rushing toward her. They melted together in an embrace, and when Max finally pulled away, Ted pulled her to him. They had only seen each other once since the Marceau wedding in Champagne, when they had all been devastated by the murders of Chloe's aunt, and then her uncle. Chloe had told Max when she and Ted flew into New York on the way to visit his family that they had been living together for two years. The couple turned to Olivier and exchanged embraces.

The civil ceremony was short and sweet, and her tribe of wedding attendees were all there. Bottles of Joséphine champagne were brought out, the signature label of the Joseph Perrier house, the very same that was served at Chloe's wedding, and Max's favorite. Max raised her glass as her father toasted her, and drank. Isabelle served a luncheon of poached salmon and salad. Anne's *premier cru* wine was perfectly chilled.

Afterward, everyone went to rest. Max fell into a deep sleep, and dreamt of flying over fabulous landscapes in a hot air balloon. She awoke feeling like her old self, and smiled when her mother opened her door and entered, holding up Caroline's wedding gown. It had been custom-made years before for Anne, and hand sewn. Juliette hung it on the door. The fabric was organza, and the train wrapped around the waist and opened in the front over the long, full skirt. Juliette pointed out the embroidered silk daisies, each petal cut from a piece of fine silk, then sewn onto the plastron.

"It's a bit much for such a small wedding," Max said.

"A dress of this magnitude carries with it a certain energy," Juliette explained. "The work is so painstaking that the seamstresses enter into a state of bliss, I believe, and this is conveyed to the wearer."

"In that case I might never take it off."

Juliette stood on a little stool in order to lift the dress high enough to go over Max's head.

Anne's house had been transformed into a garden of yellow roses and jasmine. The mantle of the great fireplace was breathtaking, with flowers cascading off it. A long, elaborately decorated table was set, the silver sparkling under the chandelier. "Oh, Anne," Max said. "I couldn't have imagined anything so beautiful."

"Oh, it's nothing." She looked up at Max. "I feel that I have this one more opportunity to fulfill my daughter's wishes. The dress is perfect on you. I know that Caroline is smiling down on us right now." She rushed off when someone called to tell her the local priest had arrived. Max stood alone and inhaled deeply. Hank entered the room, and jumped back. "You look ravishing, Detective Maguire," he said. "More like your mother every day."

Lucy came in with Carlos, and Max and Hank exchanged glances of hilarity, but knew they had to keep it under control. Carlos was wearing a suit and a red bowtie, and Lucy was decked out in a dress that they wouldn't have thought she'd ever wear in a million years. Cherry red. The skirt was short and poofy, with a tight-fitting top and short, flouncy sleeves. She had replaced her white sling with a red scarf. Once she was in New York, Hank and Juliette were taking her to a doctor they knew who supposedly performed miracles with injuries of this nature.

Max smiled at her. There she was, the girl on the red Vespa. "Look at the two of you," Max said. "My team." Carlos leaned up and kissed her.

Lucy stood spellbound in front of Max. "You're an absolute princess."

Max laughed. "Don't tell Hank. He doesn't allow that kind of talk."

Max stood in the doorway as the music of Mendelssohn swelled. "What a sound system," Carlos whispered. "What a castle. The Bronx, it ain't."

"Ready?" Hank asked. Max took his arm and they walked out to their awaiting family and friends. Across the parquet floor they went, until they reached Olivier, whose gaze didn't waver as Hank stepped back, and Max took her beloved's hand. They exchanged vows in French, then in English. The wine started to flow as soon as the ceremony ended and the couple had exchanged a long kiss that brought applause. Waiters brought in trays, and Isabelle's and Juliette's delicacies were displayed on large tables. The *foie gras* with fresh figs was accompanied by a Sauternes. Max looked around, realizing that the people she loved most in the world were all gathered right here.

Olivier came up to her, she kissed him, laying a hand on his chest, and turned back to Ted, who was telling her of a new wine he had discovered. In an hour they moved into the dining room, where tall, white candles placed in silver candlesticks were lit. A row of yellow roses in short vases occupied the center of the table that was covered with a white damask tablecloth. Olivier whispered to her as they took their seats, "This wine is going to be a thrill. It's Gevrey Chambertain 1er cru Les Chapeaux 2003."

"I remember you discussing it with the woman in Beaune," Max said with a smile. The main course was *canard sauvage*, or wild duck, surrounded by morel mushrooms. A dish of braised spinach and another of new, spring potatoes was placed in front of them.

Max looked to her hostess at the other end of the table chatting with Hugo, who seemed quite enamored of her. She tapped Olivier's knee, and indicated with her eyes that something might be going on at the other end of the table. "Projection," he whispered, and she laughed. Lucy sat on Hugo's left in her red dress and next to her was Carlos, who gesticulated wildly, fork in hand, as he spoke.

Anne stood and welcomed everyone once again, and wished a good life to the newlywed couple. To her right, Jean-Claude raised his glass, as did everyone else. Max breathed in the fragrance of the deep red wine, detecting a berry scent. She sipped, and swooned. Olivier turned and kissed her. "It's such a cliché but this is the happiest night of my life," he said. "The happiest day. I don't want it to ever end."

Hank sat next to Walt, whose wife had died two years ago, and for the first time Max realized she was looking at an aging parent. After the honeymoon, her plan was to fly back to New York for at least a month. A fabulous array of cheeses was brought out. And after another lengthy, restful pause, a waiter walked out carrying a *croquembouche*, her favorite cake in all the world. Literally meaning "crunch in the mouth," it was a tower of cream-filled puff pastry balls piled into a high pyramid and encircled with caramelized sugar. This was a surprise to her. She got up and went to Anne, giving her a kiss to everyone's applause. "It has the vanilla-bourbon cream icing that all the brides want these days," she said, glowing with pride.

"It's perfect," Max said, returning to sit with Olivier. Suddenly, everyone at the table was holding up the traditional *scintillants*, small sparklers, and music was playing. Olivier turned to her, proffering a hand, "Dance with me?"

She arose from her chair as if in a dream, and he led her in a waltz that she never thought she could manage, but with him it was effortless. So much about being with him felt that way. Effortless. She glanced at his parents, who were smiling, and she could imagine a smart little boy named Olivier, the man she was with now, adoring them, and trying hard every day to please them. "You smell divine," Olivier said, "in fact, my olfactory senses are blocking everything else out. Except the visual. *Je t'adore.*" Max put her head on his shoulder. Another waltz came on, and Max and Olivier watched as Hugo stood and invited his daughter to dance. Max said, "Olivier, I'm going to cry."

"So am I."

They stood back, and Hugo, who had arrived with a cane, put his arm around the tiny waist of Lucy-in-red, which is how Max smilingly referred to her, and slowly began to move gracefully around the room. Max recalled reading that the tremor in Parkinson's disease patients often stopped when they danced or rode bicycles. Lucy gazed up at him, and Max was amazed that she knew how to waltz. Carlos stepped near Max and Olivier and asked, "Is it rude to cut in?" He was looking at Lucy and Hugo.

Max laughed. "You don't know how to waltz."

"I've been watching YouTube."

He marched over and tapped Hugo on the shoulder, and Max looked on in astonishment as he led Lucy gracefully around the room. As if that wasn't enough, Olivier said to her, 'look,' and she saw the tiny figure of Anne in Hugo's arms. Olivier led Max back to the floor, just as Hank swept Juliette onto her feet. Max began to laugh, and Olivier said, "What's happening? Did Lucy sprinkle pixie dust all over the room?"

Olivier excused himself and walked over to Isabelle, and asked her to dance. She seemed to hold back, then said, "*Bien. D'accord.*" Max stood on the sideline, transfixed. Isabelle danced as though she had been doing it all her life.

The evening went on. And on. And Max thought, I *am* a princess, but I would never admit that to anyone. Ever in my whole life. Suddenly Lucy was at her side. Max put her arm around her, and squeezed.

The music switched to techno-pop, and Max's favorite band, AaRON, that was taking France by storm once again, drowned out conversation. The singer of the group, Simon Buret, sang songs of hope, of loss, of joy. Max waved to the DJ, and put a thumb up, as she and Ted hit the dance floor. Hours passed, and at two in the morning, Max and Olivier fell exhausted into bed.

"Tomorrow our lives change," Olivier said. "We'll see your parents and the others off, and later in the day I have a staff meeting, if you can believe it. There are concerns about new terrorist cells being discovered."

"People are just relaxing from the Paris attacks."

"I worry, though, that we are not being vigilant enough. Justice, police, and administration must communicate more with each other."

"Olivier, it's our wedding night."

"You're right."

"We'll be in our new apartment." The old friend of Olivier's had offered it to them.

"You'll be the one deciding if it's going to be home."

"It's in the Third Arrondissement, which I'm happy about. But I don't like the eight hundred thousand-euro price tag."

"We won't find anything in this area for less, I'm afraid."

"My mother inherited a small fortune from Ellen Jordan after she was killed. She's insisting that she put up half of the asking price."

"We couldn't accept that."

"Hank said we must. Ma feels it is what Ellen would have wanted."

Olivier chuckled, "We have another angel floating around over our heads? It's awfully busy up there."

"There are never too many angels."

"I just don't want them competing."

Max turned and drew him to her.

Chapter Thirty-four

It was a long, tearful leave-taking at the airport, as Juliette, Hank, Walt, Carlos, and Lucy boarded their Air France flight back to New York. Olivier felt a great sense of relief that he and Max could now begin their new life together, though taking a honeymoon trip to Australia for two weeks meant another long delay before he was functioning fully as an anti-terrorist judge. He had already spoken with the interior minister, who was now head of France's anti-terrorism operations. Before he departed, he was due to meet with one of the other six investigative judges who formed the anti-terrorism division to discuss if it was absolutely necessary for him to have a bodyguard once he began his job.

"I feel desperate for a life of routine once again," Max said. "I'm glad it wasn't my fate to be an actual princess in this life."

Olivier laughed. "I don't think you would have lasted as long as you did in Burgundy without a crime to solve." He passed the car in front of him, and entered Paris.

"It's just been proven to me that the countryside isn't as peaceful as we pretend. But okay, I'm ready to admit I'm a city girl. And I adore this city beyond all others. Why don't we go to the apartment and from there we can plan the rest of the day?"

"I have meetings set up, and you need to meet your new bosses at Interpol. Your official ID should be in the mail."

"Don't get ahead of yourself. Can't we be newlyweds for an afternoon?"

"There's a special agenda for newlyweds?"

"Use your imagination. I told Chloe and Ted we could meet them later in a little café for a bite to eat."

"Oh, Max."

"I know. But they are leaving for two weeks and so are we. It's on rue Alibert. We can walk there."

Olivier was just getting to know the area that abutted the rapidly changing moneyed Third Arrondissement. The Tenth and the Eleventh arrondissements were working-class communities, just now becoming gentrified, and Max was enchanted by the "mixte," where neither class or race seemed to matter. It was here where the November attacks had occurred, the terrorists intentionally targeting the hip professionals in their twenties to thirties who started their weekends in the bars and cafés, and attending concerts in the theaters like the Bataclan, where so many died. Looking around, Olivier saw that the cafés were crowded again, which gave him hope.

They passed Place de la République on the way, and Max stopped. "Look at the sunlight on the statue of Marianne. Pull over and I'll take a quick photo."

"You're kidding," he said.

"I'm the new kid on the block."

"Thank God they've taken the tents down," he said. "I really never liked the idea of the Place becoming an encampment. Ever since they changed the entire landscape here, it's become a place of perpetual protest. I'd hate to be living there," and he pointed up to a beautiful apartment building overlooking the scene.

Max said, "I've heard people talking about how awful the traffic was a few years ago."

"It still is, and I miss the small public gardens and fountains." He had swung into a parking space and they both got out. "There she is, our statue of liberty." He gazed up at the massive statue. "Symbol of the French Republic, like her or not. And many do not."

"What's the head gear?" Max asked.

"The Phrygian bonnet. It matches those worn by the ancient Roman slaves and much later by the French street wives in the 1789 uprising." Max took a picture with her phone, and they got back in the car. Olivier reminded her that Place de la République connected the Third, Tenth, and Eleventh arrondissements.

The apartment had an elevator, but they walked up the stairs, and Olivier unlocked the door to the apartment they had only seen once, but had fallen in love with. They paused at the doorway, and Olivier swept Max up in his arms. "Here we begin our new life together," he said, planting a kiss on her upturned smile.

CPSIA information can be obtained
at www.ICGtesting.com
Printed in the USA
BVOW03s1745120817
491804BV00004B/7/P

Russell Kirk's Concise Guide to Conservatism